"A . . . . ver
by a la . . . . nly
one av . . .

"Wh . . . . os-
ing the distance between them, clutching at his black velvet
lapels. "I have no idea what to advise Elizabeth."

"Well, now . . . as to that . . . ," Robert murmured. "That
is, indeed, a problem."

Slowly, the viscount lifted one finger to trace the delicate
curve of her lower lip, his gaze sweeping repeatedly over the
cherished contours of her face. Then, with the utmost care, he
trailed his touch across her flame-gilded cheek, at last ensnaring it within the soft golden aura the fire had made of her
tangled hair.

"I suppose, then, that you shall just have to find someone . . . of rank, of course, as that would only be proper . . .
to explain it to you first."

"Someone of rank? But . . . that only leaves . . . *you*,
cousin," Tia gasped.

Very slowly, Robert smiled.

"Yes, it does, doesn't it?" he answered, tunneling each of
his fingers into her hair, gently drawing her face upward toward his. . . .

"Rising star Jenna Jones bursts into full bloom with a warm
and vibrant love story that will make you sigh with delight.
A keeper that will bring new pleasure with each reading, this
delicious Regency romance is a treasure indeed."

—ROMANTIC TIMES

"Jenna Jones creates warm and lovable characters . . . one
of the best regencies I have read this year."

—AFFAIRE de COEUR

Books by Jenna Jones

A MERRY ESCAPADE

A DELICATE DECEPTION

TIA'S VALENTINE

Published by Zebra Books

TIA'S VALENTINE

Jenna Jones

Zebra Books
Kensington Publishing Corp.

http://www.zebrabooks.com

ZEBRA BOOKS are published by

Kensington Publishing Corp.
850 Third Avenue
New York, NY 10022

First Printing: February, 1997
10 9 8 7 6 5 4 3 2 1

Printed in the United States of America

For my own Valentines:
Roger, Leigh, Rob and Mark . . .
Not one of them nasty, insulting,
or given to vengeance!

Prologue

Whitby, North Yorkshire
January, 1803

A tiny spark leaped from the abraded edge of a chip of flint, snagged within the snarl of wool encased in a silver tinderbox cupped within the Leader's veined, crepe-skinned hand, and began to glow. Encouraged by a softly blown breath, it swelled and strengthened, growing hungry in the thick darkness like a nest-bound fledgling. It was all that was visible to them—those of the Black Mask Society gathered together in the frigid, cavelike room deep within the twisted viscera of the Whitby ghauts—until the Leader next lifted a single candle to the smouldering fibers and lit its shriveled wick.

Light blossomed then, wan and feeble in the winter cold, but enough to illuminate the ten of them sitting around the room's only accoutrements: a circular table and a complement of rudely constructed chairs. The candle's glow ended abruptly within the arc of their cloak-clad shoulders. They were light-suffocating, these men. Each was clad completely in black; each head beneath its black *chapeau-bras* was hooded, except at the mouth and eyes, by a feature-conforming black mask.

"Well, gentlemen, are we all here, then?" the Leader asked on the heels of a rather tentative harrumph, pooling

wax into the bottom of a shallow dish as he waited for a
response.

Suddenly the door opened, and another of their number
entered. The Leader acknowledged him with a nod, then
held the candle into the congealing pool for a moment before, with his newly freed hand, he reached up to scratch
with some desperation just beneath the edge of his mask
where it covered his chin.

"Yes, finally, all of us," answered a more corpulent
member of the group in tedious tones, "now that Digby
has at last consented to join us. Get on with it, Walmsley."

The newcomer uttered a huff of annoyance. "Must I constantly remind you, Fullerton," he inserted in a high tenor
as he took the empty seat to the man's right, "that I am not
the Earl of Digby in this Society, but am to be called
'Fox'?"

"Just so," the Leader affirmed, not unkindly. "And I
must insist upon being referred to as 'Leader,' as well. This
is a secret Society, after all."

"And who called whom 'Fullerton' just moments before?" asserted the other in mild affront. "Am I not to be
accorded the same deference as the rest of you?"

"Yes, of course you are," soothed the Leader.

"Very well, then, you may call me 'Raptor.' See that you
all make note of it."

"*Au contraire,* sir!" argued a palsied figure seated beside
the Leader. "You cannot have 'Raptor,' Fullerton. Not two
weeks past *I* chose that designation."

"Ah, but three weeks past I *thought* it, Walpole," Lord
Fullerton snapped. "Therefore, I have prior claim."

"Oh, I say . . . !" objected the quivering mouth as the
body beneath it thrust forth a shaking, cadaverous finger.

". . . Gentlemen, gentlemen," interrupted the Leader. "I

must say, I cannot see that our cause is aided by this bickering. We must stand united in these troubled times, don't you know. Fullerton, I suggest you take the name 'Lion' for your own."

"Lion?" parroted the other, cocking his black-clad head.

"Exactly so. Just think how it suits you, Harry," the Leader said. "Tall . . . commanding of form and voice . . . besides, not one of the others of us has your thick mane of hair."

"Lion, hmm?" Lord Fullerton considered, tapping a sausagelike finger against the several folds beneath his chin. "Well . . . perhaps there is a resemblance—"

"There is, of a certainty. We shall consider the matter settled," the Leader broke in. "Henceforth, Harry is to be known as 'Lion,' fellow brothers of the Black Masks."

"Whilst *I* am to be 'Raptor,' " asserted the ancient voice beside him.

"Most certainly, Nelson," the Leader responded patiently. "Now, as we are finally all present, gentlemen—"

"Of course, a case could be made that we are not," interjected a new voice. When all eyes turned toward him, he sank slightly in his chair. Timidly, he offered, "Well, it is true, is it not? The Enforcer is not yet here."

"God help us, Falcon, whyever would you wish that upon us!" breathed Fox, his hand rising to finger the frogs on his cloak.

"I did not wish it!" claimed Falcon in a rare assertion of his opinion. "I merely noted that it was so."

"Lud, gentlemen, it is not as if we actually have something to fear from the man," attempted the Leader, sounding altogether unconvinced. "He is one of us, is he not? . . . a Loyalist dedicated as we are to eradicating these damnably irritating Radical Societies which have been springing up all over England since the revolution in France? He has aided us with our missions in defense of the monarchy against the North Yorkshire Freedom Brigade each time he has appeared in our midst, has he not? Has he ever given us reason to question his loyalty to our cause . . . to our dear King George?"

"Well, no . . . ," replied Falcon, "he has never done so to my knowledge, but—"

"But his eyes!" interrupted Fox. "They burn into a man so!"

"And the way he just . . . appears!" added Lion, his own voice lacking its usual bravado. "One moment he is gone, sometimes for weeks at a time, and then suddenly, like a phantom, in the dark of night or the dimness of this very room, he is simply . . . there."

"Well, my objection is that we do not know him," added Raptor, his strident voice wobbling. "Each of us knows the others of us. We have been neighbors all our lives . . . gone to school with one another . . . married into one another's families. There is a trust that exists because of it. Yet we know nothing of him."

"Here, here!" Lion agreed. "Even you must admit, Leader, that in the company of the Enforcer there exists a certain . . . shall we say . . . apprehension."

"Apprehension? Hah!" barked Raptor. "Call a spade a spade, Fullerton. What exists is fear!"

"There can be no denying that what you say is true," the Leader nodded, scratching his forehead. "Yet the simple fact remains that when he is with us, gentlemen, we succeed in our efforts. When he is not . . ."

". . . We fail," sighed Fox, exhaling deeply as he subsided back into his chair.

"And that is precisely why I have called this meeting of

the Black Masks this evening," the Leader told them. "It has been a great while since we have seen the Enforcer . . . well over a month."

"Obviously," concluded the hitherto silent Wolf while tucking a strand of his pure white queue back inside his hood. "Not one of our forays against the Freedom Brigade has succeeded since."

"Just so," the Leader nodded, using two fingers to rub quite fiercely aside the bulge of his nose. "I vow, gentlemen, our every effort has been a mistake . . . deuce take it, worse even than not allowing Mrs. Reynolds to construct my hood out of silk bombazine as she suggested instead of this deucedly itchy Cheviot! I cannot conceive of why we have made such mice feet of our attempts to root out the Radical scoundrels. There seems to be no explanation for it. One would think it a simple thing to slip over the moors to Seave Green and set fire to Ethan Burnside's barn."

"Indeed. Our approach was without remark," Fox agreed, shaking his hooded head. "Yet when we reached the target . . ."

" . . . The tent of the heavens opened and most uncomfortably poured down upon us," Lion reprised dejectedly. "Such a river of water descended that I was quite washed away, don't you know."

Again Raptor poked aloft his bony finger. "And *I* became quite addlepated by a monstrous piece of hail!" he told them with indignation, afterward reaching up to rub at the offended spot on his pate and as a result completely misaligning his hood's eyeholes.

"And what of our plan to bring ruin to Hiram Bottonby by stealing his flock of Scottish blackface?" reminded Falcon. Around the table several brows dropped within view through several eyeholes, riding upon scowls.

"Mercy! His sheepdogs *were* a bit tenacious," commented Wolf.

"A bit!" complained Fox in a voice that was decidedly ruffled. "The spotted one put a period to the best of my black breeches!"

"And mine," sighed Falcon.

"Mine as well," admitted the Leader.

"Perhaps we just should have shot the beast," suggested Lion.

"The devil you say!" Fox erupted, jumping to his feet.

"A dog of such loyalty? Such dedication to duty?" warbled Raptor, struggling to rise.

"Gentlemen, calm yourselves," placated the Leader, poking a finger inside his left eyehole to rub at a particularly annoying itch. "Harry merely spoke in haste. We all know the value he places on well-bred flesh. Is not his kennel the pride of the county? Come now, let us try to stick to the point."

"What *is* the point?" questioned Wolf in his soft, airy voice.

The Leader relieved another itch inside his other eyehole and then scanned the circle.

"That we *must* contrive to do something, gentlemen, to reverse our rather dismal record of late."

"But the Enforcer has ordered us to do nothing when he is not present," Fox argued.

"Gammon! We are not under his thumb," countered Lion, buffing his nails on his cloak. "As witness," he added quite smugly, "we have done so anyway."

"And now find ourselves a laughingstock as a result,"

claimed Raptor, pounding his skeletal fist upon the table with a soft thump.

"Laughingstock!"

"Raptor is correct," the Leader sighed. "Obviously you are not aware of it, Lion, but even the peasantry has been bruiting about the Freedom Brigade's latest slander against us."

"Which is . . . ?"

"That we should abandon the name 'Black Masks' in favor of 'Slack Tasks' instead."

"Why, the scurvy traitors!" stormed Lion, pounding the planks himself with a much more resounding whack as he ponderously hefted himself to his feet. "We shall show them!" he cried. "We shall strike a blow for king and country! We shall do something fearful to drive those scoundrelly rascals completely from the county, no matter that the Enforcer shall probably tweak our twiddle-diddles for it!"

"Heaven forfend!" squeaked Wolf quite breathlessly, flourishing a handkerchief of emerald silk. "Never say that such a blatant confrontation should become necessary!"

Shocked by his own rhetoric, Lion melted back against his chair. "Well, I . . . that is . . ."

"Yet the Leader is right. Lud, we must do something, gentlemen," Fox reminded them.

The Leader threaded his fingers, then rested his elbows upon the rough table. "I had a thought," he replied, dropping his black-clad chin upon the lattice.

"Indeed," Lion commented, taking firm grip upon his corpulence. "What?"

The Leader slipped a thumb back to once again scratch at his neck. Finding ease, he then shrugged. "It occurred to me that perhaps you gentlemen might like to blow up a bit of the Penfield mine."

His suggestion was met with slack-jawed silence.

One

It was a most peculiar sight. Each day the cormorants came . . . sometimes only one or two, sometimes a whole community of them . . . but each day they appeared to hover over the delicate tracery of the eastern tower of Whinstone Abbey, riding the cold, unpredictable gusts coming off the ocean, hanging suspended where, until the sixteenth century, a great bell had daily called the faithful to their celebrations of prayer, to vespers or perhaps matins.

The Abbey stood on a high bluff overlooking the River Esk where its calm flow cut through the town of Whitby to form an hourglass-shaped harbor before emptying into the frigid violence of the North Sea. For over a thousand years it had faced the constant northerlies with defiance, thrusting its tall spires and long, lancet windows skyward against a force that had etched and crumbled lesser things.

And always, the great black birds came.

It was said by the scant populace that the cormorants were the souls of centuries of moor-spawned women who, finding themselves beyond hope of marriage, had fled for solace and a life of service into the sheltering arms of the nuns who had inhabited Whinstone before Henry VIII's reformation and the Abbey's subsequent dissolution. To the townsfolk, it was a lovely, albeit practical, legend, worth a smile or a soft sigh at least once a week as the satisfying supposition crossed one or another of their minds; especially as the tale had also come to be accompanied by a rather enticing curse over the course of its history.

It was the nuns' doing, of course, the populace had long ago agreed . . . an apt revenge those godly ladies had willed upon the descendants of the Abbey's usurpers. Like the souls who had come to the Abbey for safe harbor, in all the generations since Henry's decree, not one of the daughters of the house, for one reason or another, had ever married.

That an outsider might occasionally express the notion that the legend was perhaps a bit less than credible was, to the townsfolk, not to be borne. To even countenance it must certainly bring discredit to Whitby, not to mention unmerited embarrassment to these descendants, the Earls of Walmsley. Usurpers their ancestors might have been, but they were *their* usurpers, by God; therefore no ignorant ne'er-do-wells from England's soft underbelly had best even think to drift into town and say otherwise!

Besides, the earls had proved, on the whole, to be decent overlords. Indeed, if the truth were told, the fishermen and shipbuilders who lived at the base of the bluff—the more well-to-do in the neat houses introducing rows of long, narrow, ancient burgage plots; the poorer in the ruder, slumlike dwellings stacked up the hillside behind them in a jumble known uniquely in England as the Whitby ghauts—were rather proud of their current lord.

Brumley Hilton, the present earl, arrogant and aloof as a boy, had, quite to everyone's surprise, actually grown into a kindly sort of fellow. To the town's delight, he had made some notable improvements in both the Abbey and the community since his rakehell elder brother, Horatio, had died and he had come into the title. And the way he had allowed his brother's wife and daughter to remain a part of his household when they had been left with scarcely two coins to rub together, why, it had been a fine gesture indeed, not to be denied. He was all right, that Brumley, the villagers decided. The town was satisfied.

And so, aside from the recent activities of a few pesky secret societies which everyone knew were but insignificant grains of sand in the hourglass of England, the town of Whitby clung to its legend and passed its days in contentment, pausing over a pint each afternoon to regard the faithful cormorants above the tower, enjoying having the speculation to pass down to their children and to the few outsiders who made their way to the town by sea or across the snow-bleak moors; enjoying, too, the measure of distinction the legend brought to the men's rather isolated lives . . . more whimsically, the touch of romance to the women's.

And it was a day for romance. Valentine's Day. The most exciting day of the year for Walmsley's niece, Lady Horatia Hilton. The one day of the year she allowed herself to dream of love; for, as everyone knew, Tia Hilton had some years before quite emphatically and uncompromisingly placed herself, too, on the shelf, becoming yet the latest of the Walmsley daughters to succumb to the Abbey's ill wish.

"Horatia, do get down from that chair," requested Sophie, Countess of Walmsley, from one of the settles bracketing the fireplace centered within the Abbey ballroom's large inglenook. "Such a breach of behavior is most unseemly in the presence of your guest."

Her duty concluded, the countess again turned her attention toward her needlework.

From her perch across the room, Tia emitted the tiniest of sighs, then glanced toward her mother, yet her gaze did not tarry long. Almost immediately it drifted past the countess's serene countenance to the fireplace's heavily carved oak mantel, where, just beyond her ladyship, above several rounded rows of gleaming, gold enameled Italian tile, more than a dozen valentines had been put on display, each one unique in its personal construction by its sender, each beautiful in its combinations of rare feathers, shells, cut-outs, ribbons, semiprecious stones, or ruffles of expensive, spider wrought lace. Instantly the scold was forgotten. Tia smiled at the sight; another soft sigh removed the vexation furrowing her brow.

Suddenly one of the cards toppled forward, caught on a whimsical updraft of the warm fire current and pirouetted onto the settle beside the countess. Under Tia's wary gaze, the lady paused in her stitching to briefly regard the mantel's offering with a *moue* of distaste. Then, after glancing once more toward her daughter, she coldly signaled to an attentive footman to set the valentine back in its place.

"Horatia," she repeated with just the slightest bit more emphasis, "I believe I did ask you to get down, dear."

Across the room, Tia's nose wrinkled, more in response to her mother's action than because of her second reprimand; but she remained where she was, choosing instead to tuck another pink silk streamer into the hand clutching several others in place against the room's ivory damask-covered wall.

"I shall get down in a moment, Mama," she told her, tying the streamers together into a lavish bow, "I am sure that Margaret—"

"Horatia!"

Again Tia softly sighed. "Very well, I am sure that Miss Tutweiler—"

Suddenly the door burst open to reveal the sounds of a bustling disturbance welling up in the hall. As Tia braked her remaining words and turned toward the cacophony, Mrs. Reynolds, the Abbey housekeeper, hurried into the room through the vaulted oak entrance, her simple gown of matte black bombazine susurrant against her black-clad legs, her unadorned hem excitedly aswirl.

"Oh, do look, Miss Horatia!" she cried animatedly. " 'Tis a lifesaver, I should think! Flowers have just arrived from the Bainbridge Castle greenhouses. And none too soon, if you ask me. Our own order from London has yet to arrive, and your Valentine's ball is tonight!

"Here now," the woman interrupted herself, abruptly turning back toward the door to gesture toward the gathering of laden footmen awaiting in the darker hall, "bring those baskets right in and put them on that table." Almost immediately she reversed direction again, then pointed toward two mobcapped maids in white muslin gowns. "Mary, you and Dab begin arranging them right away in the Sèvres sconces. Gracious! There is so little time!"

After brief curtseys, the two maids hurried to do as they had been bid. Just behind them, the row of footmen entered, parading basket after basket of blurred red and pink petals past Tia's excited exclamations, quickly filling the table.

"Oh, how lovely!" Tia cried, bouncing enthusiastically atop the morocco leather seat of one of her Uncle Brumley's Chippendale side chairs. "Only see the colors, Miss Tutweiler," she breathed, glancing down at the slight, blond-haired lady seated nearby on a matching chair.

"Lovely, indeed," murmured the young woman whose

gloved hands were at the moment most delicately occupied with a Wedgwood cup and saucer. Returning Tia's regard, Miss Tutweiler smiled and then separated her plush, pink lips to sip the steaming Earl Grey.

"Trust Robert to have roses blooming in February," Tia continued. "And how dear of him to worry about the preparations for my ball, though he has been up to Town for more than a fortnight! I tell you, Miss Tutweiler, you shall like Bainbridge immensely."

On the heels of the departed Bainbridge footmen, another bumblebroth sounded in the hallway. Mrs. Reynolds clapped a palm to her cheek.

". . . Sixes and sevens, I tell you; sixes and sevens . . . ," she murmured with a harried look, again bustling from the room.

"I shall be most honored to meet your cousin," Miss Tutweiler stated after the room fell into relative silence again, her smile sweet, her lashes fluttering about her wide blue eyes.

"Excellent!" Tia vowed with a nod that dislodged several curls from the confines of her *coiffure à la grêque*. "He has the most remarkable eyes, you know. They are quite the most astonishing hazel hue."

"Quite like yours, I perceive," Miss Tutweiler observed, broadening her smile.

"Oh, dear me, no," Tia laughed. "There is a resemblance, to be sure, as Robert is my second cousin, but I fear my eyes are quite ordinary. His, however, are . . . a collection of colors," she described, assessing them again in her mind's eye, "like the woods in autumn. I have no doubt you shall find them most attractive."

"Perhaps, but I—"

Again the ballroom door swung wide and Mrs. Reynolds bounded into the room.

"That was another messenger, Miss Horatia," she called excitedly, striding forward across the polished dance floor, drawing forth two slim packages from the large pocket of a white apron set off startlingly against the somber black bombazine.

Within the inglenook, the countess lowered her needle. "Mrs. Reynolds, a measure of decorum, if you please," she chided, using the interruption to take a sip of tea.

"Beg pardon, milady," Mrs. Reynolds apologized with a quick curtsey in the countess's direction, "but just look at these, Miss Horatia. Two more valentines just come from more of your admirers. Oh, isn't this the most exciting of days!"

"Do calm yourself, Mrs. Reynolds," instructed the countess in an evenly controlled voice, again returning her attention to the drum of fabric stretched over the curved mahogany of her tambour frame. "I cannot credit that anyone should find a day given over to the excesses of so-called 'romance' exciting, nor can I approve of my staff becoming caught up in it in any way. Now, do go about your duties, if you please. Our guests for this diversion shall be arriving for dinner in less than six hours. I do not wish for my daughter's occasion to become a blot upon my brother-in-law's reputation or social standing."

"Of course, milady," Mrs. Reynolds replied, dipping into a much more humble obeisance. "I shall go at once to see to the finishing touches in the ladies' withdrawing room." Without looking up again, she quickly exited the room.

"And do get down from that chair, Horatia."

The request flattened Tia's smile. Turning toward the wall, she swallowed twice.

"Well," she said at last, turning back toward Miss Tutweiler, expelling the huge breath she had drawn in to renew her spirits and revitalize her good-natured grin, "I wonder who these might be from." Perfectly aware that all manner of fragile ornamentation might be wrapped inside, she broke the seal on the topmost missive with the utmost of care and began to remove the valentine's outer covering. "I have already received one from the Lords Pershing and Dudley in the Dales," she told her guest with growing enthusiasm, "and from Peterman, Dashwood, and Framworth near Middlesbrough as well. Oh, I know!" She suddenly grinned, eyeing her wide-eyed guest most mischievously. "Perhaps this one is from Robert. Ah, me," she sighed. "I suppose after tonight I shall have to reconcile myself to the fact that this will most likely be the last valentine I shall ever receive from him."

"Oh, surely not!" exclaimed Miss Tutweiler, her blue eyes moist with concern.

"Oh, indeed, yes!" Tia vowed. And then her grin widened. "I should not be at all surprised, Miss Tutweiler, if, after tonight, they shall all be arriving for *you!*"

"Goodness, Lady Horatia!" Miss Tutweiler responded, shaking several side curls of her simple style *à la Madonna* in denial while clasping the ends of a warm Norwich shawl more closely about the ruched bodice of her morning gown. "Your cousin is a viscount. I cannot imagine that a viscount would deign to look at such as I. If you recall, I am only the daughter of a squire."

"Fustian," Tia pronounced, her emphasis causing her to wobble slightly as she handed the footman, Wil, the valentine's wrapping paper to discard at a later time. "You are just Robert's style," she said, repositioning her slippered feet upon the firm leather. "Why, look at you! You are the pattern card of the modern beauty . . . lovely blond hair, blue eyes, wondrously plump cheeks . . . I tell you, he shall adore you. And who should know better than I? We have known one another all our lives, after all, growing up side by side together right here in Whitby. We are the best of friends, Robert and I.

"But, oh, do look at this, Miss Tutweiler," Tia said, touching the card's delicate ornamentation almost reverently, then turning it for her guest to see. "Why, each leaf is made of green parrot feathers, and the flower petals are of mother of pearl! Oh, and see?" she said, opening it. "Do look, Mama! It is from Uncle Brumley, and written in his own hand. Oh, how dear of him! And he has made up his own verse. Listen . . .

> My dearest Horatia,
>   To the apple of all my Valentines,
>   To the pearl beyond all price,
>   You have become to me a daughter,
>   And I think that rather nice.
>
>   So accept, on this day, a small token
>   And a little bit of advice.
>   Sip the nectar from my flower,
>   Then rethink your choices twice."

Tia chuckled with delight. "Dear Uncle Brumley," she murmured, touching fingertips to the parrot feathers. "He is the most wonderful of uncles, Miss Tutweiler."

"Rather the most odd," the countess corrected, pausing

in her needlework to refresh her cup of tea. "That last couplet is most esoteric, Horatia."

"Yes," Tia responded with a soft smile, staring at the words, "I suppose so. Nevertheless"—she suddenly chuckled brightly—"there is nothing esoteric at all about the token he has promised me, nor his hint that I must sip the flower's nectar to get it." Cautiously, Tia inserted her fingers between the layers of mother of pearl and pried open the flower petals, careful not to break the thinly worked plates. "Oh!" she gasped, when a large pearl pendant fell into her gloved hand. "Oh, Mama, look! How magnificent!"

"Quite lovely," the countess agreed after having looked up from her stitch, then returned her attention to completing it again. "Brumley has given you your aunt's come-out pendant it seems. She was wearing it the first time he met her."

"Was she? How very romantic," Tia murmured, holding the pendant up to the light.

"Romantic?" the countess repeated. "Hardly. Not a year later, Elizabeth was dead."

Around the vast room, sounds dulled against the sudden thrum that began to pulse within Tia's ears. Her hand formed a tight fist around the pendant; slowly her chin dropped to touch against the soft ruffles of her chemisette. The air thickened in her throat as she bit at her upper lip. And then she drew in a very deep breath.

"Who might this other card be from, do you suppose?" she at last murmured, somewhere discovering yet another smile. "Might this one be from Robert? Surely it must. His has not arrived as yet, and he always sends me one." Quickly, she opened it and gave Wil the second of the outer wrapping papers. "Oh, it is from Parkenham. Goodness,

Miss Tutweiler, look at this! There is a cluster of tiny rubies circling Cupid's brow!"

"Rather ostentatious, if you ask me," the countess commented. "Shall you read it, Horatia?"

Several seconds passed while Tia perused the inscription. "No, I think not, Mama," she replied, a slight flush rising to stain her cheeks. "This particular poem is a bit more personal."

"All the more reason to read it, I should think," responded the countess more firmly.

"I am of age, Mama," Tia countered with a gentle smile. "I am allowed my secrets." When the countess stiffened perceptibly, she added, "It shall be on the mantel with all the others in just a few moments, Mama. You may read it, or any of the others, at any time you choose."

The countess's back arched. "I do not read valentines," she stated, carefully separating each syllable.

"That is your choice, of course," Tia responded, her smile never altering. "Of a certainty, however, I shall be sharing it and all my valentines with Miss Tutweiler when we have gone to our beds after the ball. I warn you now, Miss Tutweiler, I plan to keep you awake until dawn discussing each detail of the evening . . . everything that happened, each eye that was cast in another's direction, each word that was said . . . saving the greatest of detail, of course, for the congress you have had with Robert."

"The viscount?" Miss Tutweiler gasped, a slim hand sliding upward to touch the hollow at the base of her throat. "But I understood that he was in Town!"

"He is," Tia replied happily, signaling to Mary to fetch one of the small urned sconces she had just arranged with Queen Anne's lace and several of the delicate roses reposing in the nearest of the large wicker baskets brought by

Robert's footmen. "Or, more precisely, he was. He has been there of late on some bit of business, but he shall be here for my ball. He knows I shall ring a ghastly peal over him if he should even think to miss it. I am not concerned, however. Before he left, he promised me he would be here in time no matter what, and he always keeps his promises."

"But he is . . . a viscount!" the lady beside her breathed.

"Yet, I assure you, the most docile of lambs," Tia reassured her. "Not that he does not have his strengths, of course," she corrected under Miss Tutweiler's doubtful blue gaze. "But on the whole, a most manageable young man. And ever so handsome . . . broad shoulders, a strong chin . . . why, I know for a fact that none of his stockings need wadding. And he has fine brown hair, straight, even brows . . . altogether the most regular of features. You shall find him most satisfactory."

"But . . . my family and I have been such a short time at Airy Hill," Miss Tutweiler began. "I had thought to let a bit of time pass before engaging—"

"Not a bit of it," Tia insisted, holding the sconce in place against the wall just above the knot of the bow. "Believe me, Miss Tutweiler, we must strike while the iron is hot."

"S-strike while the iron is hot?" gasped the lady, her eyes growing round.

"Yes, of course," Tia told her with a puzzled look. "My cousin is a most desirable *parti.*"

"A-and you have thought to pair him with me?"

"Assuredly," Tia told her with a bright smile.

"Horatia, do not browbeat the girl," the countess warned. "And do get down off the Chippendale."

"In but a moment, Mama. You must believe me when I tell you, Miss Tutweiler, that the two of you are perfect for one another."

"But he is a viscount," Miss Tutweiler reiterated with soft sensibility. "Surely he might look higher than the daughter of a squire."

Tia held her fingers aside while the footman hammered the sconce into place, then shrugged slightly. "Yes, of a certainty, he could," she answered honestly. "The problem is, he doesn't, you see. Or won't. One or the other." She sighed softly then. "Whichever it is makes no difference, however. I have taken it upon myself to help him . . . to nudge him in the proper direction as it were. And I am not without experience in these matters."

"You are not?" Miss Tutweiler responded in a tone that left little doubt as to her thinking.

"Just so." Tia grinned with satisfaction, gathering a generous section of her sky blue muslin skirt into one matching kid-covered hand, then bounding lightly down from her makeshift ladder.

Several more of her soft, brown curls loosened, then joined the others now hanging limp and straight over her shoulders as she reached the floor, but she ignored them. Instead, she began to drag the chair after the footman to where he was already gathering several new streamers, at the same time motioning for Miss Tutweiler to follow.

"It has been my privilege over the five years since my come out to introduce several delightful couples to romance," she added proudly, showing a good deal of trim, olive-stockinged ankle as she mounted the chair again. "Why, not one couple whom I have assisted thus far has failed to make their wedding vows."

"But I understood that you . . . ," Miss Tutweiler ventured softly.

". . . Were on the shelf?" Tia laughed.

"Oh, no! Oh, dear, Lady Horatia, I meant no offense!" exclaimed the other beneath raspberry cheeks.

"Of course you did not," Tia stated, "and what you have heard is quite correct. But, I assure you, it is by choice. You see, I have no interest in marriage myself. Uncle Brumley provided for me quite generously in my father's stead after Papa's death several years ago left Mama and me in straitened circumstances. As a consequence, I have no need for a provider."

"Forgive me, Lady Horatia . . ."

". . . Tia."

"Tia," Miss Tutweiler whispered, glancing at the countess, blushing above a sweet smile. "I do beg your pardon, but do you not consider your personal feelings concerning matrimony and your activities on behalf of romance for others somewhat contradictory?"

Tia's light, answering chuckle warmed her corner of the room. "It does seem so, does it not?" she asked, her amusement fading into a smile. "Yet the odd fact is that there is not a woman in all of England who enjoys seeing two dear friends find happiness with one another as much as I. I cannot explain it. It is just so."

"It is most unusual," Miss Tutweiler responded.

"I cannot deny it," Tia affirmed cheerfully. "On the one hand to adore love, to live for the most romantic of all celebrations, Valentine's Day, and on the other to believe that the estate is not for me . . . it is a remarkable inconsistency, I quite agree, Miss Tutweiler. Or may I call you Margaret now that you know such a marvelous secret about me?"

"On a mere sennight's acquaintance? Horatia, really," the countess chided from the settle. "That would be most rag-mannered. And, dearest, do get down from that chair."

Tia's gaze drifted momentarily up to the spidery tracings of the room's ancient fan vaulting, and then she charged into the breach.

"I am sensible, of course, Mama, that our acquaintance with the Tutweilers has not been of long duration since the squire and his family only recently moved to the Grange in Airy Hill," she said, again motioning to a passing maid to hand her a sconce of flowers. "But I feel most positive that Miss Tutweiler and I shall become fast friends. Margaret, do you not agree?"

"Oh, yes," Miss Tutweiler nodded, clutching at her shawl with her pink-gloved hands in order to still their trembling. "I should like it above all things."

"There, you see, Mama?" Tia asked, once more rising up to her tiptoes to hold a second sconce in place for Wil to affix. "Now it cannot be improper. We shall be Margaret and Tia . . . the best of friends." And then she smiled down into Miss Tutweiler's huge blue eyes. "Perhaps even more," she added, her hazel eyes sparkling, "as I shall be introducing her to Robert at my first opportunity."

As Miss Tutweiler grew radiant, the countess sighed. "So you have definitely settled upon Robert again, have you?" she asked, adjusting the tambour frame until it was more comfortably close to the heat flowing out from the fire. "La, Horatia, I vow that this whole idea of arranging grand romance, not to mention the unaccountable passion you have developed for celebrating Valentine's Day, is beyond anything. And do get down from that chair."

Something shifted within Tia as her mother spoke, and as quickly as it had come, her vexation faded. Glancing quickly toward Miss Tutweiler, she responded guardedly.

"I am sensible of your circumstances before Papa's death, Mama, and I have said that I would not marry, that

I would not place my life in the same . . . situation . . . within which you found yourself bound. But surely the ideal of love might be celebrated on one special day, though the reality of it does not exist. And is it so wrong to help others to find it who are better suited to take the risk?"

The countess anchored her needle, then motioned to a footman to warm each of their cups of tea. "I should think you would spurn this day, Horatia. You were witness to—" and here the countess, too, glanced briefly toward Miss Tutweiler before finishing *sotto voce*—"what I endured." She smoothed the bodice of her sea green morning gown then, and in a more confident voice asked, "Miss Tutweiler, do let Mary bring you one of Henri's jam tarts. He is quite renowned for them. And you, Horatia, kindly get down from there, if you please."

"I cannot, Mama," she responded, shaking several more curls into the exodus. Refusing to allow her pleasure in the day's excitement to be doused, she widened her smile and concluded, "How shall Wil fasten the urns to the wall without my aid?"

"We shall call another of the footmen to assist him, of course," her mother stated, completing a leaf with her next stitch.

"Oh, Mama," Tia replied on a soft chortle, again adjusting her fingers so as to avoid a descending stroke of Wil's hammer, "what would be the point? It is the same every year. I become much too excited to allow even Mrs. Reynolds to supervise the decorations for my Valentine's ball. You know that I cannot help being in the thick of the preparations. Everything must be absolutely perfect for tonight. Should I even try to sit before the fire taking tea as you and Margaret are, of a certainty I would only begin fidgeting and complaining until I ended up on a chair again."

"A lady does not behave in such a fashion," the countess gently argued. "Especially one who has chosen the path of spinsterhood, Horatia. I do not disapprove of your choice, of course; but it is a bold decision for a woman, my dear, and it does place you in a somewhat tentative place in Society. Therefore, you must conduct yourself in a manner that is above reproach."

"I cannot be a hoyden, is that what you are saying, Mama?" Tia laughed.

"No you cannot," the countess answered. "And it is no laughing matter, Horatia."

"I know, Mama, and just as soon as these decorations are finished, I shall be utterly transformed into the highest of sticklers."

"Only when Newcastle runs out of coal," chuckled a deep, commanding voice from the doorway. "And, Tia, before you break something quite lovely, my dear, do get down off the chair."

Not even hesitating for a moment, Tia did exactly as she was told.

Two

"Robert!" Tia cried, bringing her hem up over the crook of her elbow in order to also avoid breaking something lovely as she rushed headlong into his outstretched arms. "You've come," she breathed, throwing herself against him, burying her face into the warm curve between his neck and broad shoulder, thoroughly ruining his already travel-weary white silk Mailcoach.

"Of course I have," he murmured into her hair, enfolding her within his strength, pressing her tightly against his sable brown cutaway. "When have I ever missed your Valentine's ball? And what is this?" he questioned, drawing away a bit to gaze down upon her, bringing up a York tan-gloved finger to toy with an escaped, ramrod-straight tress. "You look like the mother of twelve. Make yourself presentable, Tia," he ordered, placing a kiss on her forehead before turning to gesture behind him. "I have brought someone I would like you to meet. Dex, come and make the acquaintance of the scapegrace side of my family."

As Tia gasped and used Robert's body to block her hasty repairs from the newcomer's sight, his unregarded companion stepped into the room. Seizing several curls, Tia peeked over Robert's shoulder to assess him. Slightly shorter than her cousin, he was still a well-favored man. Dressed in a dark blue cutaway, white waistcoat, and buff inexpressibles, he was actually quite nice looking, she thought as she abstractedly pulled at one of her ribbons. Not nearly so handsome, of course, as Robert, she considered, jabbing at a particularly unruly strand. Yet still quite attractive. Perhaps, she thought with newly elevated brows, he might be just the one for Miss Alicia Evans.

She glanced at Miss Tutweiler next, anxious to gauge her friend's reaction to her cousin. Miss Tutweiler was staring quite intently in the direction of the two gentlemen—obviously taken with one of them as her lovely countenance now quite closely resembled that of a gasping trout—however, since Robert and his friend were standing quite close together, which one had become the object of her goggle-eyed regard? For the life of her, Tia could not tell.

Behind Robert's back, chagrin flickered at the corner of her mouth. Fiddle! she thought as she shoved another errant strand up under her coiffure's binding, at the same time allowing several more to escape. Just what she needed. Competition from another quarter.

Suddenly Robert turned and tucked her up beneath his arm, startling a slight squeak out of her before she recovered enough to look up at him and notice that his eyes were narrowed knowingly.

Tia glowered back at the familiar expression as she had always done.

Her cousin pursed his lips. Slowly his gaze rose to regard her hair. Tsking softly, he slightly shook his head.

"Keep working on it," he whispered down into the silky disarray.

"Varlet," Tia whispered in return, at the same time reaching up toward her curls to try again.

The viscount broke into a soft chuckle.

"Come make your leg to the countess, Dex," he commanded, turning away from Tia to capture his friend, too, with another hand settled just below his neck. "Her ladyship only sounds like a dragon," he whispered loud enough for the countess to hear, beginning to propel both of them toward the inglenook. "I give you my word as a gentleman, however, that you shall be safe. In all the years I have known her, she has never set fire to anyone."

"So you have found your way home once again, have you?" the countess greeted, offering her fingertips after he had removed his gloves and bowed low beside her tambour frame.

"As you see, cousin," he returned pleasantly, touching his lips to her gloved hand. "But where is cousin Brumley at this hour? I expected to find you all together."

"At one of his endless meetings, I suppose," the countess sighed. "Brumley finds any excuse to shun such preparations, you know. Pity I did not realize it when I agreed to remain at Whinstone to serve as his hostess. It has been a grave responsibility all these years . . . one which weighs quite heavily upon me."

"Yet no one could have borne it with greater sublimity," Robert told her, his next kiss inspiring a wan smile. "And see what I have brought along for your entertainment . . . ," he added, nodding toward Dex, "a friend to help me regale you with all the latest London *on dits*. May I present to you Mr. Dexter Clark of Sunderland. Dex, I give you Sophie, dowager Countess of Walmsley."

"An honor, ma'am," the young man replied, extending one white silk-clad calf while his lips hovered the requisite distance above her hand.

"Mr. Clark," the countess repeated, eyeing her guest appraisingly. "Of Sunderland, did you say? The Clarks who own the Penfield mine?"

"The same," Dex confessed. "As a matter of fact, I am traveling there now. I see word of our trouble has preceded me."

"What trouble?" Tia asked from Robert's opposite side after finally managing to muscle the last wayward tress into a decidedly untidy twist.

"Horatia, you have not been introduced," the countess scolded.

"A breach of etiquette easily remedied," Robert said, again perusing Tia with a wry smile. "Cousin, may I present my friend, Mr. Dexter Clark. Dex, Lady Horatia Hilton."

"A pleasure," Dex responded, giving the same care to Tia's bow as he had to the countess's.

"For me as well," Tia answered warmly, extending her hand. "And may I present to you *my* friend," she said brightly, quickly turning to draw the hesitant Miss Tutweiler to her side. "Margaret, allow me to introduce you first to my cousin, Viscount Bainbridge . . ."

" 'Service, ma'am," Robert responded, bowing low.

Margaret's gaze hovered for only the twentieth part of a moment upon Robert's clean-shaven chin before, as she sank into a deep curtsey, it dove like a cormorant for several loops of the Brussels carpet.

Above her, Tia sighed.

". . . And his friend, Mr. Dexter Clark," she finished with considerably less enthusiasm, staring down in dismay at the neat center part bisecting Miss Tutweiler's head.

Slowly Miss Tutweiler rose. Extending a trembling hand, her remarkable blue gaze elevated, touching upon the deep brown softness of Mr. Clark's, locking into place.

"H-how do you do?" she breathed at last from lips left dewy after a nervous flick of her tongue, surrendering her fingers into his.

For the life of him, Dex could not think of a suitable answer. He was caught in a snare of blue filaments; blue talons sank sweetly into his abdomen. A remarkable blue fog rolled across his cognitive processes. He swallowed hard, then did so again.

Like a paper boat on a ruffled pond, the knot of his Mathematical lifted to ride the uneven swells.

Tia regarded the phenomenon with growing alarm.

"I . . . well . . . r-rather well, I suppose . . . ," Dex finally, awkwardly, responded.

"What a relief," Robert commented with a laugh, releasing Tia to stroll casually over to the Chippendale dining chair. Briefly looking the situation over, he mounted it, then motioned for another sconce from Mary. "I might suggest, though," he continued, holding the sconce to another of the bows and beginning to hammer it in place, "that since by your own admission you approximate good health, it might be a good idea to cease trying to support yourself by clinging to the lady's hand."

"What? . . . Oh!" Dex exclaimed, jumping back as if he had just touched an electricity machine. "I . . . beg your pardon, Miss . . ."

". . . *Tut*-weiler," Tia growled, skewering Dex with the best of her glowers. "Miss Margaret Tutweiler, lately of Airy Hill."

Across the room, Robert glanced toward the sound of his cousin's vexation before remounting the chair just beneath the next grouping of streamers farther down the wall. Seen from his perspective, Dex and Miss Tutweiler looked like twin braziers framing his cousin's glare. Biting into his cheek, the viscount only just staved off the urge to climb back down again, stride purposefully over to his cousin's side, and whack a well-aimed palm most firmly against her lovely posterior. He had known from the moment he had walked into the ballroom what she was about, of course . . . that he had undoubtedly arrived just in time to stave off yet another of his cousin's manipulations, this time involving Miss Tutweiler . . . and it rankled.

Yet it was Tia, he acknowledged; therefore nothing in the situation was unexpected.

Finally, relaxing, he shook his head. Let her do her damnedest, he challenged with a soft smile, once again turning to fit another sconce to its companion bow. She had no idea of the strength of his immunity, after all, nor its source. But he knew that even the best of her efforts were doomed to fail.

Dex and Miss Tutweiler, on the other hand, altogether ignorant of any of the undercurrents soughing all about them, continued their self-absorbed stare.

"Miss Tutweiler," Dex finally repeated in a voice of prayer.

"Mr. Clark," Margaret breathed, her features softening with pleasure.

"The deuce," Tia mumbled, her gaze flitting back and forth between the two of them, her toes soon taking up the rhythm beneath her soft blue flounce.

Yet dogged romantic that she was, she quickly recovered. "La, I am persuaded that this misfortune in your family must take you away from us before we have barely become acquainted, Mr. Clark," she suddenly stated, mustering a sweet smile as she seized his arm and began ushering him toward the door. "What a pity it must be so."

"On the contrary, cousin," Robert called cheerfully above the sound of hammering. "Dex is a friend of long-standing. Quite naturally, I have extended my hospitality to him for the night. He shall not be leaving for Sunderland until the morrow."

Tia's smile abruptly changed direction.

"What a pleasant happenstance," she managed to say quite politely, releasing her captive so that she might slip another drooping strand behind her ear. "And how very good of you, cousin."

"Yes, it is, is it not?" Robert allowed, exercising no control whatsoever over his grin as he again relocated the chair. "And just think of the added benefit, Tia."

"There must be many, of a certainty," she declared, turning her glower upon him, her eyes beginning to spark fire. "To which are you referring, cousin dear?"

"Why, to the fact that you are forever complaining that you lack enough gentlemen for your occasions," he told her with a positively wicked shrug. "Now, however, with Dex staying over in Whitby tonight, we shall both of us be available to attend your Valentine's ball."

"If I might do so without imposing, of course," Dex hastened to interject, allowing only a moment away from his concentration upon Miss Tutweiler to glance toward the other two.

Tia had already prepared her set-down for Robert, and her scold for this . . . this scoundrelly usurper of affections and befuddler of plans, and had even opened her mouth to do so, when the countess suddenly motioned to her.

"My dear," she whispered after she had taken Tia's arm and pulled her close, "I very much fear it would not be appropriate for you to encourage Mr. Clark's attendance at the ball this evening."

"Why?" Tia responded with eagerness, feeling her hopes begin to rise upon the possibility that her mother was about to provide the perfect excuse.

The countess's glance flicked toward Robert's friend. "Horatia, you are quite old enough by now to know that a gentleman's . . . associations . . . are allowed to be less restrictive than a lady's."

"Mama," Tia whispered in return, shaking her head, "how does that signify?"

"It signifies, dearest, because while it is disconcerting that Robert has befriended a man such as Mr. Clark, it is not unheard of. We, however, owe it to the Walmsley title to remain above reproach in our associations. My dear, we cannot extend an invitation to Mr. Clark."

"Mama, you still have not explained . . ."

"Then let me speak plainly," the countess hissed. "Mr. Clark must not be invited because his father is in trade."

Tia straightened abruptly. After some moments in which she stared down at her mother, she then glanced toward the absorbed couple. At last, she dropped her gaze to the knot of fingers she had clasped just below her waist. Not the twentieth part of a moment later, she again elevated her chin.

"You would not be imposing at all, Mr. Clark," she finally told him with a warm smile, crossing to extend her hand. "I should be honored to have your presence at my ball tonight."

Behind her, the countess expelled a noticeable sigh.

And then Robert was standing before her, his eyes a smile, his countenance affirming and proud.

Suddenly he winked at her.

Tia swallowed a very unladylike squeak. Varlet! she thought as her spine lengthened. He knew very well that by introducing Mr. Clark into their society he had just made her task twice as hard as it had been but an hour before. And from the grin threatening to permanently separate his chin from the rest of his face, she knew that the bounder was quite proud of the fact. In answer, she cast him a returning glower, yet she did not yield to an impulse to poke her tongue out at him as she might have in years past. She was three and twenty now, after all, and such behavior was, of course, quite beneath her.

Instead, she looked down the length of her nose.

"Mr. Clark," she stated, suddenly the pattern card of the perfect hostess, "you were telling us of your family's recent difficulty. I would be most interested in hearing about it. Perhaps there is something we might do to help."

Reluctantly, Dex again drew his gaze away from Miss Tutweiler. "I very much doubt it, Lady Horatia," he responded quietly, "though I appreciate your kind offer. You see, a sennight ago I received a letter from my father summoning me home and informing me that someone, for some reason, had blown up our mine."

"Heaven forfend!" Miss Tutweiler exclaimed. "Was anyone hurt?"

"By the grace of God, no," Dex told her gently. "The mine was between shifts . . . even the watchman was away from the office building on rounds. But the charge used was enormous. Everything collapsed except for the deepest of the tunnels."

"But who would do such a thing?" Tia asked, shaking another curl loose.

"Who, indeed?" Dex responded, his voice growing hard. "I can only say that at this point I have no hard proof. But rest assured, milady, I shall get it. Nothing on the face of this earth shall prevent me from bringing to justice those who have ruined my family."

Tia wondered for several moments after Mr. Clark's vow why her cousin was suddenly no longer smiling.

Three

"Begging your pardon, milady," cut a deep apology through the rustling silence that followed Dex's vow.

"Yes, Wardle?" the countess responded, looking up at the tall butler who now stood just inside the room.

"Mrs. Reynolds has asked that you come at once, milady," he informed her, staring straight ahead at a point on the opposite wall. "Henri has flown into a pelter again."

The countess sighed heavily. "What is it this time?" she wearily asked.

"Several of the lobsters that were delivered for the patties are dead in the water, milady," Wardle answered in a monotone. "As your ladyship is the only one who seems to be able to appease Henri during such crises, Mrs. Reynolds requests that you endeavor to speak to him, and then inform her whether you still wish to use the lobsters or would judge it safer to substitute boiled turbot in its stead."

Again the countess sighed. "La, I wonder sometimes if it is a requisite for French chefs to take classes in volatility! Very well, Wardle," she told him, securing her needle aside the delicate pink shape of a lily before gracefully rising. "Tell Mrs. Reynolds that I shall meet with her shortly." Then, turning toward the others, she added, "As for you, Horatia, I ask . . . nay, I urge you to reconsider your decision. Gentlemen, Miss Tutweiler, if you will excuse me . . ."

Atop his chair, along with Dex, Robert bowed deeply. Near Tia, Miss Tutweiler dropped into a curtsey. When the countess had departed, all around them, the room relaxed. Robert affixed the last of the Sèvres urns to the wall, then lithely jumped down.

"I would very much like to know what you learn about the explosion, Dex," he said, striding over to stand beside his friend.

Dex nodded briskly. "I shall stay in contact, then," he replied. His gaze then flicked toward Miss Tutweiler. "Sunderland is not far."

Robert smiled, his regard, too, wandering briefly in the young woman's direction. "Not in the least. I shall look forward to seeing a great deal of you in future. But now, I wonder if you and Miss Tutweiler will excuse my cousin and me for a short time."

Suddenly he reached out and snared Tia's elbow in a firm grip. Before she could muster an objection, he turned her resolutely toward the door.

"Matters of a family nature have arisen which need to be discussed," the viscount added, his voice drowning out Tia's sputter as his energetic pace ate up the distance to the door, his hand easily controlling her wriggles of affront.

"Do help yourself to the Armagnac, Dex," he called as they reached the doorway. After unfastening Tia's quick snag of the carved oak frame by several slippered toes, he concluded from the corridor, "It is warming above the mantel, I believe."

Dex and Margaret stared for several moments at the empty doorway after Tia and Robert had disappeared without. And then they stared at each other. And then, instantaneously, their gazes leaped apart.

"H-hasn't her ladyship decorated the ballroom beauti-
fully?" Margaret tentatively asked as several of the maids
began clearing away the remains of the streamers, baskets,
and clippings of flowers that had been strewn about the
floor. "It was once the nun's gallery, I believe," she commented, watching as more clusters of footmen began arranging the refreshment area, while others carried in
armfuls of fine linens or scurried to precisely line the walls
with chairs.

In response, Dex let his regard wander over the room's
embellishments, his perusal sliding along the red, pink
and white swags of streamers to each flower-burdened
sconce, the whole of which were displayed to beautiful
advantage by the wide panels of ivory damask spanning
the spaces between columns of ancient Yorkshire sandstone. Parlor palms delineated the orchestra and refreshment areas, their bases concealed behind lush displays of
arranged roses, each splayed frond affixed with rows of
tiny candles waiting until the final moment to be lit. And
everywhere there were valentines . . . every one that Tia
had ever received . . . layered upon the walls over great
heart-shaped silken cut-outs that had been scattered here
and about. It was an interior created by an incurable romantic. Dex smiled, trying to reconcile that fact with the
woman he had just met.

"It is quite nice," he commented, beginning to make his
way toward the inglenook.

"Yes . . . Lady Horatia seems to take great pleasure in
the occasion," Margaret added as she followed him toward
the large cove's captured warmth.

"Seems?" Dex questioned, taking glass and decanter
from a small silver tray and pouring himself a measure of
the costly smuggled brandy. "You sound as if you do not

know of a certainty . . . as if you have not been long in her acquaintance."

"I have not," Margaret confessed. "My father, Squire Tutweiler, only recently inherited a second estate in Airy Hill. It has been but a sennight past that we took up residence. However, from the moment her ladyship heard of our new situation, she has offered me her hospitality most generously. She has even . . . oh, dear," she hesitated, thinking better of her comment, dropping her gaze as she delicately drew in her lower lip.

"She has what, Miss Tutweiler?" Dex asked, sensitive to her discomposure. Quickly he shoved his snifter back upon the mantel so that he might step closer to her. The glass brushed one of Tia's elaborate valentines, sending it fluttering to the floor. Dex ignored it, instead reaching out to touch lightly beneath Miss Tutweiler's fingertips.

Blushing prettily, Margaret's eyes flew to his. "I-I feel that I would be speaking out of turn, sir," she replied softly.

"Never," Dex declared. "Besides, you may say anything you like to me. Now what were you going to say?"

Margaret's color deepened, touching upon even the bits of flesh Dex could see between the loops of her Norwich shawl. He drew in a breath and stepped slightly closer. Margaret grew even rosier.

"I was going to say that it seems her ladyship has even undertaken to . . . to f-find me a . . . a suitable *parti*," she told him in a gush of release. "I am persuaded that tonight's occasion is to be the launching of that endeavor."

"A husband? Indeed," Dex responded, his dark eyes flaring with an odd gleam. "And who is the fortunate man

Lady Horatia has in mind?" he asked, slipping his fingertips up to touch against her gloved palms.

"Her c-cousin!" Margaret gasped, reflexively tightening
her fingers around his.

Dex quite suddenly laughed out loud.

"Robert?" he questioned when his laughter had dis-
solved into chuckles.

"The very one!"

"My dear Miss Tutweiler," he said comfortingly, rubbing his thumb back and forth across her knuckles, "I
shouldn't worry if I were you. I very much fear for Lady
Horatia's intention that Robert has a mind, and prospects,
of his own." Dex then grew more sober. "I would know,
however," he said softly, ". . . does this intelligence blue-
devil you?"

"Goodness, no!" Margaret replied with alacrity, releasing his hand to clutch her shawl even more snugly about
her generous curves.

"Then you have formed no *tendre* for him as yet? The
idea of a match with him does not appeal?"

"Not in the least!" Margaret vowed, and then she red-
dened all over again, suddenly aware that she had allowed
her inflection to elevate beyond proper bounds. "That
is . . . I . . . I am sensible, of course, of the great honor that
her ladyship has bestowed upon me, and do concur with
her that the viscount is a well-favored man, but . . . but,
Mr. Clark, he is a viscount!"

"Most would consider such a match quite a feather in a
woman's cap," Dex commented, the casualness in his voice
belying the intensity with which he regarded her.

"Yet I cannot conceive of it," Margaret responded, shaking her head quite firmly. "I have no wish to move in the
circles of the *haut ton,* sir. Why, if I should ever have to

give a party in which the sole measure of my husband's
success in Society for the rest of his life depended upon
my making no mistakes in precedence as I arranged our
guests for the parade into dinner, I should die . . . I should
simply die!"

"Surely it is not so desperate as that," Dex chuckled and
soothed all at the same time.

"It is, I assure you!" Margaret said. "Why, I should soon
be like—" and here she cast her gaze about the inglenook—
"like that valentine!" she pointed out, stooping to pick up
the forgotten object from the flagstone floor.

"Like this you say?" Dex said gently, taking the card
from her and replacing it upon the mantel. "Oh, yes, I quite
agree," he murmured, still regarding the valentine's unique
delicacy. "Of a certainty, you are fragile, just as it is . . .
and pink . . . and quite exquisitely lovely . . ."

"Oh!" Margaret gasped, again blushing rosily.

". . . But also a good deal more powerful than you
think," Dex added, turning to once again face her.

"Powerful?" she repeated, blinking appealingly.
"Against the wishes of a viscount? . . . even more, against
the daughter of an earl?"

"Just so," Dex replied, leaning against the mantel as he
crossed his arms over his well-muscled chest. "No one can
force another into marriage, Miss Tutweiler," he informed
her calmly. "If you do not wish to wed Bainbridge, simply
say no."

"No?"

"No."

"Oh," murmured Miss Tutweiler.

* * *

As Dex and Margaret fell into comfortable conversation

before the fire, and Tia was being propelled in a most improper fashion along a wide corridor that had once led to the nuns' dining hall, two figures drew near to Whinstone Abbey and the town of Whitby just beyond, having set out earlier in the morning along the clifftop footpath leading up from Robin Hood's Bay, a smugglers' haven cut into the coastline about six miles to the south.

The two had been wary in their passing, their eyes constantly shifting in their watchfulness as they had hunched into the collars of their many-caped drab coats against the steady sea wind. For the most part they had traveled the path in silence; yet occasionally, one or the other had ventured a short phrase when they were certain it could not be overheard by the inhabitants of the several scattered sandstone farmsteads appearing along the route, each glowing rusty-orange against the dark humus of the moors in the afternoon sun.

"We'll be late again," the one called Beale had just finished muttering into the face of a bone-chilling gust, his narrowed gaze sliding to a pair of cormorants hanging their drying wings out on one of the rock outcroppings far below at the sea's edge. "Best pick up our step."

"Aye," his companion, Wilson, returned, mustering a faster stride as the path curved around a skirting of small thorn trees shying away from the relentless wind. His coat flapped in response to his quickened pace, snagging on one of the landward branches as those seaside had been eaten off even as they had budded by the unending etch of salt and sand. Giving a quick glance about him, he pulled it free and hurried to catch up to Beale. "Will they go through with it, do you think?" he asked when he had again gained his partner's side.

"Unless someone stops them," Beale replied, pursing

his features even more as he breasted a low hill and the towers of the Abbey came into sight.

Burrowing even more deeply into his collar, Wilson hesitated, then responded, "The Enforcer."

Beale momentarily slid his slitted gaze in his companion's direction. "Aye," he responded in a low rumble before fastening his gaze upon the Abbey's tall towers once again.

The two moved even more quickly now, hastening into the frosty shadows of the oak trees lining the avenue leading up to the ancient cloister's thick, crossbarred entry; a broad road that began where the footpath divided, the one branch going to serve the Abbey and the other continuing on to cover the remaining distance across the moorland before it tumbled over the edge of the Esk estuary in a set of one hundred ninety-nine Yorkshire sandstone steps called the Church Stairs, then swept on down the cliff face into the midst of the huddled dwellings of the town. It was this latter path that Beale and Wilson took after one last furtive glance up at the Abbey. Settling their beaver brims much lower on their foreheads to make themselves as inconspicuous as possible, they passed out of the Abbey's shadow and hurried on.

Neither of them spoke again. Instead, doggedly, they pushed on across the remainder of the sparse, sea-scoured moor until at last the precipice overlooking Whitby appeared just to the front of them, and, after a few more steps, they were standing upon the edge of it. They paused then, momentarily scanning the jumbled stack of rippled pantiled roofs that hugged the harbor below, concentrating on the bustling activity taking place in the town, alert for the slightest motion that might be unusual.

There was nothing. Nodding their agreement that all appeared to be safe, they quickly began to descend the stairs which carried them in a wide arc down the cliffside to deposit them, panting and windblown, into Church Street near the Market Tollbooth.

It was market day. The street teemed with traffic, yet again nothing seemed out of the ordinary to the two men. Once more content that they had been unobserved, they next slipped inconspicuously into the ebb and flow of the shoppers and began to make their way toward a modest, well-groomed brick house fronting on the harbor, a sturdy dwelling whose pantiles, warm and welcoming under a soft glaze, undulant atop the brick facade in attractive, terra cotta waves, had once been brought into Whitby, along with the brick used in its construction, as ballast on one of the Hanseatic League's tall-masted merchant ships.

The house was ancient. Having been built by one of the town's original shipbuilders on the long, narrow burgage plot granted to him by an equally ancient Walmsley earl, it stood shoulder to shoulder with the others of its kind in a long row down the street, each of the neatly kept houses heading a plot that stretched out behind like an index finger, then rose more than a hundred yards up the side of the rugged cliff.

It was against those cliffs at the back of the burgage plots, in a rude collection of houses stacked one atop the other as if at any moment the whole construction might collapse, of impossibly narrow stairs branching into even narrower alleys with logic-defying twists and turns, of tunnels between dwellings that leaned against one another, closing each other off from the sunlight, shunning the welcoming skies, that the poorest residents of Whitby lived. It was here, too, that Beale and Wilson headed, slipping, after a single backward glance, into the side yard of the neat brick dwelling, then back toward the first in a series

of writhing stone steps disappearing into the worst of the
ghauts. Without pausing, they quickened their pace, beginning to climb; turning first to the left, then to the right,
then to the left again before they at last disappeared into
the black maw of a tunnel that took them deep into the cliff
face.

They were almost running now, but it would make no
difference, of course. They had already missed a good portion of the meeting of the Black Mask Society.

"Devil a bit, Wilson," Beale panted as a low, rough-
planked door finally separated itself out of the dank gloom
not too far in the distance. "Get on with it, man! God save
us if we are late and the Enforcer has chosen to be in attendance!"

Four

The library of Whinstone Abbey had once been its Lady Chapel, that is, one which had been dedicated at its completion to the Virgin Mary. Over the years since the Dissolution, the Earls of Walmsley had changed it little; niches still held their original gold-enhanced statuary, and each lancet window still supported the finely wrought intricacy of its original stone tracery. Only the highly polished oak shelving for each earl's addition to the store of books lining the wall on either side of the fireplace was new, if by 'new' it is understood that the construction went back several centuries.

At one end of the room, a large table stood before two eighteenth century Mortlake tapestries which had been commissioned by an earlier earl to help warm the room by buffering it from the two large expanses of cold stone standing between the wall's three pediments. A fireplace stood opposite the tapestries, modernized in the previous century from its original massive stone simplicity to a more delicate gilded Italianate; above, a large oval mirror hung in ornate splendor, reflecting the rich, muted colors of the tapestries and adding an elegance to the wall. Before the fire, two gilded chairs turned toward one another in conversation, almost excluding the round table and oil lamp that stood between them. It was toward these chairs that Robert directed Tia after the two of them had entered and he had closed the library door quite solidly behind them.

"Tia, this has got to stop," Robert stated before she had even come to a halt before the fire.

"What, Valentine's Day?" she laughed, looking back at him over her shoulder while holding out her hands to warm them over the welcoming flames. "Never say so!"

"No, not Valentine's Day," Robert said, emphasizing each word, "and you know exactly what I mean."

"Ah, my ball then. Have you at last tired of being dragged home for it each year? It does not signify in the least, you know. I shall not stop my celebrations even for you, Robert, *and* I shall still expect you to come." Her features softened then. "I think it is all that is wonderful. Have you seen the valentines that have arrived for me so far?"

"You are trying to change the subject," Robert growled.

"Not at all," Tia blithely replied. "I am merely making sure I provide you with ample opportunity to present me with your offering this year."

Robert broke into a soft chuckle. "You are quite incorrigible, you know," he told her, taking a small parcel from his vest pocket. "Very well, here you are," he said, extending it toward her. "Happy Valentine's Day, Tia."

Tia's face glowed with pleasure as she accepted the parcel into her hands. As Robert watched, golden firelight bronzed her cheeks, shading them to a delicate peach while forming flickering, impish sprites deep within her hazel eyes. She smiled her joy up into his own expectant grin, then began to break the package's seal. Another curl slipped from its casual binding as she did so. Spontaneously, Robert reached out and took it between his fingers just as he had always done since before either of them could remember. This time, however, he savored its soft silkiness for just a moment before gently securing it behind her ear.

"I cannot conceive of what you might have brought me," Tia said, glancing excitedly up at him, her voice softly animated. "It is too small for a card."

"You shall soon find out," Robert murmured, moving a bit closer so that he might share in her pleasure. Relaxing, he leaned his shoulder against the gilded mantel.

"It is quite soft," Tia informed him as she slipped the outer wrapping aside. "Oh! It is of velvet!" she noted, looking up at him with a huge, radiant gaze. "Robert, what have you brought me?"

"Open it, widgeon," Robert laughed. "Look and see."

Tia immediately did so. "Oh!" she cried. Instantly her eyes puddled as she stared at the two matching, delicate diamond and ruby teardrop earrings nestling in the palm of her hand. "Oh, Robert, how beautiful they are! Oh, goodness, I am quite put out of countenance!"

"Never say that I have actually managed it at last," Robert commented wryly.

"Varlet!" Tia laughed, putting a handkerchief to the corners of her tear-spangled eyes. "Oh, Robert, thank you . . . for these . . . for the flowers . . . for everything!" she cried as once again she exuberantly threw herself into his arms. "You are the best of cousins," she added, once more nestling her chin in the notch of his neck, ". . . the very best of friends."

Robert did not respond as he again drew her slim length tightly against his own. Yet above her curls, his eyes slid slowly closed. Tenderly, as Tia leaned against him, pressing into his warmth, his hand rose to cup her head. With the subtlest of motions he turned it, bringing the smooth roundness of her cheek in contact with the exposed flesh of his neck. For only a moment, he held her thus, relishing the feel of her feminine softness before lowering his own cheek to brush briefly against the soft, warm curve of her ear. Then, ever so slowly, and with great savor, he inhaled, drawing in her essence, mingling himself with her.

"I am gratified to hear you say that," he told her, setting her back from him a bit. "Remember it, please, as I am about to cut up stiff with you."

Tia sighed through lips twisted with chagrin. "Back to that, are we?" she responded with a playful pout before stepping fully away to pick at a fleck of gilding protruding from the back of one of the chairs. "I thought that I had managed to divert you this time."

"Well, you have not," Robert replied awfully. "Tia, I mean it this time. It really has to stop. I must insist that you cease trying to play your little match-making games with my life. I know you mean well, but as I have told you repeatedly, I prefer to choose my own bride."

"But you do not, Robert," Tia insisted. "That is the whole point."

"Therefore, you, of course, feel compelled to assist me."

"That I deny!" Tia stated emphatically. "It is not a compulsion. It is rather a . . . a pleasurable duty, to my mind."

"Which you seem to think you can perform better than I," Robert challenged, again leaning his shoulder against the mantel as he crossed his arms before his broad chest.

"I do know you better than anyone else, Robert," Tia justified, straightening her spine. "Yes, I believe I know exactly the sort of woman who would suit you."

"Indeed," Robert replied, his lips thinning beneath an increasingly deep frown. "A sort like Miss Megwith, I suppose?"

"Miss Megwith was all that is proper, Robert," Tia defended, crossing her arms beneath her breasts as well. "She would have brought credit to you as your viscountess. Yet in spite of her obvious interest, you did not dance with her once during last year's ball."

"Oh?" Robert responded, one brow cocking in question. "Was she in attendance?"

"What sort of question is that?" Tia scolded, tipping her head with her glare. "You know very well she was!"

"Hmm, perhaps you are right," Robert said thoughtfully, reaching up to rub his chin. "She might have been present at that. Hard to say, though . . . deucedly difficult to find Miss Megwith under all that white lead."

"Robert . . ."

". . . and mouse fur."

"Robert . . ."

". . . always put me in mind of a rather large badger," Robert reminisced.

"Robert!"

"So this is a woman you think appeals?"

"Oh, very well," Tia groused. "I can be honest about this, Robert," she conceded. "Perhaps Miss Megwith was a mistake on my part . . . but what of Miss Dresher? Now there was an Incomparable . . . lovely in all ways. Surely you cannot deny it?"

"No, I must admit that I cannot," Robert agreed. "Impeccable breeding, as I recall . . . a delightful form . . . quite a lovely face."

"And yet you did not exchange five words with her during last Season's house party," Tia complained.

"Because four words proved to be all that she knew," Robert countered.

"Robert, really!"

"Each of which was continually rendered in that damnable lisp."

Tia paused in her argument to pace the floor.

"Miss Parkenham, then," she suddenly cried out. "I defy you to find fault with her."

"Egad, cousin, how can I?" Robert chuckled in reply. "I have always considered creaking corsets, false teeth, and a mouth full of wax to be all the crack. Everyone knows it."

"She has a good heart," Tia grumped.

"Unfortunately, a man has to wade through a great deal of flesh before he can find it."

"Robert, that is an unkind thing to say," Tia chided.

"Yes, it is," he responded softly. "Unforgivably so. Have I convinced you yet that you do not know as much about me as you think?"

Tia clasped her hands before her and took the few steps that again brought her close to the fire. When she had warmed herself, she turned to smile impishly up at her cousin.

"No." She grinned. And then she sighed. "Oh, Robert, what I know is that you need someone . . . someone who shall bring credit to your title, who shall give you children and be your companion so that you shan't be lonely as the years go by."

"It does sound rather nice," Robert responded, nodding on a soft sigh, bending slightly toward her, his gaze intent upon her golden, fire-flecked eyes.

"Someone who shall make you laugh once in a while."

"An agreeable trait," he concurred, his gaze drifting down to rest upon her full lower lip.

"Someone you can love."

"Mmm . . . yes," Robert breathed.

"Perhaps I did err just the tiniest bit before," Tia stated on a soft breath which moistened the end of her cousin's nose.

"You did," he murmured, fascinated by her upper lip's delicate bow.

"I admit it, cousin. And I also state that you may rely upon me now," she told him.

"Mmm?" he replied, intrigued by the way the down covering her cheek glowed in the firelight.

"I shall not do so again. You can, after all, see now that I do know what you need, can you not?" she whispered, her eyes glimmering up into his with tiny slivers of excitement, of fire. "That now I really do understand?"

"Mmm," he murmured, mesmerized by the new light rising in her eyes, his voice rough and deep.

"Good. Because now I am certain exactly who it should be," Tia told him, nodding firmly, her gaze now filled with purpose, her body now very close to his.

Robert blinked. "What . . . ? What did you just say?"

"I have decided upon your perfect mate, Robert," Tia replied, tipping her head to the side in remonstrance. "Do pay attention, if you please."

Robert rolled his shoulder away from the mantel. "Tia . . ."

"It can be none other than Miss Tutweiler," Tia stated, smiling up at him broadly.

Robert's spine grew half again in length. "Hah! I thought so. Tia . . . ," he reprised in a low and menacing growl.

"Now, Robert, just think about it for a moment," Tia argued, holding both hands up to ward off his encroaching chest. "Miss Tutweiler is all that is lovely, well-mannered . . ."

"No, Tia, absolutely not!"

"She is sweet and kind . . . ," she continued, shoving slightly against Robert's cutaway until the backs of her knees bumped up against one gilded chair.

". . . Tia, so help me . . ."

Tia's index finger shot up into the air. "She wears no artifice of any kind!"

"Tia, for the love of . . . !" Robert bellowed in exasperation. "Have you heard nothing that I have said?"

"Well, of course I have!" Tia replied with unladylike volume. And then she released her vexation on a sigh. "Oh, Robert, I only wish to see you happy," she told him softly. "You are more than my cousin, you know."

Robert's gaze sharpened.

"Am I?" he questioned, his gaze searching hers.

"Of course you are," Tia replied, patting his Mailcoach. "You are my oldest and dearest friend."

The viscount released his captured breath.

"As you are mine," he acknowledged. "Yet that changes nothing, Tia. I still must insist that you cease continually foisting women upon me. You still do not understand what I am looking for."

"What then?" Tia quickly countered. "What sort of woman are you looking for if not the ones I have found for you?"

Robert's woodland eyes took on a mischievous gleam. "One just like you, of course," he answered, tapping a finger upon the bridge of her narrow nose.

Tia burst into laughter.

"Indeed!" she chuckled, her eyes dancing with merriment. "I beg to differ with you, sir. I know better. I am only too aware that for three and twenty years, you have been thanking all the powers that be that there are no others like me."

"Happy evidence," Robert replied loftily, capturing her hand to tuck it into the crook of his arm, "that the Almighty does indeed answer our prayers."

"Varlet," Tia giggled, poking him in the stomach.

" 'Servant, ma'am," Robert responded with a polite bow.

Laughter was their escort as, arm in arm, the two walked back to join the others.

"It was merely a slight miscalculation, I tell you," Lion insisted tersely, the light from the meeting room's single candle glistening against the stubble peppering his sweat-beaded lips.

"You said you knew all about explosives!" Fox cried, throwing up his one functional hand.

"And so I do!" Lion roared in self-defense. "During our little tiff with the colonies, was I not ordnance officer under Burgoyne?"

"So you keep informing us *ad nauseam*," Fox responded, rising to begin a painfully halting pace. "Telling, is it not, that Burgoyne was forced to surrender?"

"Zounds, sir!" Lion cried, levering himself to his feet with a leather-padded crutch. "Will you blame that on me?"

"Gentlemen, gentlemen . . . ," the Leader interrupted wearily, scratching at his ear.

"Well, why must Digby keep rowing back and forth over the same pond?" Lion complained, fitting the device under his arm. "It's coming it a bit too brown, don't you know. I did, after all, accomplish the task. I *did* destroy the mine office."

"Who can tell?" Fox shouted. "As a result of your expertise, the building's entire remains sank into the ground!"

"Did I, or did I not, accomplish the plan?" Lion bellowed, attempting to maneuver closer and in so doing, sending his chair crashing to the floor.

"You blew up everything!" Fox shouted in the direction of Lion's shadowed mass.

"Gentlemen, do calm yourselves," the Leader again interjected.

At his remonstrance, Lion subsided, though his nose elevated just the slightest bit. "Very well," he replied in a hurt voice, motioning to Wolf to right his chair before once again lowering himself into it. "But I *did* destroy the office."

"There certainly can be no denying it," the Leader agreed. "Now, Fox, I really must ask you to cry peace and sit down. We have business to discuss this afternoon."

Still glowering ferociously, Fox paced for only a moment more, then deigned to comply.

"Well, gentlemen," quavered Raptor from the Leader's side when all had quieted again. "I assume that the purpose of this month's meeting is to decide upon our next exercise. Have you something in mind, Leader? What shall we all have the opportunity of making a mull of this time?"

"I do not account sarcasm to be especially helpful at this particular time, Raptor," the Leader chided softly, burrowing a scrabbling finger beneath his *chapeau-bras*.

"How is it to be avoided," the wrinkled voice insisted, "as the whole purpose of our last endeavor was to restore our countrymen's esteem of us and we have hardly done that? . . . nay, if anything, we have sunk even further. Why, not two days ago near Cholmley's Tollbooth I heard some mutton-head call us the Cracked Flasks!"

"Yet we must try, try again, Raptor," the Leader responded with great cheer. "Sooner or later, we shall succeed . . . sooner, I am persuaded," he added in a conspiratorial voice and with eyes that twinkled mischievously, "especially as I now have a devilishly brilliant maneuver in mind."

"You do?" Falcon breathed above the following murmur of softly gabbling voices, intently massaging a row of bruises riding one prominent rib. "Indeed!"

"Lud, what next?" Wolf murmured to no one in particular from farther around the table.

Lion leaned heavily toward Fox. *Sotto voce* he asserted, "I *did* blow up the mine office. You cannot deny it, Digby."

"What have you in mind?" Raptor asked on behalf of the assembly.

Before the Leader could answer, however, the door suddenly opened, and two barely discernible shapes moved inside. All twenty eyeholes turned immediately in the newcomers' direction. The Leader blinked.

"Ah, excellent!" he soon said, finally recognizing the men during a bandaged finger's relief-giving run around the rim of his mouth. "Come in, Beale . . . Wilson . . . ," he invited, rising to gesture toward two vacant chairs reposing just across the table from him. "Do sit down. You are just in time."

"And not one soul was killed," Lion insisted, gushing warm air against Fox's hood with a firm nod.

Fox's gaze rose heavenward within the circles of his eyeholes. "Lud!" he sighed.

"Black Masks," the Leader continued, "you will of course recognize our two informers, Beale and Wilson, who have worked so tirelessly on our behalf within the

Freedom Brigade . . . and at great peril to themselves, I might hasten to add."

Appreciative murmurs of "Here, here!" and "Well done!" rumbled about the small room.

"I was just about to reveal our plan to the Society, gentlemen," the Leader continued, turning his attention toward the two when the accolades had faded. "Before I do, however, I would have your report."

"Of course," Beale stated, clasping his hands above the table. "Wilson and I just come from London, milord. Our contacts within the larger Radical Societies confirmed what the Home Secretary said. He is indeed coming."

"Excellent!" the Leader cried, scratching his chin.

"Who is coming?" Raptor quavered.

"In a moment, Raptor," the Leader replied. "Was Pitt able to gain an audience with the king?" he next inquired of the two informers.

Beale shook his head. "The king has no liking for Addison, you comprehend," he told the Leader, "but His Majesty still be put out about Pitt's support for Catholic Emancipation."

At that bit of news, the Leader drummed his fingers upon the tabletop. Twenty eyeholes slewed back in his direction.

"Then we cannot count on support from that quarter," he finally assessed, staring into the darkness. Suddenly he collected himself, nodding as he pursed his lips. "Well, so be it," he pronounced, flattening his palms. "It simply means that we are on our own."

"On our own in what?" Raptor queried impatiently, tugging upon the Leader's heavy wool cloak.

Beneath his hood, the Leader wiggled his nose against its covering Cheviot and smiled.

"In the undertaking of the most monumental, most audacious scheme we have ever perpetrated against the Radicals," he told them in a taut, excited voice. "Gentlemen, this is the opportunity we have been waiting for. When we have accomplished this deed, we shall not only have routed the dastardly Freedom Brigade in our own county, but I am persuaded that Radical Societies everywhere shall be so demoralized that I daresay we shall have put a period to every one existing in England!"

"Mercy from above!" Wolf gasped, wafting one black-gloved palm in front of his mouth hole while the other aimlessly flourished a trembling handkerchief of lavender silk shot with golden thread. "Whatever can you be thinking? Tell us quickly, Leader, or I shall fly over the boughs!"

"Yes," harrumphed Lion beneath beetled brows. "I say, Walmsley, what's toward this time?"

"A kidnapping, my fellow Black Masks," the Leader responded, tenting his fingers in front of his nose.

"Odso!" Fox commented over several gasps. "A kidnapping. Whom are we to snaffle?"

The Leader suddenly rubbed a finger violently over his cheek. When he was at ease again, he slowly looked around the circle of his compatriots, nodding with his understanding of their foibles after a lifetime of acquaintance, content that this time he had planned their next endeavor with a care that had been lacking in the past, certain that this time his compatriots would not make ducks and drakes of his brilliantly conceived plan.

"Gentlemen," he finally responded, "it is my intention for the Black Masks to capture Mr. Thomas Paine."

There followed a heart-pounding pause that slowly settled and thickened like dust over the occupants of the room.

"Never say so!" Wolf finally breathed, raising a fluttering hand.

Five

"Thomas Paine . . . !" Raptor warbled softly, slowly allowing his ancient shoulders to sag.

"Are you daft, sir!" Lion bellowed, again sending his chair crashing to the floor.

"Not a bit of it," the Leader declared. "Think about it, gentlemen. What could be a more perfect way of undermining the Radicals in our beloved England? Why, the man is practically their patron saint!"

"But how . . . ?" Falcon broke in. "The gentleman ain't even in the country, is he?"

"No," the Leader replied with a smile, "but . . . Beale, you have been the one responsible for gathering the intelligence in this matter. Perhaps you would care to explain."

"Aye, milord," the informant responded, rising to his feet. "Most of you know, I believe, that although Mr. Paine were born an Englishman, he became a naturalized American during the time of the colonies' rebellion against us."

Murmurs of "Yes, yes . . . totty-headed, if you ask me," and "Damn fool!" ricocheted around the room.

"Most likely you also know, then, that not long after this occurrence Mr. Paine invented a new sort of bridge . . . ," Beale continued, "an iron one designed to span particularly dangerous rivers. The bridge had no piers which had to be fixed in place in the middle of the torrent, you might collect, but instead sported a single arch supported on each shore. You could dismantle it, too, milords, then cart the thing off and reassemble it wherever it was needed."

"I remember the model he built about ten years ago," Fox interrupted.

"Odso . . . set it up in Paddington Green, did he not?" Lion reminisced. "At Lisson Grove. Charged a shilling a head to view it as I recall. Scandalous amount, I vow."

"The model were his, milord," Beale responded. "But before that, Mr. Paine spent years, both here and in France, trying to find someone who would give him the money to manufacture the full-sized span. Edmund Burke were his companion during that time. He were the one introduced Mr. Paine to the Walker Brothers of Rotherham, who eventually agreed to cast the iron, and to an American merchant living in London, Mr. Peter Whiteside, who gave him financing. It were this that consumed him until the fall of the Bastille."

"And then?" Falcon queried.

"Then he were captured, milords," Beale answered levelly.

"Captured?" Fox parroted.

"By the revolution, sir. By its ideals . . . by his Frog comrades' fervor. Mr. Paine completely lost interest in his bridge. Why, he were so taken by his new cause, milords, that his own arrangements for the bridge's construction took a tumble. The man didn't even seek reparations either when, years later, another man saw his design, stole his patent, and built a bigger version of the bridge than even Mr. Paine had dreamed over the River Weir near Sunderland. No, milords, Mr. Paine's new interest were fixed. He spent the next three years traveling constantly back and forth between our country and France, making friends with the revolutionaries across the Channel, latching onto their ideals, then returning to England to stir up a hornet's nest of our own bastards, teaching them how to form the Radical Societies. In truth, milords, he were the world's greatest missionary for revolution."

"Wrote that rubbish, *The Rights of Man,* during those years, did he not?" Lion growled, righting, then sitting down on his battered chair again.

"That be correct, milord," Beale responded. "Prime Minister Pitt tried to suppress it, but copies of the book were easily smuggled into England and reprinted on unlicensed presses. Mr. Pitt had no choice but to put Mr. Paine on trial after that. After all, the man were advocating treason."

"La, Mr. Beale," Wolf commented, crossing his legs until each of the sixteen lavender bows at his knees pressed untidily against one another, "little good it did. Mr. Paine was safe in France at the time he was convicted and declared an outlaw."

"True," the Leader responded, grinding a knuckle into the concavity beneath his cheek. "However, at least he was not here. And his conviction did mean that he could never return to this country to preach his seditious flummery again on penalty of death. It put a rather nice period to his scurrilous endeavors, do you not agree?"

"I never heard what happened to him after that," Falcon commented.

"Excellent," the Leader responded, "because now the story becomes much more relevant to us. Beale, do continue, if you please."

"Very well, sir. When Mr. Paine found out about his conviction here in England, he went for help to the friends he had made among the members of the French Revolutionary Convention. With their aid, he took up residence in France."

"He did not return to America?" Fox questioned.

"No, milord. England were blockading the French sea lanes at the time, you collect, but my thought is that more were involved in Mr. Paine's wish to stay in France."

"Do continue, sir," Falcon urged.

"My guess is that Mr. Paine were addicted, sir."

"Addicted?"

"Aye, milord. To the excitement going on all about him," Beale answered. "I believe that the bastard couldn't stand the thought of being out of the thick of things. Course he were broke, too, by that time as the plans for his bridge had . . . forgive the pun . . . all but collapsed. So his friends got French citizenship for him and a seat in their Convention, and this gave him rank, milords, and an amount to live on, and a ringside seat to what were happening in the cradle of the revolution . . . more'n enough reason for him to remain."

"What happened next?" Lion asked, caught up in the tale, cupping the folds beneath his chin within the palm of his hand.

"The government of France got overthrowed again, milord," Beale responded. "Mr. Paine's friends fell to the blade, and he were arrested."

"Egad!" Fox exclaimed from beside him. "Arrested? Whyever would they do that?"

"Because he were considered by the new government to still be an Englishman, milord," Beale told him. "It were not but a year later that he were released, and then only because the American secretary of state, and France's ally, Mr. James Monroe, demanded it on the basis that Mr. Paine were neither English nor French, but in reality an American."

Nearby, Falcon began to chuckle softly. "The veriest tug-of-war!" he laughed, shaking his head. "What happened then?"

"He were sick, milord, and deep in Dun territory. Mr. Monroe nursed Mr. Paine back to health, then saw that he got back his seat in the Frog Convention. After Mr. Monroe left France, Mr. Paine took up residence with a Monsieur Nicolas de Bonneville, where he lived off that gentleman's kindness until last October's Peace of Amiens between our two countries made it safe for him to leave France. My sources tell me he wants to live out the remainder of his life on the small farm the colonials provided for him near New Rochelle."

"Ah, I believe that I am beginning to understand," murmured Fox, relaxing back into his chair. "One, since there is no longer an English naval blockade to stop him, two, Mr. Paine is planning to leave France."

"You have the right of it, milord," Beale affirmed.

"And three . . . soon, I'd wager," Raptor added in a tremulous vibrato.

"Aye, sir," Wilson could not help but excitedly add.

"But how does that aid our cause?" Fox asked.

Suddenly his countenance abruptly altered as comprehension came to him. "By Jove, that's it, is it not?" he finally breathed, the shape of his eyes slowly conforming to his eyeholes as his gaze slid toward the Leader. "The addlepate is coming here, ain't he? Devil take it, the deuced fool is not going directly to America at all. He is going to try to sneak back into England!"

"Ho, Digby, you have the right of it!" the Leader exclaimed with a wide grin that set him to scratching his mouth hole again.

"But why?" Lion reiterated in befuddlement.

"Why?" Fox exclaimed, striking the other's bruised back. "The bridge, of course!"

"Huzza thrice!" cried the Leader, pounding in turn upon one of Fox's assorted abrasions. "He sails in four days, gentlemen," he told them with a hush of excitement in his voice. "I have it directly from Portland, our Home Secretary, that Mr. Paine cannot tolerate the thought of returning to his adopted country without setting his old eyes one last time upon his iron bridge."

"So he really will be coming!" Wolf gasped, placing a gloved palm to his cheek.

"To Whitby?" Lion queried.

"To Sunderland," the Leader corrected enthusiastically, ". . . where his bridge is. Just north up the coast from our own fair town, and past which snug harbor he has no choice but to sail if he is to get to Sunderland. And we, fellow members of the Black Mask Society, are going to take advantage of the opportunity he is flaunting in our faces. We, my brothers, are going to kidnap the traitorous bounder."

"Heaven hide our eyes!" Wolf exclaimed, biting into his lower lip.

"Lud, Leader," Fox added as the room again swelled with murmurs, "kidnap him? Why is that necessary? He is still a convicted traitor, is he not? Why do we not just have him arrested by the magistrate?"

"But . . . but then he would be hanged!" Wolf cried, brandishing his lavender handkerchief beneath the tip of his nose.

"Surely we do not wish to see any real harm come to

Mr. Paine, Leader . . . do we?" agreed Falcon, his eyes growing round.

"Of course not, gentlemen," the Leader affirmed. "That is not our aim. Besides, what would be the advantage to us if Mr. Paine should be put to death for his crimes? He would only become a martyr, don't you know. No, gentlemen, this way he becomes a tool for us to use. With Mr. Paine in our possession, we can use threats against him to force the Radical Societies to disband."

"But they would only be threats, would they not?" Falcon again asserted. "He would not actually suffer at our hands?"

"Heaven forfend," soothed the Leader. "You are sensible, I am sure, Falcon, that I take great pride in the fact that not once has our Society ever actually drawn blood. Why, such abhorrent behavior must be unthinkable! However, our dear king needs us, gentlemen. Therefore, let us commence with a discussion of how we are to do the deed. I propose that we hire one of our own sturdy Whitby colliers to sail out at Mr. Paine's approach, waylay his ship and take the man prisoner, then secrete him here in the ghauts until our negotiations with the Radicals convince them to cease their advocacy of the overthrow of our most time honored traditions. Do you agree?"

"Well, yes . . . I suppose," Falcon spoke into the hesitation. "Yet earlier in the meeting, Leader, Mr. Beale reported that Mr. Pitt was not able to gain an audience with the king."

"That be correct, milord," Beale affirmed with a brisk nod.

"Obviously, then, His Majesty is not aware of our plan," Fox concluded.

"True," the Leader responded with a small sigh. "That I cannot deny."

"Then, lud, Walmsley, under the circumstances, do you think it wise to proceed?"

"Proceed with what, gentlemen?" hissed a soft, susurrant voice from the doorway before the Leader could respond.

Instantly every eyehole swiveled toward the sound.

"Well?" the newcomer asked again in a voice that buffeted each ear like the passing of the wind, his gaze as he slowly directed it around the circle a searing instrument that he wielded expertly, cauterizing each tender bud of courage as it swelled.

His only answer was the whispered antiphonal sigh of his own swirling black silk cloak as it drew into a restless stillness over the polished darkness of his Hessians.

And then Wolf shakily drew his lavender handkerchief up to dab one corner at the moisture beading just below his left eye. "Sweet sugar sticks!" he moaned almost to himself. "The fat is in the fire now, my lovelies. The Enforcer has arrived."

Tia lay beside Margaret beneath the high chintz canopy above her bed watching a late afternoon shadow creep inexorably across the items on her rosewood dressing table like a polishing cloth grey with use . . . one, she thought with a half smile, being slowly dragged by a ghost, perhaps, over the silver-backed brushes, mirror, and comb that were spread over the richly inlaid surface in disarray, rendering them bright and sparkling in the wan sunshine at the chore's end.

Her smile widening with contentment, she then tugged

her attention back onto the patterned chintz of the canopy above her, letting her gaze slide down just after to idly peruse the length of her body. It was nice enough, she assessed, noting the feminine curves beneath her wrapper of soft gold silk, bound about her waist by a matching tie, the whole protecting her thin petticoat from the abuses of her nap; though most, she supposed, would consider her form too thin.

Not that it mattered, of course. She had no need for the bountiful flesh Society deemed necessary to attract a man. Yet, she had to admit, she took a certain pleasure in being admired. And she would be tonight, she thought with an expectant grin, turning her head with a soft rustling to look toward the ball gown awaiting the completion of her toilette next to her garderobe. The gown was all that is lovely . . . a sheer, white Valenciennes lace confection over a pink chemise ordered several months ago during the Little Season from Madame Fouchard, its bodice capped at the bared shoulders by tiny puffed sleeves and bound beneath the breasts by a ribbon of deep ruby red. Drawing in a deep breath of happiness, she stretched long and languidly, leaving her arms draped up over her pillow when she had finished.

The rustling sounded again. In vexation she drew up a hand to pluck at the large white cap holding several dozen curling rags tightly against her head; another of her maid Nancy's noble attempts to inflict a measure of decorum upon her rag-mannered hair. She looked next at Miss Tutweiler lying still and silent beside her, her face turned away toward the opposite wall, her golden curls spread in glorious profusion over her pillow. It isn't fair, Tia thought, even the simplest movement producing an irritating soughing all about her ears. It simply is not fair.

And then she smiled.

"Margaret," she whispered after a brief moment in which she chided herself for her envy. "Margaret, are you awake? Margaret?"

In response, Miss Tutweiler drew in a deep breath. "Yes," she soon whispered back, placing her fists beside her cheeks in a small stretch before turning slightly toward Tia.

"Did you get enough rest?" Tia asked, ever the thoughtful hostess.

"I believe so," Margaret replied with a sweet smile. "Though it was indeed difficult. I fear I am quite over the boughs."

Tia's hazel eyes lit with pleasure. "Hah! I misdoubt there is a need to ask why! So . . . what did you think of him?" she asked with an expectant smile, reaching over to poke Margaret in the shoulder of her blue silk wrapper.

"He seems very nice," Margaret responded dreamily, letting her gaze drift to the window just beyond Tia's dressing table, raising a hand to separate several strands from the rippling blanket of gold covering her shoulders, then entwining them about her fingers.

"Nice?" Tia exclaimed, twisting her head on her pillow with another flurry of rustles so that she might look at her new friend. "You think that he is merely nice?"

"Of a certainty," Margaret sighed with a secretive smile. "Well . . . oh, very well, perhaps he is more than nice."

"Just so!" Tia affirmed, her rags again murmuring as she looked up toward the gathered chintz of her canopy, feeling quite justified in her mild indignation as she crossed her arms beneath her breasts.

"Are you angry, Tia? Oh, do not be!" Margaret cried, reaching over to take Tia's arm. "In truth, Tia," she then confided, her blue eyes dampening most alluringly, "it is my feeling that he is all that is wonderful . . . no, more. He is strong, and kind, and so handsome that when I look upon him I think that I shall simply die!"

Tia's heart began to pound in pleasurable expectation. A smile germinated . . . a blazing one that began to well just at the corner of her lips, the one that had been hovering behind her teeth all day awaiting just such a declaration from her friend since the moment she had introduced her to Robert. Like a bubble, it bulged against her cheeks for only the twentieth part of a moment . . . and then it simply died.

If Tia had not been lying down, she might have stumbled from the surprise of it. Again she stared up into the canopy. What in the world had happened? This was the reaction from Margaret that she had been waiting for, was it not? So where was her joy in the moment?

Again she tried to muster an excited grin. Nothing happened.

Disconcerted, she blinked her eyes. Margaret had just told her she was top over tails for Robert, had she not? Where was the exhilaration she should be feeling at this first indication of her plan's ultimate success . . . more, why was she feeling instead . . . good heavens, there could be no other word for it . . . why was she feeling instead just the tiniest trifle vexed?

"Die, eh?" she finally commented, awash in her most peculiar feelings, thoroughly at sea over the fact that her brows had now drawn into quite the most inexplicably solid straight line.

"Oh, yes," Margaret breathed, clutching the bodice of her wrapper with one small fist, with the other reaching over to take Tia's hand. "And quite the most mannerly of gentlemen. Do you not agree?"

"There can be no question," Tia affirmed, her scowl deepening. "Handsome . . . and mannerly. Of a certainty."

"Yet quite the most outrageous flirt," giggled Margaret, letting go of her bodice to touch her lips before resting the back of her wrist upon her forehead. "Do you know, Tia, when no one was around he quite improperly took my hand!"

Tia's eyes became sudden saucers. Heat prickled at her neck; her rags muttered. One by one, her vertebrae aligned themselves.

"Indeed," she murmured, beginning to drum her fingers against the counterpane.

"Yes, he did," Margaret chuckled, her laughter softening into a radiant smile. "And he quite turned my head with the loveliest of compliments."

"Compliments?" Tia parroted, her mouth now set in a rigid line.

"Oh, yes! He told me that I was fragile . . . and pink . . . and exquisitely lovely . . ."

"Not just 'lovely'?" Tia interjected, her skin now beginning to flush. "He said, 'exquisitely lovely'?"

"That is exactly what he said," Margaret told her with a soft sigh. "Of course it was not at all the thing," she allowed, turning to look at Tia, "but still . . . ," she added, her gaze once again growing distant and dreamy.

"Still, it was most improper," Tia insisted above the pounding in her ears and, of course, the persistent rustle of her curling rags. "And on your first acquaintance, too, Margaret. The man should have his ears boxed. Rest assured, dearest, that I shall rip up at him upon my first opportunity!"

"Oh, must you?" Miss Tutweiler replied, again seizing Tia's arm. "I am sure Mr. Clark meant no offense."

The world suddenly came to a clattering halt.

"Mr. Clark?" Tia cried, sitting bolt upright, flinging several curling rags down the length of her embroidered coverlet to land upon Nancy's cot.

"Why, yes," Margaret replied with huge eyes. "What did you think?"

"Nothing," Tia finally remarked, subsiding back down upon her pillow. "Absolutely nothing. Mr. Clark."

"Oh, yes," Margaret happily sighed. "He is all that is wonderful, is he not?"

Tia thought that she probably should make some sort of response, but, in truth, she did not know quite what to say. As a result, the two soon fell into silence, their hands still clasped together, their eyes staring up into the canopy once again, each consumed by decidedly different thoughts as they awaited the time when Nancy would arrive to bathe them and dress them for dinner.

Deep shadows slowly climbed the bedposts, then began to drift like charcoal smudges across the canopy. Tia watched their relentless advance, her eyelids growing heavy; not quite understanding why she had reacted in such a baffling way, not quite understanding, either, why she could muster so little vexation toward Miss Tutweiler when the lady had just planted a rather large hurdle in the way of the accomplishment of her plan. She should have been using these moments remaining before dinner to deliver a jaw-me-dead to Margaret while she argued Robert's case. Yet she was not. Even more unsettling, she had no wish to. Tia could make no sense out of it. She had vowed to help her cousin find his perfect *parti,* and would continue her efforts tonight, no matter what the hurdles, she knew. But why was she not even now working to dissuade Miss Tutweiler from her obvious *tendre* for the wrong man? Goodness, one would think from this odd reaction that the *tendre* belonged to *her* instead!

"I asked you a question," the Enforcer again asserted through the thick atmosphere that had suddenly congealed in the Black Mask meeting room at his appearance, his soft voice taut and raspy, each word like a footstep over shattered glass. Slowly he started across the room, gliding in ghostly silence, his cape rippling apart as he moved, revealing the thick black belt dividing his black shirt from his matching inexpressibles, and the oily coil of the whip lashed to it with a braided black leather thong.

The Leader swallowed, suddenly becoming numb to every prickly itch. "Well, we . . . that is . . . we . . ."

". . . Were about to proceed with something, I believe," the Enforcer rasped with slow precision, coming to a halt before them. He stood looking down upon the circle of wide-eyed men then, a mirthless smile slightly stretching his lips. "Is it possible, gentlemen, that you planned to do so without me?"

"Why, no! . . ." the Leader vowed. "That is . . ."

The Enforcer tsked softly, crossing his muscular arms before him, beginning to slowly circle the table, his piercing gaze never seeming to disconnect from any of their eyes. "I would have thought, gentlemen, that you would have learned your lesson after the fiasco at the Penfield mine."

"You knew about that?" Lion asked, his dumbfoundment overcoming his fear.

Instantly the Enforcer's burning gaze snapped to Lion's eyeholes.

"As does most of the civilized world!" he lashed out in

tones as brittle as autumn leaves, rounding on the trembling man, impaling him with such a heated glare that before their eyes a good deal of his lordship's corpulence seemed to deflate. "Was it truly your intention, sirs," he ground out in a rustling hiss, straightening to again take them all in as he planted both fists on his hips, "to shift a good measure of public support toward the Radical side? Or were you merely acting with your usual competence?"

"Here now, you young cock!" Raptor sputtered bravely, struggling to unkink his spine. "Who do you think you are? I shall give you a taste of my fives—"

"Save your strength, old man," the Enforcer interrupted in a soft husky tone. "And as for the rest of you," he warned in a deeper growl, "I give you the same warning I gave you before. Whatever you are planning, end it now. Do nothing without my approval and attendance."

"We ain't any of us in leading strings, sir!" insisted Fox, taking heart in Raptor's defiance to find within himself a particle of courage. " 'Pon rep, what makes you think we need a nursemaid to wipe our arses?"

"Perhaps because you keep sitting in shit," the Enforcer quickly fired back. "Here me, gentlemen," he then bit out, casting his fire-flecked gaze about the circle of wan white holes. "I mean what I say. Do nothing until I speak with you again. Go against my orders just once, and the next time one of you might be killed."

"Heaven forfend!" gasped Wolf, his fingertips drifting up to cover his mouth. "Killed?"

"Precisely," the Enforcer responded, staring dreadfully at each of them. "If not by your own efforts or those of the Freedom Brigade, then in all likelihood . . . *by me*. Think it over, Black Masks . . . ," he told them, turning away, before their eyes seeming to melt into indistinctness within the darkness permeating the room.

Seconds later his final word came to them in a whispered rasp from far down the silent passageway.

". . . Carefully . . ."

"Well, what do we do now?" Fox asked when it was obvious that they were alone again, and the tension that had been quite palpably pressing down upon them eased.

"Call the blighter out, by Jove!" exclaimed Lion, slapping a fleshy hand upon the table.

"Now, now, Harry," the Leader responded, scratching at his nose again. "I hardly think that necessary."

"Then what are we to do?" Wolf asked.

"What choice have we?" Falcon answered. "We must give up our plan."

"Oh, I hardly think so," the Leader corrected. "No, gentlemen, I am certain that the Enforcer believes he has the right of it, but he cannot, of course, know how well-conceived my plan is this time nor how imperative it is that we act without delay. It might, after all, be weeks before he returns to us again, yet there is less than a sennight before Paine's ship passes Whitby by."

"Then you suggest . . . ?" Lion rumbled.

"I merely suggest that we do as we have always done," the Leader replied, "and ignore the Enforcer's warning. What say you, sirs?"

"Time does seem to be of the essence," Falcon commented with a nod of his head.

"And we shall never have a better opportunity to strike a blow against the Radicals," Raptor reasoned in a quavering vibrato.

"Or one that has greater significance," added Fox, beginning to nod as well.

"Or one that shall send more perfectly delicious tremors throughout their dastardly Societies," Wolf noted, giggling slightly as he dragged his lavender handkerchief through a circle made of his thumb and index finger.

"Just so," the Leader affirmed.

There was a pause then, while the arguments imbedded themselves in the noblemen's brain cells.

"Lud, gentlemen!" Fox suddenly groaned after a time. "Only think what we are saying. It was one thing to carry out a plan against the Radicals when we had not seen the Enforcer for weeks. It is quite another to fly in the face of his orders when we know he is here in town!"

"And to do so under threat of death!" Wolf added, his own meager courage wavering. And then, leaning toward Fox, he whispered, "That *was* a threat of death, was it not, Digby? Would you not agree?"

"Undeniably, that is one interpretation," Fox murmured back. "Of course, perhaps it was just an exaggeration. Hard to tell with the Enforcer, don't you know. In my opinion—"

"Gentlemen, the topic at hand, if you please . . . ," the Leader admonished them. "Now," he said when he had again gained their full attention, "the simple fact remains that I *am* the Leader of this Society, if you collect, duly elected by you all and installed by proper secret ceremony."

"Here, here," several voices concurred.

"Therefore, while I am sensible of the . . . er, rather strong sentiments offered by the Enforcer," he continued, the assurance in his voice wavering noticeably, "I am persuaded that the decision as to our maneuvers against the Radicals is still mine to make . . . would you not all agree?"

"True, true," and "Undeniably," rattled about the tiny room.

"Well . . . all's right and tight, then," the Leader concluded, scratching furiously behind his ear.

"Nay, he shall kill us," Falcon uttered dejectedly.

On that sobering statement, the room again quieted.

"Yet, it is an extraordinary opportunity," Raptor offered some moments later.

"Which must be undertaken in but four days," added Lion, poking a finger into the air.

"And we have no idea when the Enforcer might return," Fox interjected.

"Not to mention the fact that the man *is* supposed to be on our side," Raptor quavered.

"And I *am* the Leader," the Leader insisted, folding his hands.

"Well, then . . . ?" Wolf asked tentatively, casting a quick glance about him.

"Think all of you that we should . . . ?" Falcon queried timidly.

Once more the room sank into silence.

And then the Leader heaved a shaky sigh. "Devil a bit," he exclaimed softly, digging a finger under his hood where it covered the nape of his neck, then swiping at a trickle of perspiration dangling from one eyehole. "I do believe, gentlemen, that in all of our existence as a Loyalist Society, we have never faced such a crucial test of our will. Are we, or are we not, the king's defenders?"

"We are, by God!" Lion bellowed.

"Then what are our lives compared to that?" the Leader asked quite reasonably. "Gentlemen, our greatest opportunity lies before us. We have no choice but to proceed as planned."

"And the Enforcer?" Falcon reminded them, pressing back into the depths of his chair.

The Leader's forehead slumped against the heels of his hands. "I suggest we pray, Black Masks," he responded, his voice muffled amid the ruffles at his wrists. "This would be a devilishly good time for a miracle."

Six

The orchestra leader tapped his six musicians to attention behind the buffer of light-spangled potted palms in the Whinstone Abbey ballroom at precisely eight o'clock that evening. Tia turned at the sound, hesitating in her acknowledgment of Viscount Pershing as he approached her in the reception line just long enough to reach behind her mother's silver-grey silk train and tug upon her Uncle Brumley's plum-colored tails.

"Uncle!" she whispered loudly behind her mother's shoulders, causing the countess's brows to arch in dismay. "Monsieur Fournet is about to begin the minuet. We must go at once to open the dancing."

"Horatia, dearest," her mother implored *sotto voce,* "the orchestra shall await our pleasure or they shall not be paid. Do turn your attention back to your duties, if you please.

"Ah, Pershing," she then greeted as the young man released the Earl of Walmsley's hand to step before her and make his leg. "So kind of you to join us on such a frosty eve, and from such a distance as Richmond."

" 'Pon rep, milady," the viscount said, his gaze shifting sideways to sweep over Tia's length, returning to hover at her bodice, narrowing slightly as it sought to penetrate the gown's layers of pink silk and delicate lace, "I would have come from Land's End for a dance with the Lady Horatia at her Valentine's ball. Ain't a trial, though, by any means. Several of us have put up with Parkenham for the duration, don't y'know."

Even before the viscount finished speaking, his hands stretched out for Tia's. Smoothly he stepped in front of her, raising her fingertips to touch against his soft, moist lips, his blue eyes, outlined in black, staring into hers raptorially.

"La, how you flatter me, sir," Tia smiled, gently removing her fingers from the viscount's ever-increasing grip.

"Now that is impossible, my dear," the viscount disagreed, his gaze sinking to her *décolleté*. "Even the highest accolade becomes as dung when describing you."

Tia's eyes widened, then fluttered disconcertedly.

"Indeed," she commented, swallowing a sudden urge to giggle. "What a lovely thing to say, Elbert."

"Do you think so?" the viscount replied, beaming. "Then wait until you read this," he told her, taking out a slim package from the depths of his waistcoat.

"Oh, a valentine!" Tia exclaimed, taking the package from him. "How very dear of you, Elbert. And what a beautiful card," she complimented after unwrapping it and appreciating the time and thought that had gone into the arrangement of hearts and cupids cut from pattern books and applied in a rather jumbled collage.

"Read it," the viscount commanded, leaning even closer to watch her eyes scan the cherished lines.

Tia did so. And then her face colored all the way to her toes.

"Aloud," the viscount breathed, curling the paper's edges with moist warmth as he again reached for Tia's hand.

"Oh, I could not," Tia said quickly, drawing back her fingers before sweeping gracefully around him to take her uncle's arm. "Some things should remain private between two people, do you not agree?"

Pershing tipped his head in a slight bow of conspiracy. "A great many things," he answered, barely moving his lips.

"I am glad that you agree," Tia stated with alacrity. "And such sweet sentiments they are, too, Elbert. Shall we read them together later, do you think? Perhaps you would put your name on my card beside a rigadoon after Uncle and I have opened the ball. We shall sit out our dance, shall we? We shall speak of valentines . . . and love . . . and romance . . . *and* discuss in the greatest detail how you manage to 'put up' with Parkenham. I declare," she laughed as she began to tug Walmsley toward the dance floor, "I have yet to figure that out, and I have known the gentleman for years!" After gaily wiggling her fingers back in Pershing's direction, she and her uncle strode to the center of the gleaming flagstone floor to take their proper places at the head of the other dancers.

"Deftly done, Tia," Walmsley told her with a proud smile as the music began and they undertook the first of the stately, rigidly choreographed steps.

Tia chuckled softly. "Thank you, Uncle," she replied, bowing slightly toward him, in spite of the fact that the next step called for a stiffly erect spine. "And thank you, too, for Aunt Elizabeth's pendant," she told him, squeezing his hand as she reached up to finger the large, luminous pearl. "It is beautiful. I shall wear it at each and every one of my Valentine's Day balls from now on. I vow it."

The earl laughed then, and shook his head. "Tia, Tia . . . ," he said softly, "always so impulsive . . . always so ready to make rash promises."

"Why, Uncle!" Tia responded, executing a perfect turn

before regarding him with wide eyes. "I thought that you might be pleased with my sentiment. And speaking of rashes, do not think that I am not sensible of the one circling your neck. Where has it come from, Uncle, and what are you doing for it?"

"It is a trifling reaction to something, I am sure," he responded dismissively, "and I am laving it constantly with Mrs. Reynolds's camomile cream. And as to your sentiment, my dear, I *am* pleased," he added gently. "I would be more pleased, however, if you would do a bit more to please yourself."

"Myself? But I do, Uncle," Tia insisted with a grin. "Do I not demand that you pay for this ball each and every year?"

"You do," the earl agreed, nodding his neatly combed head of steel grey hair. "Yet answer me this, Tia. If what you insist is true, why are you wearing diamond and ruby earrings this evening with a pearl solitaire? They hardly complement one another, my dear, and the precision of your usual mode of accessorizing does not allow me to believe that this rather glaring *faux pas* was merely an oversight. No, never mind, do not bother to respond," he said, interrupting Tia's imminent explanation. "I already know the answer to my question, and it makes my case and point. You are wearing the earrings because they were given to you by an admirer and you cannot bear to hurt the young man's feelings."

"Not quite," Tia laughed. "The earrings were given to me by Robert, Uncle . . . hardly an admirer. And for your information, it pleases me to wear the pieces together tonight because both gifts mean so much to me. You two are the dearest people in the whole world to me, you know."

"Well, I am gratified, to be sure," the earl stated gruffly.

"Nevertheless, the point remains. My dear, you must follow your own heart more often. I would not see you spend your life unhappy and unfulfilled."

"Dearest Uncle Brumley," Tia said with a soft smile that raised moist sparkles in the depths of her hazel eyes, "is that what you meant by my valentine poem's last line?"

"Just so. Rethink your choices twice, my dear Tia. And speaking of Robert," he stated in a disconcerting change of subject, "where is the bounder, do you suppose?"

Tia laughed delightedly as the strains of Mozart came to an end and she dropped into a curtsey before her uncle's low bow. "En route, or I shall have quite a crow to pluck with him," she warned upon rising. "He has a houseguest with him this year. I expect the two of them will be arriving momentarily."

"A houseguest, eh?" Walmsley remarked as he led his niece on a slow stroll around the room's perimeter. "And who might that be?" he asked, stepping back so that Viscount Ingram might put his name beside another minuet before giving Tia a valentine of painted porcelain as thin and delicate as a flower petal.

"A Mr. Dexter Clark," Tia told him after thanking the viscount. "Oh, look, Uncle," she whispered as she unwrapped the valentine and read the intricately pleated offering.

Lord Dallings suddenly bowed before her then, startling her as he slipped his own valentine atop Ingram's, afterward entering his name on her card next to a *contra* dance, or "country" dance as the corruption had come to be called not many years before. Tia watched the lines on her card fill, smiling her pleasure as her face flushed with new excitement. She particularly liked the lively country dances in which the two partners faced one another across the space between them, unlike the minuet where couples paraded stiffly side by side. Because of this, and because the dancers would have much more opportunity to stare into one another's eyes, and because it was her ball, after all, she had requested that the orchestra leader include more than the usual number of them. Oh, yes, she thought as enthusiasm rivered through her, it promised to be a lovely night.

"Robert met Mr. Clark in Town several years ago, so he told us this afternoon," she finally finished telling her uncle, nodding as Dallings politely took his leave. "He has extended his hospitality to him until he leaves on the morrow for his home in Sunderland. Poor man! A great deal of trouble awaits him, I am afraid."

"Trouble?" the earl queried in an odd tenor. "In Sunderland, you say? And his name is Clark?"

"Yes," Tia responded, suddenly finding herself surrounded by gentlemen vying to put their names to her card. Laughing at the surprise, she turned slightly away from her uncle, chattering with each as he took her card even as she attempted to continue her conversation. "His family owns the Penfield mine," she said over her shoulder toward the taut silence behind her. "Have you heard what befell it, Uncle? Someone set a charge to it and collapsed it entirely! Mr. Clark has been summoned home to give comfort to his father and to try to discover who might have done such a terrible thing."

Beneath the impeccable folds of his Waterfall, Walmsley's Adam's apple rose and fell. One slow trickle of perspiration eddied down the narrow length of skin between his thick, grey sideburn and the foothill leading up to his right ear.

"Indeed," he replied in almost a whisper.

"Oh, yes," Tia responded, shaking a teasing fan beneath the nose of a persistent gentleman who was about to sign his name to the dance she was reserving just in case. Laughing, she withdrew her arm. "He is quite determined to uncover the villains and see them brought to justice. And who can blame him? Why, his family has lost everything, Uncle, and—"

"Viscount Bainbridge and Mr. Dexter Clark," interrupted Wardle's booming announcement over the milling sounds of the assembly.

"Oh, at last! Uncle, here he is!" Tia cried happily, suddenly relaxing muscles that she had not even known she was tensing. For the twentieth part of a moment she wondered at the unusual occurrence, but in the end set it aside to turn instead with the others in the room toward the ballroom entrance, watching as her cousin's broad shoulders filled the opening within the carved oak door frame. Again she took her uncle's arm.

"Yes, indeed," the earl murmured, focusing not upon his cousin, but upon the young man standing just beside him, an impressively powerful young buck resplendent in a cutaway of bottle green velvet, a white silk waistcoat, matching inexpressibles, and black dancing pumps.

"And it seems our cousin has learned in Town to be fashionably late, I see," Tia added, her smile widening with amusement as she watched Robert pause, then arrogantly raise his quizzing glass to observe the dancers' slow parade around the furniture before granting the room at large the pleasure of his presence in their midst.

She noticed, too, the black velvet cutaway he had chosen for the occasion, its expert cut, tellingly from Schweitzer's in Cork Street, clinging elegantly to his form without a sign of a wrinkle. He was certainly in looks tonight, she thought as a disconcerting sensation negotiated her nerve endings and an odd weakness set her head tilting slightly to the side. Whatever? she pondered, clasping her hands at her waist just as the viscount dropped his quizzing glass back down amid the folds of his intricate Mathematical, allowing its black satin ribbon to once again frame a pristine collar whose points touched just beneath his clean-shaven chin.

Quite unconsciously, Tia's gaze followed the glass's downward fall. It did not stop at the limit of the black ribbon leash, however, as did the glass. Instead, it continued even farther in its descent . . . down to skim over the row of diamond studs fastening Robert's waistcoat . . . down again to focus upon the garment's tailored hem peeking out just below his cutaway, and then down once more . . . ever so slowly down . . . sinking lower and lower along the seam of his inexpressibles until it paused, hovering, sharpening, just . . . there. . . .

Suddenly Tia's breath caught as she realized where she had been staring. Instantly her gaze veered away, fluttering upward toward the ballroom's fan vaulted ceiling where, caught like fireflies tethered to waxen chains, the flickering light of hundreds of candles bent, broke, and dazzled as it danced over the sparkling facets of six Waterford crystal chandeliers hanging in opulent magnificence from the ancient stone. She swallowed then, battling the insistent color staining her cheeks; yet, perversely, her regard sank toward Robert again.

White silk inexpressibles gleamed in the candlelight, bound just below the knees by several white ribbons drawing the eye downward even farther to the viscount's magnificently muscled calves. As Tia watched, even as Robert stood calmly waiting, ridges of muscle bulged and ebbed within his pair of costly clocked white stockings. As Tia concluded her appraisal at Robert's black dancing pumps, she found herself quite unaccountably damp.

It has to be a touch of the quinsy, she thought, raising a palm to her forehead when sudden chills skittered over her heated skin. Or dyspepsia. Perhaps the ague . . . yes, that was it.

And then she gave her head a slight shake, loosening one soft brown tress as she took her sensibilities in hand. It was the excitement of the ball, of course, she finally concluded with a soft laugh. Reassured, she again drew her gaze upward, smiling at her folly. It was then that she made full contact with her cousin's woodland eyes.

He was staring at her. As if she were one of his favorite cream cakes. And he were ravenous.

Typhoid fever!

The idiocy exploded in Tia's mind just as the most inexplicable tremor frolicked over her skin. She blinked rapidly.

He was still staring at her, the varlet! Worse! . . . As she watched, the subtlest of smiles curved the corners of his lips.

Good heavens! Tia exclaimed, clamping a hand over her lower abdomen as it grew alarmingly unstable. And, la, she was feeling damp again!

"C-come, Uncle, you must meet Mr. Clark," she suddenly stammered before she could completely liquefy, beginning to pull the reluctant man forward. "And you shan't mind doing the pretty for me once you have made his acquaintance, shall you?"

"Doing the . . . ? Oh, I say, Horatia!" the earl blustered, applying more resistance to their forward progress. "Never say you intend to abandon me . . . !"

"Well . . . yes. But only for the nonce, Uncle," Tia vowed, again attempting to swallow away her perplexing feelings as she dragged him a bit farther.

"But . . . but, my dear, where shall you be?" objected Walmsley, finally yielding as he had begun to perceive that they were quite imprudently drawing their guests' notice, not to mention his sister-in-law's.

"Baiting the parsons mousetrap," Tia ground out with determination, looking back over her shoulder toward the room at large. "If, that is, I can cut Miss Tutweiler out from amongst all our local North Yorkshire cheese."

The two quickly came to a halt before Dex's curious regard and the rag-mannered grin that Tia was persuaded her cousin could have learned nowhere else but in St. James's Street.

"Uncle, this is Mr. Clark," she introduced brusquely, glowering up at Robert as she gestured back and forth between the two men. "Mr. Clark . . . my uncle. Now, if you will excuse me . . ."

Before Mr. Clark could even bend at the waist, Tia had spun about and disappeared. Only a remnant of lavender remained to mark her former place.

"Well, er . . . that is, Horatia . . . ," stumbled Walmsley into the void left by his niece's departure, avoiding eye contact with Dex as he gestured somewhere behind him.

"Let me guess," Robert interrupted, widening his smile. "She has gone to fetch her friend."

"Has she indeed?" remarked Dex, brightening.

"Er . . . so she said," the earl affirmed, clasping his hands behind his back while he rocked on his heels. "So she said. In any event, er . . . welcome to Whinstone Abbey, Mr. Clark. Do come in, sir," he continued, nervously sweeping one hand back toward the room at large, only to connect rather solidly with the ample bosom of the strolling Mrs. Hortense Fortenby-Smythe.

"Oh, I say, I do beg pardon!" Walmsley cried, spinning about while his fingers convulsively clutched quite deeply into one breast's soft, springy depths. "Dear me!" he gasped, receiving the spluttering matron's hearty shove, and as a result springing backward against Dex.

"Well, I never . . . !" gasped the lady, smacking Walmsley upon his head with her folded fan.

"Oh, but my dear Mrs. Fortenby-Smythe . . . !" the earl cried, casting his feet and arms about, reaching in vain toward her retreating affront.

"Here, sir, let me help you," Dex offered while several noble appendages flailed against his cutaway.

"Cousin, take hold of yourself," Robert urged, reaching over to help Dex finally get the earl set back aright.

"Oh, lud," Walmsley muttered when he had regained his balance. "Do forgive me, if you will. Quite a pother, what? Most mortifying, I can tell you. I am quite put out of countenance. Do you think Mrs. Fortenby-Smythe was overly offended?" he asked Robert with worried eyes.

"I am persuaded the lady will find your error highly flattering when she has had time to consider it," Robert soothed with a smile.

"One can only hope . . . ," the earl mumbled into the cravat he was intent upon reordering. "Oh, but do come in, Mr. Clark," he then repeated, giving up on his task. "I have been most remiss, have I not?" he apologized, taking Dex's elbow and leading him forward.

"Not at all, sir," Dex told him politely.

"Nevertheless, I am persuaded that you must be stamping at the bit to dance with our local lovelies, Mr. Clark, and, I must say, Horatia's Valentine's ball does attract the cream of the crop.

"Lud, Robert, will you look at my Waterfall!" the earl babbled on. "I vow it looks more like a weed-choked pond. Well, there is no help for it, I suppose. I must go have Brice change it.

"Oh, but do come in and partake of the Abbey's hospitality, Mr. Clark. Robert will escort you to a table, won't you, cousin? But, of course, you must feel free to ask the countess for the proper introductions," he said, turning and beginning to amble agitatedly away. "No, no, of course you would wish for a bit of refreshment before you seek out a partner. Cousin," he called back, waving over his shoulder, "do act in my stead and offer your friend a nice cup of explosion, won't you?"

Moments later, the earl was out of sight.

"Explosion?" Dex questioned, glancing up at Robert.

"Potion," Robert easily replied. "No doubt 'potion' is what Cousin Brumley must have said. Henri is renowned throughout the moors for his party potions, after all."

"Ah," Dex responded, again turning to look out over the dancers.

"Best not to have too much, though," Robert warned after a few moments of silence had passed. "A single cup has put many a man in his altitudes."

"A good reason to stick with what I know," Dex replied with a laugh.

"And, perhaps, with whom?" Robert questioned, gesturing with his quizzing glass toward the approach of Tia and Miss Tutweiler.

"Mmm. Considering the determined look your cousin is giving you," Dex sighed, "I doubt I shall be allowed."

Robert burst into laughter as the two women drew to their side.

Seven

"I am gratified that this evening finds you in such good spirits, cousin," Tia said, coming to a stop before Robert with Margaret in tow, her smile a little too bright and far too wide.

"As it happens, I am in the best of spirits, my dear," Robert responded, bringing her fingers up for his kiss.

"Then you will be the perfect partner for Miss Tutweiler," Tia responded enthusiastically.

Beside her, Margaret dragged her avid gaze away from Dex to stare at her in dismay. "Oh, no, really, Tia . . . ," she began, touching gloved fingers to the delicate yellow muslin tucks at her bosom.

"Now, Margaret, there is no need for polite protestations," Tia countered, squeezing her friend's hand. "I insist. Besides, Robert is well aware of how difficult it can be to establish oneself in new social situations. I am persuaded that he shall be delighted to partner you, shall you not, cousin? After all, one dance with you shall guarantee Margaret's success in our small Society. Why, once the gentlemen see the regard you have for her, I misdoubt Margaret's card shall be full within seconds of the last steps."

"I think you give Miss Tutweiler far too little credit, Tia," Robert replied, smiling pleasantly as he made his leg in the direction of Margaret's petrifaction.

"Oh?"

"Oh, indeed. And I shall prove it to you. Dex," Robert said, turning his attention toward his friend, "you are an unprejudiced observer in all this, are you not?"

"Absolutely," Dex replied with the appropriate sobriety.

"Then enlighten us, if you will. As an average man who might happen to be seeking an obliging partner for . . . oh, say for the country dance that is just about to begin . . . would you hasten to sign the card of a lady such as Miss Tutweiler?"

"With no hesitation whatsoever," Dex stated with no hesitation at all, quickly seizing Margaret's card. "As a matter of fact . . . ," he continued, demonstrating the truth of his statement by placing his name beside that dance, the supper dance, and, quite shockingly, a third dance at the conclusion of the evening, "one can easily see that the concept is giving me no difficulty at all. I am pleased to report that I am experiencing no knee-knocking whatsoever, no rising of the gorge, not even a lip curled in distaste . . . no, there is nothing. Except, of course, that now," he added, looking up at Margaret with a satisfied grin, "quite by the most pleasant of circumstances, I find that I am to be Miss Tutweiler's partner for a good part of the evening. Shall we begin, my dear?" he asked, dropping the card back at her wrist, then obligingly offering her his arm.

"I should like that above all things, Mr. Clark," Margaret murmured, smiling up into Dex's eyes.

With great care, Dex led Margaret away to join the fifteen or so other couples forming the line.

Tia inhaled the deep breath of the neatly foiled, then curled her fingers into fists.

"That was really too bad of you, Robert," she chided, tapping his forearm with her fan.

"Oh, I think not," Robert breezily replied. "Of the four of us, three of us are quite satisfied. Come now, cheer up. Who is to be your partner for this set?"

"I haven't one," Tia grumped as the music began. "I left it open in case you flew into the boughs over having to dance with Margaret and I needed an excuse to spirit Mr. Clark away."

Robert chuckled softly. "Poor Tia. Well, judging by the numbers in the line over there, this dance is going to last the better part of an hour. Let's go find you a glass of champagne, shall we? We shall drown your sorrows in no time." Appropriating her elbow into his gloved hand, he soon directed her toward the inglenook, all the while trying very hard not to break out into chuckles again.

The fire was just what was needed . . . soothing and heartening, Robert thought as the two entered the almost room-sized space and Tia immediately made herself comfortable on one of the adjacent settles. It was a good thing, too, he continued to consider, signalling to a passing footman for one of the champagne flutes balanced expertly upon his silver tray, especially as his cousin was not exactly known for the tranquility of her temperament and so far he had managed to frustratingly parry every one of her thrusts in this deuced fencing match.

He would be careful, therefore, he determined, letting a show of settling into the stiff cushions mask his surreptitious study of Tia as she went about smoothing her lace overskirt beneath her and tugging correctness back into the sagging ends of her long white gloves between sips of the champagne in her glass. Raising his glass, he accepted her warm smile, then watched as she grew comfortable within one of the easy silences their years together had made proper between them, and allowed her attention to wander into a contented perusal of her current year's crop of valentines, a feathered, beaded, and bejeweled collection sparkling across the mantel in the candlelight like a row of bright new debutantes in the best of their finery awaiting their introduction to Queen Charlotte.

Breathing silently, evenly, he sated himself, letting his eyes touch upon each fire-burnished plane of her face, each drooping curl, each flaring curve of suggested womanliness beneath the Valenciennes lace.

Finally, when he became persuaded that he could no longer contain the words threatening to burst from his chest, he allowed himself release. Moistening his lips against their dryness, he spoke but a sentence of the volumes within, a foretaste of the lifetime of words that he had stored in his heart awaiting the time when they would finally find acceptance.

"You look beautiful tonight," he said with practiced casualness, settling back to lazily swirl the costly brandy around in his glass.

Tia's gaze jumped to his at the sudden breaking of the silence, snagged just long enough to widen slightly under his stare's compelling intensity, and then flickered back toward the flames.

"Thank you, Robert," she responded as her eyes filled with suspicious sparkles. "You have never failed to tell me that since the first of my Valentine balls."

"On the contrary, cousin, I have never failed to tell you that since the first of our Valentine's *Days,*" Robert corrected, again raising his glass to her with a one-sided grin.

Tia laughed then. "Yes, that's true, isn't it?" she said when her merriment had subsided. "I have always been able to count on you to make this day special for me, have I not? Will you always do so?"

"Always."

Tia's grin turned mischievous. "Even after you are wed to Miss Tutweiler?" she asked, peering toward him out of the corner of a very impish eye.

"Tia . . ."

"No, really, Robert," she interrupted, "she is perfect for you, and I shan't stop telling you so until you come to see things as I do."

"Deuce take it, Tia, why do you not expend all this energy seeing to your own future happiness?" Robert cried, bounding up from the settle to stand, forearm upon the mantel, before the fire.

"I have!" Tia responded, rising just as quickly to stand beside him, her loosened tress finally drooping all the way down to touch upon her bare shoulder. "Do you not see, Robert?" she asked, placing a reassuring hand upon his biceps. "This *is* my happiness."

"An annual ball celebrating the *idea* of romance?" he queried, rounding on her in astonishment.

"Yes!" she responded with a warm smile.

"Engaging in the manufacture of love between anyone you can get your hands on?" he continued, adding a bit more volume.

"Well . . . yes, if you wish to see it that way," Tia answered as her smile slipped somewhat.

"And why not yourself?" he posed again, finally pushing away from the mantel to face her at his full height. "Why have you made yourself the exception?"

As Robert watched, Tia's gaze softened, then dropped toward her clasped hands. "You know what my father was like," she stated just above a whisper.

"I know what your mother never fails to take every opportunity to tell you," he responded, hanging on to his control.

"Robert, she suffered terribly at his hands," Tia said, again looking at him. "You must not fault her for her bitterness. Anyway," she added, stiffening noticeably, "I do not wish to discuss the subject further. The matter has already been settled. I have made my choice."

"Your promise, more likely," he countered from between his teeth.

"It was *not* a promise, cousin, and I'll thank you not to ruin my evening practically at its onset."

Beside the warm fire, Robert sucked in a deep breath. "And I'll thank *you,* cousin, not to ruin your life," he parried softly. Then, carefully setting his brandy glass down on the table, he bowed deeply. "But you are correct. This is not the time or the place for an argument. Please accept my apology."

"Robert . . ."

"Enjoy your evening, cousin," Robert said tightly, turning back toward the ballroom. "If you will excuse me . . ."

"Robert, wait! . . . Oh, fiddle! You have no right to question my choices," Tia directed toward his retreat. "I am of age, you know," she said as he reached the inglenook's arch, "and it *is* my life."

Robert paused then, turning slightly so that he might look back at her. "You are right, of course, cousin," he replied, his voice deep and void of emotion. "Do forgive me again for objecting to your idiocy."

In the next moment, he was gone, leaving Tia to huff at the empty arch in vexation.

Quite suddenly, however, he returned.

"Yes, cousin?" Tia asked, elevating her chin when she

had gotten over her surprise, drawing her spine into rigid self-possession.

"Lower your nose, Tia," Robert told her, striding purposefully forward. "I returned only because I forgot something."

"My acceptance, I misdoubt," Tia responded loftily. "Very well, Robert, I forgive you and accept your apology."

"You accept . . . ! Well, that's the dandy! *You* accept *my* apology," the viscount muttered as he drew very near. "I swallow my pride and come back in here," he continued, reaching out for her, "and you . . . Hell, Tia, you cut up my peace! And, deuce take it, hold still a moment, will you?" he admonished when she began backing away from his ire.

"Whyever should I?" Tia cried with rounded eyes, dodging again when once more he reached for her. "And what are you doing, Robert?"

"What I came back in here to do," he told her between his teeth. "Now stop wiggling so I can fix your bloody hair!"

Clamping one strong hand around the back of Tia's neck, Robert soon seized the lank, soft fugitive into one hand, deftly twisted it and fastened it into place within her coiffure, then spun about and again disappeared.

"I am *not* an idiot," Tia said to no one in particular. But an unsettling wavelet had set up its rhythmic motion somewhere inside her stomach, and for the first time in her life, Tia began to wonder if it might indeed be true.

It was a notion she decided must quite quickly be muzzled. Wasting no further time in introspection, she left the inglenook just as the country dance was drawing to a close, then began to search for Viscount Pershing, her partner in the *louvre* due to begin in the next several minutes.

"There you are, Pershing," she said with mustered gaiety after she had found the viscount among the sad crush trying to put pencil to Margaret's card.

From the corner of her eye she saw Robert clap a hand upon her uncle's shoulder, share an amusing word with him, then, after a burst of laughter, follow his elder cousin across the dancing area into the card room. Again Tia's lips thinned.

"Can it be?" Lord Dudley suddenly remarked beside her, materializing out of the crush to raise her fingertips to his lips.

"Can what be, sir?" Tia asked with a distracted smile.

"Can it be that you have granted Pershing a dance? Never say so, my dear! Why, you shall come up positively bruised."

"Shall I?" Tia responded, laughing delightedly, feeling the wavelet begin to dissolve. "But this dance is promised to Lord Pershing, sir," she said, fluttering her fan before her bosom. "What do you suggest I do?"

"Elope with me, of course," Dudley told her conspiratorially. "Only say the word, my lovely, and we shall seize our cloaks and be off for Gretna Green."

"What, and leave my guests without a hostess?" Tia giggled in horror as her muscles further relaxed.

Dudley frowned then. "Mmm. You have a point. The gazebo, then!" he suddenly offered, thrusting one finger skyward.

Tia's eyes danced with humor. "In February?" she questioned, looking at him askance.

"We could share a cloak," Dudley suggested in a whisper.

"I think not," Tia laughed, raising her spread fan to mask

the slight evidence of her embarrassment as Viscount Pershing joined them to claim his set.

"But what of your toes?" Dudley finally wailed, throwing up his hands.

Tia placed graceful fingers atop Pershing's blue kerseymere sleeve and then shrugged slightly. "I shall do what necessitated dear Uncle Brumley's employment of nine different dancing masters for me over the time of my social training, of course," she told him, fluttering her lashes above the arc of her fan. "I shall simply step on top of his."

All around Tia, her guests joined with her in warm, bubbling merriment.

And it was what she needed, she realized as she left behind his lordship's low chuckling and followed her partner onto the floor . . . lovely music, a pleasurable fatigue after lively dancing, and, most of all, bright, carefree hours of flirtation and joyous release. This was *her* night, after all, she thought, a bit of pique rising to again slightly displace her smile. How could Robert think to put her out of countenance on this of all days? How could he think to spoil her one evening of romance? Even worse, how dare he take a pet and hie off to the card room when he knew she expected him to dance with Margaret twice?

There was only one thing to do, Tia concluded quickly. If she were to rescue her evening, the ultimate sacrifice would have to be made. No matter what schemes she had envisioned for Robert and Margaret this evening, for the nonce . . . well, until the morrow, anyway . . . she would have to set them aside. It was not that she no longer cared for their welfare, of course, she acknowledged in counterpoint to a twinge of guilt; but she only had this one night, after all. She could not let her cousin's potty-headed refusal to see what was good for him negate what had come to mean so much to her. There was no other time for her, and never would be. It was her only chance in the year to brush against the wonderful, mysterious feelings others could at any time fully embrace.

So she would ignore him utterly. It was decided. Her cousin could spend his entire evening in the card room for all she cared. She would set aside all thoughts of his vexation with her—most certainly all the misplaced sensations she had suddenly found springing up within her since his return—and she would make the most of her Valentine's ball. She would enjoy it as she had never enjoyed it before. To the fullest. And not once would she think of Robert. From this moment on, Tia determined, curtseying to Pershing as the first strains of the music began to flow, as far as she was concerned, the varlet was not even there.

Tia kept her promise. For the better part of the remainder of the evening she relished the occasion, holding court in the midst of an attentive crowd of dandies, dispersing her favors with laughter and a great deal of flirtatious fan wafting, dancing as if each step were the last she would take. Not one approached her orb of devotees without being pulled inside and matched with his perfect partner; not one was left to sit out a dance alone and ignored. The supper was consumed, the music swelled and ebbed; a dance of subtle, deft maneuverings on Tia's part matched pair after pair after pair. And always, a recollection of Robert's censorious gaze ate at the edge of her gaiety.

He had not appeared in the ballroom again after the scold he had given her in the inglenook, but she had seen him once during supper when he had been filling a plate for himself. For a moment only, he had caught her glance; muscle had rolled at the corner of his jaw. Tia had thrust the sight of it away, turning her back upon the condemning shake of his head before stalking toward one of the supper room's small tables ahead of her partner. That had been over an hour ago. She had not seen him since.

Tia ended the final *Pas de Basque* of *La Polonaise* and accepted Baron Wrightville's arm for a stroll past the ranks of chairs and twinkling palms, stopping several times along the way to contrive more partners for the upcoming rigadoon before returning at last to the embrace of her awaiting court. She rejoined them gladly, yet felt oddly separate from them. It had been so since the supper hour. But why? Tia placed a hand upon her unsettled stomach. Her reaction made no sense to her . . . unless, of course, her mother really should have opted for the boiled turbot instead of the lobster.

The thought brought a welcome smile. And then Tia slowly looked at each distinctly different face forming a circle around her, her presence apart and yet in their midst, observing as from a distance as each gentleman took his turn inserting himself nearby to turn what witty phrase had occurred to him in an effort to gain her attention. Each was just as solicitous as before, just as eager to please; yet now her smile of acknowledgment did not radiate quite so brightly . . . now finding the perfect pointed response was infinitely harder.

It was Robert's doing, of course, she thought as peevishness welled up into her throat. Behind her attentive smile, Tia began composing the blistering set-down she intended to give him the very next time she saw him . . . if, that is, she ever spoke to the bounder again in her life.

"Is something troubling you, Tia?" Margaret asked as Dudley brought her back to Tia's side at the rigadoon's end.

"What? Oh . . . no," Tia responded, drawing her con-

templation back away from plotting murder and mayhem.
"Not at all."

"You do look a bit Friday-faced," Dudley observed. "My
dear lady, I am persuaded that what you need is an imme-
diate change of scene."

"Indeed," Tia commented, fluttering her fan as a bit of
sparkle returned to her eyes. "What do you have in mind?"

"The stables," Dudley murmured, raising his quizzing
glass but not his gaze. "And don't tell me again that it is
February. It don't signify. Consider that we shall be as warm
as toast amid all that lovely hay."

"And quite compromised amid all those lovely stable
boys," Tia pointed out with a laugh. "Besides, that is hardly
a change of scene. I am in the stables several times a day."

"Ah, me, then I fear that only leaves London," his lordship sighed. "I shall write to my staff at once to open my
little town house in Soho."

"Goodness!" Margaret gasped, staring at Dudley with
huge eyes.

"You shall do no such thing," Tia giggled, once more
punishing his impropriety with her fan, "and you shall
kindly stop being such a frightful tease. You are putting
Margaret to the blush."

"My apologies," Dudley offered with a bow. "But . . .
the house?"

". . . Will have to be occupied by someone else, I fear.
As well you know, Dudley, when I next go up to Town it
shall be for the Season, and I shall stay as I always do at
the Walmsley mansion in Upper Brook Street. And the Season, if you recall, does not begin for several more weeks."

Dudley heaved another heartfelt sigh. "Then it seems
I am spurned utterly. Cursed with unending solitude.

Doomed to never being comforted by a woman's presence . . . by her charms."

"Not a bit of it," Tia countered, placing her fingers within his elbow with a ready grin. "Look around you, sir. The room is full of lovely women." She gestured, starting him toward the nearest row of chairs. "Tell me, Dudley. Have you chanced to meet Miss Alicia Evans?"

Suddenly, a deep voice beside her abruptly arrested her attempted match.

"I beg your pardon, milady."

Tia turned quickly to see the butler patiently awaiting her. "Yes, Wardle?" she smiled in response, releasing Dudley to delicately fan herself.

"This just came for you, miss," Wardle told her, bowing slightly as he held out a plainly wrapped box.

"Oh, how lovely!" Tia exclaimed, taking the box and smiling up toward his lordship. "Oh, this is most delightfully unexpected. I was certain I had received all the valentines meant for me this year."

"You must open it at once, of course," Dudley told her, turning her back toward the others. "Come look," he commanded them with a crooked finger. "Lady Horatia has received a rather intriguing latecomer to challenge our own humble offerings."

"Whom is it from?" Parkenham asked with disdain, coming up to Tia's side along with the rest of her court.

"Patience, milord," Tia laughed excitedly, her warm eyes brilliant as she removed the wrapping paper, gave it to Wardle, then nodded her dismissal. "We shall see presently. Oh, goodness, I am persuaded that this is the most exciting of all the valentines I have received today!" she commented, attempting next to work off the box's tight lid. "It is so unusual for one to be delivered this late, don't you think? I am convinced that it must be of the greatest moment. Can you not just sense that it is so? Oh, Dudley, do help me with the lid. I vow, I am too excited to remove it properly."

"With pleasure," his lordship replied, taking the box from her.

As Tia eagerly watched, he gently wiggled the cover, slipping it higher and higher over the box's corners until it at last came free and he lifted it aside. He glanced then into the box's shadowed interior. And then he grew oddly still.

"What is it? Oh, Dudley, cease your teasing!" Tia laughed excitedly, reaching toward the valentine. "You cannot keep the box, you know. It was sent to me."

Seeing her movement from the corner of his eye, Dudley quickly removed the box out of Tia's reach.

"I, however, did not receive a single one," he told her evenly. "And, after all, you *have* just spurned me utterly."

"What rubbish!" Tia laughed, stretching even farther in his direction. "Now kindly give me my valentine."

The viscount's face then sobered. "My dear lady . . . ," he hesitated.

"My *lord* . . . !" Tia countered playfully, delicately wiggling her fingers.

Dudley stared hard at Tia, then let his shoulders sag. "Very well," he relented, handing her the box. "But be careful not to put your hand—"

"Ouch!" Tia cried after she had plunged her hand down into the shadows. Instantly she drew her offended finger back into the light. Several filamentlike barbs were protruding from the tip of her glove. "Whatever . . . ? she murmured, turning the box toward one of the nearby sconces and, for the first time, peering inside.

"I assure you it means nothing, my dear," Dudley said

from beside her. "Allow me to throw the damnable thing into the fire."

"Into the fire? Oh, Tia, what is it?" Margaret asked, placing a comforting arm about her friend's waist. "Whatever can be inside?"

But Tia could not answer her. In truth, she could not speak at all. Instead, slowly, very carefully she reached back inside the box again. And then she drew out the valentine, afterward gingerly turning it toward the light. From around her spread a widening circle of shocked, susurrant silence.

The card Tia held up for all to see was entirely black. Edged with the finest of black Irish lace, spangled with loops of midnight satin ribbon fastened in place by rare black pearls and expertly worked Whitby jet, it was beautiful, enthralling . . . and like a knife to Tia's romantic heart. She had heard of other poor souls receiving such cards before, but never . . . never! . . . could she have imagined one being sent to her. She could only stare at it, glittering in the candlelight . . . an ill wish sent by someone to her on this her most cherished of days . . . a curse; malevolent, and utterly obscene.

Caught in a sudden reverberant shudder, Tia dropped the box with a muted clatter upon the gleaming flagstone floor.

"Dear heaven . . . !" she breathed, her gaze locked upon the center of the card, at the tiny jet cupid frolicking above a nosegay of dried nettles clustered around sprigs of tiny nightshade blossoms, the whole fastened to the card by more of the black ribbon interspersed with several more thin strands of jet and pearls. The cupid was glaring at her evilly, Tia thought as her heart stood still. He was glaring,

frolicking, laughing at her as he shot a black jet arrow backward from his bow into himself.

"Oh, Tia . . . !" Margaret wailed. "How shall you ever
look to see what might be written inside?"

Slowly Tia raised her shocked gaze toward her friend.

"Shall I open it for you, do you think?" Margaret asked.

Tia shook her head. "No," she responded, swallowing
back a welling of tears. "I shall do it. It did, after all, come
for me." Now set upon her course, with an ember of resolve
as shaky as her hands, she opened the delicate paper and
looked inside. Red letters gleaming like an accusation
filled the page.

My dear Miss Meddler,

Tia read with horror,

> *Thou who blithely connives*
> *To maneuver, to tamper in others' lives,*
> *May this card confront you, on this Valentine's Day,*
> *With each manipulation you have forced my way.*
>
> *May another's scheming fingers now clutch your*
>   *heart,*
> *Then thrust it at another of whom you wish no part.*
> *Please, do wear my corsage upon your décolleté.*
> *(Ah, sweet recompense!) At last to nettle you*
> *As you have callously nettled me.*

Tia dropped the valentine as if she had been burned. And
then she began to run.

He was in the card room, just as she had known he would
be, at that moment placing a wager on his piquet hand.

"Oh, Robert!" she sobbed as she spotted him.

Somehow the viscount managed to make his feet before his cousin crashed headlong into his cravat.

Eight

"Tia, what the deuce . . . !"

"Oh, Robert, it is awful!" Tia cried, clutching at his lapels, wilting his carefully constructed neckcloth with tears and moist, gusted breaths as, all around her, the reaper of avid curiosity abruptly scythed the slap of cards and humming conversation out of existence.

"What is?" he demanded, seizing her shoulders and setting her away from him, an action that precipitated the slow sag of several tresses from her *coiffure à la Tite*.

"The v-valentine," she sputtered, batting away his restraining hands to again press herself into his warmth.

"What valentine?" the viscount asked as his lips thinned. Yet before she could respond, once more he crushed her against the soft black velvet of his cutaway, nestling her against his strength. His eyes opened again just as Dex and Margaret hurried into the room.

"Is she all right?" Dex asked, his brows narrowed with concern.

"I shan't know that until I figure out what the devil is going on," Robert stated, turning Tia's face into his neck, feeling a trickle of warm tears begin to invade his shirt and pool in the hollow formed by his collarbone.

Walmsley joined them then, on Dex's and Margaret's heels, having just negotiated his way between the ranks of card tables after the commotion had diverted him as well from his nearby game of whist.

"Why, Horatia," the earl soothed as he gained her side and began to pat her back on one of the few places left uncovered by Robert's surrounding arms. "Whatever is the matter, my dear?"

"Oh, Uncle Brumley!" Tia answered, her voice muffled against Robert's neck. "The valentine . . . ," she told him, managing to point an elbow toward the ballroom.

"Why, what valentine?" he, too, asked as his eyes, along with all the others in the room, slewed in that direction.

The purposeful approach of the countess, unfortunately, blocked their view.

"Horatia, you are making a spectacle of yourself," the lady stated stiffly as she drew up before them, her patience already provoked at having to abandon a lengthy discussion concerning the base nature of anything male with Mrs. Fortenby-Smythe in order to comfort her daughter in her reported distress. "It is very bad *ton,* dearest. You must cease this display at once."

"Egad, Sophie, the child is more overset than I have ever seen her," the earl countered. "She has a right to cry. Now does anyone present know what's toward?"

"It was the valentine," Margaret breathed into the general clamor of suppositions, her huge blue eyes awash with sympathy.

"What valentine?" they all asked in a roar of simultaneous exasperation.

"The one she just received," Margaret responded. "Oh!" she cried, covering her face with her hands and turning toward Dex. "It was quite awful, I do declare."

As would any proper gentleman in the presence of a lady

in dire distress, of course, Dex immediately enfolded the suffering Miss Tutweiler into his arms.

"Yes, it was," Tia agreed in muffled affirmation, once more tightening her arms about Robert's neck. A few moments later, next to Robert's heart, she hiccoughed twice.

"Horatia, some dignity and decorum, if you please," the countess reminded her, glancing about their audience.

"Oh, I say!" Walmsley cried, throwing up his hands as word of the scandalbroth spread into the ballroom and the press against their persons intensified, each ear new to the scene pricked for the least bit of intelligence, or, failing that, at least the smallest whisper of gossip. "This is the outside of enough! Does anyone know what has happened to my niece?"

"Miss Tutweiler is our best hope, I perceive," Robert said as several of the card players rose to better hold their positions of proximity against the crush of the dancers and, as a result, jostled against him. "We would be most grateful, madam, if you would tell us what you know."

Margaret raised her head from Dex's shoulder, took one look at Tia's shuddering back and then, waving helplessly, burst into tears. Grinning above an apologetic shrug, Dex flourished his handkerchief and once again ministered to her disquiet.

Robert rolled his eyes.

"Here now, this will never do," Walmsley stated when a particularly zealous tabby, trailing behind her extended ear, pressed portions of her anatomy against his shoulder blade.

"You have the right of that, cousin," Robert agreed. "We must by all means get Tia out of this crush. Let's adjourn to the picture gallery, shall we? Dex, bring Miss Tutweiler, too, if you please. And Wardle," he commanded the hov-

ering butler over several gentlemen's heads, "convey my
request to Monsieur Fournet that he immediately begin the
next set. Oh, and see if you can find that deuced valentine
while you are about it."

He turned Tia then, and with the others following, forged
a path between their guests that led through a nearby door
and into the adjacent room.

"Well, that certainly is better," Walmsley remarked as
he closed the door behind them. "Now, my dear," he said,
appropriating Tia from Robert's arms, "you must tell us
what has overset you so."

"It was the v-valentine," Margaret explained again, using Dex's handkerchief to delicately dab at her lustrous
eyes.

"*What* valentine?" everyone shouted just as a soft
scratching sounded at the door.

"We are about to find out, I would wager," Robert responded. "That will be Wardle, no doubt. Excuse me for
a moment, will you? I am most anxious to get my hands
on this . . . *valentine.*"

Moments later, all interest was centered on the mesmerizing object reposing in Robert's hands.

"Incredible," Dex murmured, slightly shaking his head.
"I have never seen the like."

Beside him, Margaret raised her liquid gaze. "I have,"
she told them softly, catching another tear with a fold of
the richly embroidered linen cloth. "Actually, such cards
are sent quite often . . . at least they were in Dorset where
I lived until my come-out Season."

"And they look like this?" Walmsley asked, reaching
over to take the card from Robert.

"Not always. There is great variety in their construction,
of course," Margaret replied, gaining more control over her

sensibilities in her duty to instruct. "Some of them can be quite pretty, as this one is."

"Why would someone send such a thing?" Walmsley again asked, reaching over with his handkerchief to dab at Tia's eyes.

"Usually to punish one who has jilted another; but, unfortunately, they are also sent to those whom the sender considers a constant annoyance, or whom another finds repulsive . . . or to those who caused harm to the sender in some way. But the object is always the same . . . to give hurt in return."

"But who would wish to hurt her ladyship?" Dex asked, looking at Robert.

"A man," the countess answered instead. "Most certainly it is a man."

"Now, Sophie," the earl chided, "we have no proof of anything at this point."

"But we do know that dangerous deviates exist in the area, milord," Dex asserted, walking a bit apart to seize the back of a nearby chair. "Devil a bit, sir, they destroyed my father's mine!"

Walmsley suddenly fell into a spate of loud harrumphing. "Now surely it is stretching things a bit to say that the two relate. No, it is my opinion that this is just a piece of paper and a few baubles, after all. Nothing whatsoever to get in a pother about. Why, if I had received such a thing as this, I should take care of it in a trice."

"Would you indeed, Brumley?" the countess responded as one brow arched. "How, may I ask?"

"Why, I should find out the name of the knave who sent it to me and by the next cock's crow have called the blackguard out," he replied with another harrumph, and then he thrust the valentine back toward Robert.

It was Tia, however, who took it into her hands. At the suddenness of her action, all eyes swung in her direction. And paused.

It was undeniable. Unobserved by any of them over the period of their discussion, for some reason, Tia had markedly changed.

Robert bent slightly in order to look closer. All seemed just as it should be: Tia's cheeks were flushed and abraded below tear-swollen lids, that was to be expected; several loops of hair swayed against her shoulders like spavined spines, all too normal, Robert thought with a quirk of his lips. Too, she was standing as still as one of the Elgin marbles, but even that was not altogether unusual when she was hatching a match in her maggoty mind. The black valentine lay open in her white-gloved hands. And then he realized what was different . . . not one tear was poised in the corner of either of his cousin's lovely hazel eyes.

"Tia?" he questioned, continuing to study her.

"Yes, cousin?" she responded softly, glancing up at him, her eyes quite thoroughly and amazingly dry.

But filled with purpose, Robert noticed as one brow hit his hairline. Even worse . . . devil a bit, signs of the beginnings of a plan.

"Tia, are you all right?" Margaret asked before Robert could prepare his counterattack.

"More to the point, dearest, are you quite well?" the countess corrected, arching her other brow.

"Quite all right and quite well," Tia told them with a reassuring smile, again opening the card after pausing briefly to make sure her fingers did not come in contact with the prickly nettles. As the others watched, she began to scan the poem once more.

"Tia, what's going on behind those lovely hazel eyes?" Robert asked warily, his perusal becoming intense.

The countess interrupted. "I shall have Wardle bring the *sal volatile.*"

"There is no need for that, Mama," Tia told her, raising an arresting hand. "I shall not have the vapors. In fact, as it happens I am feeling much more the thing."

"Well, I, for one, would very much like to know what suddenly changed," Walmsley asked, his brows awaggle. "But a moment ago you were over the boughs."

Tia smiled at her uncle and softly stroked his cheek. "Actually, it was something you said, Uncle," she told him. "I?"

"Yes, indeed. And I have decided to take your advice."

"You have?" Walmsley remarked, his brows now beginning to wobble even more in the way Tia had considered as looking like combative caterpillars ever since she had been in leading strings.

"Oh, yes. And excellent advice it was, too, Uncle. As usual," Tia kindly told him.

"Just what advice is Cousin Brumley supposed to have offered?" Robert inserted, fast becoming convinced that the whole situation was teetering on the lip of a disaster and about to slide over the edge.

"What you, yourself, heard, Robert," Tia responded, giving him her full attention. "Uncle told us all what must be done. Apparently, I was the only one who was listening."

"But, Horatia, dear, the only comment I made at all was that I would discover the name of the bounder and call him out," Walmsley recalled.

"Horatia, I absolutely forbid you to issue anyone a challenge," the countess stated, giving her daughter an icy glare.

Tia could not help her sudden giggle. "Then, of course,

I shall comply," she replied after concealing her smile's remnant behind her fan.

"But you will attempt to discover the sender's name," Robert stated softly, at last understanding what was whirling around inside his cousin's head.

Tia affirmed Robert's conclusion with a nod. "As I see it," she said levelly, "I have no choice."

"Because . . . ?" Robert queried.

"Because once I recovered from my initial horror at what someone was thinking of me, I began to understand that whoever sent this valentine is truly suffering. Only read it, Robert," she asserted, handing it to him. "Can you not see beneath the anger to the anguish in every line?"

"Yes," Robert stated almost inaudibly, looking at her, "I can."

"Horatia, do be sensible," objected the countess. "How are you to go about an investigation of this sort? . . . a process, I might add, that should be quite beneath the comprehension of anyone who calls herself a lady."

"In truth, Mama," Tia told her with a contained smile, "I am persuaded that I already know where to look."

"You do?" Walmsley asked, dropping his quizzing glass so that it bounced askew onto plum-colored velvet.

Tia nodded. "I believe that there can be no question that the card was sent by someone whose marriage I . . . facilitated . . . with one of my personally selected *partis.*"

"Yet nothing is written that speaks of the sender's wedded state," Margaret observed softly, her own emotions now nicely settled as Tia was once again at ease. "Could the sender not be merely one who wishes . . . to be allowed to make his or her own choice?"

At Margaret's question, Tia blushed a rather guilty raspberry. "Perhaps . . . but I think not," she responded. "It is the tone of the poem, you see. No, Margaret, I am persuaded that the sender, whomever the person is, is . . . well . . ."

"Stuck?" Robert finished for her. "Leg-shackled for life? Caught in a parson's mousetrap with no escape and probably little in the way of cheese?"

Tia cast him a quelling glower. "My cousin has overstated the situation somewhat as I am certain you realize, but I must admit that essentially he has the right of it. I am persuaded that the sender is indeed wed. It follows, then, that he or she must be one of the people I have brought to the altar in past years. And I think that I might say with some assurance that it is someone who feels terribly wronged by me."

"Which one, do you suppose?" Walmsley questioned, staring into the distance as he idly scratched his chin.

"More to the point, whatever can you be thinking to do about it?" the countess added, actually raising her voice somewhat.

"I intend to set things right, of course," Tia told her, squaring her shoulders. "This valentine is a cry for help, Mama, from someone whose marriage has become troubled for some reason. I am persuaded that unable to find a resolution, the person is striking out at me. I can do no less than come to that person's aid. It was I, after all, who brought about the situation in the first place."

"But, dearest, how can you know which one it is?" Walmsley quite properly asked her.

"By visiting the several couples whom I have heard rumored as having difficulties," Tia explained with a firm smile. "I am certain that one of them is the culprit."

"Horatia," the countess uttered with tight control, "I forbid you to go about the county in the dead of winter on some fool's errand."

"Cousin Sophie is right, Tia," Robert affirmed. "It isn't at all the thing."

"Precisely why I shall take Margaret with me."

"Me?" Margaret breathed, clasping her bosom.

". . . And Nancy to see to our needs and to act as our chaperone. And you, too, of course, Robert," she added, smiling impishly up at him.

"Tia . . ."

"No, cousin, I am persuaded you shall have to stay quite close to Miss Tutweiler for her protection. And do not think to remain any longer at the ball, either," she concluded, appropriating Margaret from Mr. Clark and starting toward the door. "You had best begin making our preparations for the trip as soon as possible. I intend to set out first thing tomorrow."

"Tia, so help me . . ."

"Brumley, do you intend to allow this?" the countess asked, rounding on her brother-in-law.

"Well, I . . . why, I cannot see why not. She is of age, after all, Sophie," Walmsley replied, taking the countess's hand and threading it through his elbow. "Besides, Robert will be with her," he added, patting her hand. "You will be, won't you, cousin?" he called back over his shoulder.

So certain of the viscount's answer was his cousin that the earl felt no remorse whatsoever in immediately maneuvering himself and his sister-in-law into Tia and Margaret's wake, contentedly following along as the younger two left the room.

Robert slumped into a chair.

"How very cozy," Dex commented after a time into the fuming silence that lingered in the gallery, barely containing his mirth. "Only imagine it, Rob . . . the three of you, alone for the span of several days. Just you . . . Miss Tutweiler . . . and an irrepressible matchmaker."

"Just the four of us, don't you mean?" Robert gritted out between his teeth after glancing up at his friend.

"Four? Why, no, indeed," Dex responded, beginning to chuckle now. "You forget, milord, I am under my father's orders to return to Sunderland."

Robert's glower again slid toward the man now propped against an adjacent table.

"A command which must take precedence, to be sure. Yet here is another order, Dexter, old fellow . . . old friend; this one from a peer. You will settle matters at the mine and discover what there is to discover about the explosion as soon as possible."

"Because . . . ?" Dex urged with rag-mannered cheerfulness.

"Because it's the queen's house to a charley's shelter that I am not spending near a sennight as the sole male in the company of those two deuced females!" the viscount bit out. "I give you two days, Dex. If you do not wish to see a man strangle his own cousin, in but two days you'd damn well better show up wherever the hell we are."

Nine

Two of the viscount's traveling coaches, followed by Mr. Clark's spanking curricle and four, entered the long drive leading up to the Abbey entrance at precisely eleven o'clock the following morning, immaculate in their crisp lacquer of Bainbridge green and gold beneath a richly embossed family crest.

A very short time later, a bevy of bags had been strapped into the carriage boots, Nancy and Robert's valet, Romney, had been relegated to the rear carriage, and Tia and Margaret had been handed up to the first coach's forward-facing squabs, as was only proper considering the more delicate constitutions of ladies, of course. Immediately after, Robert and Dex settled themselves comfortably across from them. A conscientious footman then gave each of the travelers a warm lap robe and tightly closed the door.

"Do you accompany us on our journey after all, Mr. Clark?" Margaret softly asked as the robes were being distributed and snugged about their legs, thrusting her gloved hand even farther into her warm muff of white rabbit's fur.

"Only as far as the Esk crossing at Airy Hill, I regret to say," he answered with a smile. "From there I must take the road north toward Cleveland County."

Just outside, a whip sharply cracked, bringing a pause in the conversation while the four seized several conveniently placed straps and gripped them tightly. The twentieth part of a moment later, the coach lurched, then rolled into motion.

"Bainbridge has lent me one of his men to drive my curricle so that I might share in at least this small part of your journey," Dex added when it was prudent to release the straps again.

"How very kind in you, sir," Margaret responded, glancing shyly toward Robert's benevolent regard, then slowly bestowing upon him her very first smile.

Tia's fingers fisted within her sable muff, not fooled by her conniving cousin's *kindness* even a whit.

"And how wonderful that you shall be able to accompany us as far as Airy Hill!" Miss Tutweiler added brightly. "Do say that you will stop by the Grange with us and allow me to introduce you to my parents, sir. I should like that above all things . . ." Suddenly Margaret glanced again toward Robert. "H-his lordship, too, of course," she added with a burning blush.

Across from her, Robert grinned. "We should be delighted to meet them," he replied, deftly smoothing over the lady's *petit faux pas*.

On her part, Tia smoothed her features. "Such a pity that afterward you must leave us," she commented sweetly.

Dex's dark eyes assumed a suspicious sparkle. "Yes, but having only recently been reminded that one must always give proper place to precedence, Lady Horatia, I must, of course, first and foremost consider my father's needs. However, even if he had not requested my help, I would still go."

"It would be your duty," Margaret agreed.

"Yes, but it is more than that, my dear."

"More?" Margaret asked on a soft breath.

"Just so," Dex responded, sobering somewhat as the road curved toward the west and the carriage drew within sight of the bridge crossing the Esk. "Over the past several days I have been giving the matter a good deal of thought. It is no secret that my father has ties to the Radical element in Cleveland County . . . that he supports a democratic England. While still in Town, I made inquiries . . ."

". . . And have you learned something of import?" Margaret was curious to know.

"Enough to misdoubt that should I but scratch the surface of the evidence when I arrive home, I shall uncover the somewhat clumsy hand of the Black Mask Society."

"The Black Mask Society!" Margaret gasped, her face growing quite white.

"Them? Oh, surely not!" Tia exclaimed.

"I think it quite possible," Dex countered firmly.

"La, Tia, even their name is ever so ominous! Who are they?" Margaret asked.

"Our local group of Loyalists," Tia answered with a smile.

"Are they quite terrible, then?" Margaret queried, slipping a hand up to touch the bonnet ribbons at her throat.

"Judge for yourself," Tia chuckled in response. "Not too many months past, the Society attempted a bit of midnight mischief upon the Sinnington mill wheel."

"But . . . that is indeed terrible!"

"Not when you understand that not one paddle succumbed," Tia gaily chortled.

"Not one?" Margaret repeated, a small smile forming.

"Not even a splinter had been dislodged. It was discovered later, however, that the Society's costumes had."

"Never say so!" Margaret exclaimed through a widening grin.

"Yes, indeed! In the morning, searchers discovered the Seven River thick with tattered black shreds. A great deal of it. Why, whole shirts, Margaret . . . even unmentionables! . . . were found downstream snagged on the rocks and stumps."

"Oh, Tia, how very amusing!" Miss Tutweiler exclaimed, laughing softly behind her fingers.

"The greatest of jests," Tia merrily agreed as the carriage rumbled across the bridge. "Only think of it, Margaret. Dozens of men running about in the damp and dark, miles from their homes and safety, and without a stitch—"

"I misdoubt we all have the image in our minds, cousin," Robert leveled into their mirth.

Tia wrinkled her nose in the direction of the viscount, but afterward quite properly restrained the remainder of her giggles.

Across from Margaret, Dex clasped his gloved hands. "Obviously, in the assault you just described, Lady Horatia, the Enforcer was not involved," he concluded without the trace of a smile.

"The Enforcer!" Miss Tutweiler again exclaimed, her eyes once more enlarging. "I have never heard of him. Who is this Enforcer? Tia, do you know of him?"

"Everyone knows of him," Tia laughed.

"The Enforcer! Goodness, another menacing name," Margaret noted, drawing her muff almost up beneath her nose.

"As menacing as the man, so word has it," Dex seconded.

"And how do you know that this Enforcer was not involved at Sinnington mill, sir?" Margaret wondered.

"Because the Black Masks made a mull of the attack.

According to my contacts among the Radicals, that doesn't happen when the Enforcer is involved."

"And you believe this?" Tia asked with a chiding grin.

"My information comes from competent men," Dex responded. "They say that the Enforcer is an evil creature who simply . . . appears . . . upon occasion, as if released from the maw of hell itself for a time to reign over the Black Masks and lead them to success. Several in Cleveland County's Reformers speak of the man as if he had been given the power to ensorcel the Society into competence. Whatever the truth, however, the Black Masks rule the moors at such a time. I know for a fact that the Freedom Brigade will not mount a direct counterattack against the Society when they know the Enforcer is present no matter what mischief they might attempt. The Brigade fears even the sound of the Enforcer's name."

"Heaven forfend!" Margaret gasped.

This time Tia laughed out loud. "Then they run from a figment conjured up by the Loyalists to frighten the Radicals into yielding the upper hand. Surely you cannot give credence to such taradiddle!"

"I don't believe in ghosts, if that is what you are asking," Dex responded.

"Give over, then. You are alarming my friend."

". . . Who asked the question in the first place, cousin," Robert reminded her, enjoying the lively verbal combat.

"Point taken." Tia nodded in capitulation. "Very well, do go on, sir," she urged, smoothing away her smile. "I would hear what else you might tell us about this man."

"Heaven help us, Horatia Hilton is on the scent of another male upon whom to fob off Alicia Evans," the viscount interjected, his eyes rolling upward toward the carriage's embossed leather ceiling.

Across from him, Tia punished his wrist with her fan.

"I believe that the man is dangerous," Dex responded, ignoring the cousins' teasing.

"Ah, but only if he exists," Tia pointed out with an elevation of her brows.

"A sovereign says you would fail to find anyone in the entire county who did not fear him," Dex then challenged, his gaze growing intractable as he leaned forward upon his forearms.

"Except, perhaps, someone who had never heard of the man before," Margaret suddenly offered as the carriage shifted, then began to rattle over the gravel drive leading up toward Airy Hill Grange.

"Indeed, but my wager is that there is no such person," Dex argued with an indulgent grin.

"Then, sir, you would lose," Tia stated confidently, again seizing the strap when the coach slowed and pulled to a stop.

"Would I, milady?" Dex questioned just as one of the Grange stable boys wrenched the door open.

"You would," Tia responded, pausing on the step to face him again. "There are certainly two who would qualify."

"Meaning you, for one, of course," Dex stated, his eyes now alight with amusement.

"Yes, certainly me," Tia affirmed with a nod, stepping to the ground, "and Robert, too, for the other. Isn't that right, cousin? You are not afraid, are you? . . . Robert?"

Oddly, the viscount refused to respond.

Shortly after their arrival at the Grange, after the party had been introduced to the squire and his wife and entertained with tea, macaroons, and whinberry tarts, Dex took his leave.

Not the twentieth part of a moment later, Margaret had been resoundingly denied permission by her doting father to ramble about the as yet unfamiliar county on what was surely a cockle-headed errand in the questionable company of the two cousins.

Tia, as might be imagined, was vexed beyond anything.

Therefore, sooner than they had anticipated, Robert and Tia once again found themselves in the comfortable coach, very much alone this time, traveling west between the picturesque slopes of the Esk valley, or dale, toward the village of Castleton where Robert had planned the day before that they might take a meal sometime around mid-afternoon.

"You surprise me, Robert," Tia said as the carriage climbed above the northern slope of the river and the Stakesby Vale Farm drew into sight.

"Oh?"

"Yes. If it were not for the fact that you have been with me every moment since leaving the Abbey, I might suspect that you and the squire had somehow arranged for Margaret to remain behind."

"Perhaps I did," the viscount commented, his attention upon the vast expanse of dry ling heather he could see from the window stretching up and out into the rolling distance until it rose sharply into the lowering sky upon the back of the first of the high moorland riggs, or ridges, just to the south.

"You were that desperate to escape her?" Tia exclaimed. "Well, I shall not believe it for a moment. She is wonderful, Robert . . . the pattern card of everything you deserve. She is—"

"Top over tails for Dex, Tia," Robert interrupted, "in case it has escaped your notice. And he for her."

Tia's mouth snapped shut then, pausing for a moment while her thoughts regrouped and so that her lips might pout a bit in disgruntlement.

"It does not signify. You could win her in a wink, and you know it," she soon resumed.

"I could, hmm?"

"Of a certainty. You are far more eligible. And a hundred times more handsome."

"Do you think so?" Robert questioned with a wisp of a smile.

"Unquestionably. Why, look at you, cousin," Tia commanded, gesturing toward his form. "What woman would not find you the most compelling of men? Why, only consider how well-shaped your ears are . . . or that, right there," she continued, narrowing her eyes as she pointed toward his jaw. "I have always found that most appealing, Robert . . . that tiny little fold at the corner of your mouth where your lips come together . . . or . . ."

"Or what, cousin?" Robert asked, at last sliding his gaze from the scenery to slowly, steadily, purposefully, let it collide with hers.

"Or . . . ," Tia began, suddenly bemused, stumbling over her argument as twin tides of brown, green, and gold seeped into her nerve endings and quite remarkably began to drain away every shred of her intelligence.

"Yes, Tia?"

"Or only consider . . . your . . . eyes . . ."

"My eyes."

"Yes . . . they are . . . Oh, it is a ridiculous notion," she suddenly blurted out, dragging her gaze away from Robert's as she squirmed upon the carriage seat.

"What is?" The viscount smiled, his gaze still molten, moving to prop his cheek upon his fist.

"That you would plot with the squire to leave Margaret behind," she told him, restless under his relentless gaze.

"I regret having to disabuse you, cousin," he countered, his voice now soft and deep, "but it is not ridiculous at all. Not, however, because I have little desire for her company."

"No?" Tia inquired, her head tipping slightly to the side. "Why then?"

"Because I rather like being alone with you."

"You do?" she asked, her gaze once again snared quite solidly within his forest hues. "But, cousin . . . we are often alone."

"Not in the way I wish, Tia," he told her, suddenly intense in his tone, his chest beginning to noticeably rise and fall beneath his cutaway. "Nor intend to soon be. Make up your mind to it."

Confusion furrowed Tia's brow. "Make up my mind to what?"

"That it will be as I intend, and that it starts now."

"I have no idea what you mean," Tia responded, shaking her head.

In response, Robert merely smiled. "I know," he replied, reaching over to adjust his cousin's rumpled lap robe. "Just make up your mind to it anyway."

"And that is all the explanation I am to receive?" Tia asked with a downward turn of her lips.

"For now," Robert responded, turning to stare out of the window again.

One of Tia's feet began to tap upon its warming brick. "You are the veriest varlet, cousin," she pronounced, crossing her arms beneath her breasts.

"I know that, too," Robert responded with a pleasant nod, fitting himself more comfortably into the squabs.

Tia turned then to look out her window, watching as the clouds thinned somewhat and Egton Low Moor suddenly took shape ahead.

"You surprise me, too, cousin," Robert told her after a short time, effectively putting a period to her inner speculations.

"Do I?" she responded absently. "Why?"

"Because you do not fear this Enforcer," he replied.

"Ah, the Enforcer again, is it?" she replied with a chuckle, once more giving him her attention. "No, I do not fear him. Why should I? . . . assuming he exists, of course. I shall never meet the man, after all. And what should he do to me if he ever did cross my path? Do not forget, cousin, that he is one of the Black Masks. Surely you must agree that from everything that we know of our dear Loyalist Society, the reality of the man cannot possibly equal his reputation," she laughed. "Nor can this Enforcer be dangerous as Mr. Clark insists. Name me one instance when the Masks have ever been accused of doing their enemies actual physical harm."

Robert studied his cousin consideringly. "That would be a futile exercise, cousin, as it doesn't signify."

"Why not?"

"Because it sheds no light on the larger questions," Robert told her.

"Larger questions?" Tia repeated, the memory of Robert's earlier silence suddenly causing disconcerting cracks in her conclusions. "What larger questions?"

"For one, why this Enforcer comes and goes as he does," Robert responded.

"If he even exists to do so," Tia countered stubbornly.

"Sightings of the man abound, Tia," Robert argued calmly, "and by far too credible a witness for them to be in error. The questions, therefore, remain. Why is there this mystery surrounding the man? And why is it necessary to cultivate such a reputation? More, why is he not with the Black Masks each time they set out to harry someone? Where is this specter during his absences . . . and with whom? And what assurances have we that he truly is one of the Loyalists?"

"Well, we . . . have . . ."

"Rumor," Robert finished for her. "Nothing but rumor, Tia."

"La, cousin," Tia laughed, unease still at anchor in her eyes, "are you trying to frighten me?"

"Yes," Robert responded softly, reaching across to tidy a strand of hair beneath her bonnet's brim. "Have I succeeded?"

The road turned then, to make one of the several crossings of the Esk before it reached Castleton. Turning away, Tia watched the curved arch of a limestone bridge approach.

At last, she looked down at her gloved hands.

"Perhaps a bit," she quietly confessed.

"Good," Robert replied, and then he slouched more comfortably into the tufted squabs, letting his long legs quite agreeably bracket Tia's as his knees came to rest against the opposite seat.

Only moments later his lids began to droop.

Across from him, Tia's other foot began to tap. "Robert!" she exclaimed when she was certain no solution would be forthcoming.

"Yes, cousin?" the viscount replied, granting her a glance from out of one half-opened eye.

"What *are* the answers, then?" Tia asked, exasperated.

"To what?" Robert asked with a slow grin.

"To the larger questions! Certainly you have a guess as to why the Enforcer comes and goes as he does."

"Only one," Robert told her, shifting his beaver forward so that he might more agreeably settle his head, cushioning it within a depression in the deep brown leather.

"Well, what then?" Tia cried, growing even more vexed.

"I'd wager that the man must have gotten wind of *your* reputation, cousin," he said, rag-manneredly grinning as he closed both his woodland eyes. "Likely he makes himself scarce because the poor sod has learned you are to take tea that day with Alicia Evans."

"Robert, really!" Tia laughed, popping one of her knees against the taut muscles of her cousin's inner thigh. "Varlet!"

" 'Service, ma'am," the viscount murmured, his eyes closed, touching a finger to his beaver's brim.

A comfortable silence took the empty seats in the carriage then, and accompanied the cousins all the way to Castleton.

Ten

"I perceive that Falcon is not yet among us," the Leader stated, looking about the circle of Black Masks as their midday meeting settled into order. "Have none of you seen him, then?"

"Dined with him and my sister Felicity only last evening," Fox told him.

"Well, then, I shouldn't doubt he'll be along at any moment," the Leader replied. "There is no rush to begin today's meeting."

"My apologies, Leader," Beale said, his voice taut, "but there is. My news cannot wait, in fact. You all must hear it without delay."

"Odso!" the Leader murmured, peering at the spy out of the one orbit he wasn't gouging. "Tell us what you know, then, sir. We can always convey your news to Falcon at a later time."

"Aye, milord." Beside Wilson, Beale quickly stood. "Milords, I come as quickly as I could to tell you that as members of the Black Masks you are all now in grave danger . . . even more so, your families be at great risk."

"Egad, sir!" the Leader exclaimed, beginning to rub at his chin. "How so?"

Beale rested his fists upon the rough-hewn table. "It be the mine explosion, sir. Wilson and I have learned that it were no coincidence that your last two missions since then was thwarted."

"Indeed not!" Lion asserted, shifting his corpulence upon his battered chair. "But that was Digby's fault." His gaze then slewed toward the condemned. "Zounds, sir, if you had but allowed me to use both barrels of powder, the whole of the remaining west front wall of Byland Abbey would have collapsed instead of a few wretched arches!"

"Oh, pish tosh!" Fox reprimanded. "How can you state such a Banbury tale? There is no earthly way to know how much powder it would have taken to down the Abbey wall, Harry, as we never were able to light the fuse because of the ghosts. Well you know it, too, milord *Ordnance* officer!"

"Now see here, Digby . . ."

"Fox!" the slender tenor replied, leaping to his feet. "Fox is my name in this room!"

"Gentlemen, please," the Leader cajoled, scratching at a spot just above his ear. "Mr. Beale, I fear that I cannot credit what you say. It was no earthly hand that prevented our attempted display of authority. On the contrary, it was quite extraordinarily supernatural."

"It was ghosts," Raptor bleated deep in his ancient throat. "Scores of them . . . flying out from the ruins . . . from headstones centuries old . . . from the west wall's very windows. Horrifying, it was, I tell you . . . horrifying."

"Begot bumps on m'baubles," Wolf agreed from farther around the table, wafting cherry red lace.

"Forgive me, milords, but be you certain of that?" Beale asked, his gaze scanning the black-clad men. "Did any of your number remain behind to verify who were mounting the counterattack?"

"Deuce take it, sir, we did what anyone would do under

the circumstances!" Lion roared, bounding to his crutch, completely shattering his beleaguered chair. "We ran like the devil!"

"Most likely the very reason, then, why you did not discover that your ghosts was in fact men," Beale responded with great calm.

"Men?" the Leader repeated, pausing in his assault against yet another itch. "Men? Of the Brigade, do you think? Well, of course, they were! Confound it, were they the same ones who outwitted our second attempt? . . . our plan to drive Fenster Ogilvie out of business by cornering the market in Whitby jet?"

"It be a safe assumption, I think," Beale replied.

"Lud, someone, or perhaps several persons, kept dumping jet on the market," the Leader recalled, his shoulders sagging, at the moment too perplexed to chase even the new raw itchiness frolicking around his neck. "The more we obtained, the more appeared to fill Ogilvie's orders. But how? Who among the commoners of the Brigade has the funds for such an enterprise?"

"And how have the scoundrels always managed to get there ahead of us?" Raptor cried, pounding upon the table with a soft rap.

"It be precisely that, milords, that brings Wilson and me here today," Beale responded, straightening to his full height. "I fear you have been infiltrated."

"Infiltrated!" the Leader parroted, one caterpillar brow again declaring war.

"Aye," Beale replied. "I seen the evidence myself, milords. There be no doubt about it. There be one among you, sirs, who be a Radical sympathizer."

"Can it be true?" asked Lion, hopping over several chair rungs to oust Beale from his seat.

"Aye, I can verify it, sir," Beale told him, motioning in turn for Wilson to rise. "Wilson and me just come from London as we told you upon our arrival. The mood there were ugly, I can tell you. Rallies supporting the Radical cause was taking place everywhere. People was stoning windows and passing carriages. There weren't no thought given for the owners' sympathies."

"But why?" Wolf breathed, opening the raspberry scarf encircling his neck so as to allow the winter air to cool his wrinkled flesh.

"Outrage, milord," Beale answered. "Because of the mine explosion. I fear your action against Mr. Clark did not take into account the regard he be held in all over England. Because of the explosion, several of the London Radical Societies have now joined forces. Wilson and me have learned that several of their number have been pledged to deliver retribution to the leaders of the Loyalist groups."

"Lud," the Leader replied, his jaw sagging slightly.

"We can take heart, however, can we not," Raptor offered into the stunned silence, "in the fact that all Loyalist Societies are to be targeted?"

Beale shook his head. "I seen the list of the Societies named to be the Radicals' prey, milord."

"And . . . ?"

"The Black Mask Society be at the top of the list."

"Miss Molly's merkin!" Wolf breathed, his voice trembling.

"Hold, now, gentlemen," Lion said forcefully. "Do not lose heart! We are a secret Society, are we not? How could a Radical blackguard from faraway London possibly know who we are?"

"How, indeed?" agreed the Leader, brightening as, within

his red-rimmed eyeholes, his caterpillars disappeared back into their proper places.

"Milords, all they have to do is ask the Freedom Brigade," Beale responded.

"Do you mean . . . dare you say . . ."

"Aye, milord," Beale told him, taking Wilson's seat. "I seen the Brigade's secret book. They know you all . . . not only by your secret names, but by your real titles as well. And there be more, I fear."

"More?" the Leader asked, swallowing a lump of alarm.

"The Brigade also knows of your plan to kidnap Thomas Paine."

"Good God," uttered Lion, staring straight ahead.

Softly, the Leader cleared his throat. "Mr. Beale, you and Wilson have been with the Brigade for some time. You must be well trusted by now. You must know what is planned."

"I do, milord," Beale replied. "It be the Brigade's mission to . . . neutralize . . . the Black Masks."

"Lud . . . neutralize," repeated Lion.

"What does that mean?" Fox squeaked.

"It means that the Brigade intends to turn the tables, milord," Beale responded. "Just as you plan to kidnap Mr. Paine and hold him against any further activity on the part of the Radical Societies, so the Freedom Brigade intends to kidnap members of your families to hold against your attempt upon Mr. Paine. You be in danger, milords, and your families. It be my thought that you should take steps to assure your safety immediately."

"But how?" Wolf wailed airily.

"By repairing to Bainbridge Castle at once," Lion declared with a decisive thump upon the table. "We shall be safe behind Robert's portcullis."

"Gentlemen, let us try to be logical," the Leader suggested. "We are still the Black Mask Society, charged with defending King George. How can we do that from within the walls of a castle?"

"How, indeed?" Raptor agreed. "And yet we must see to the safety of our loved ones."

"Yes," Fox replied, his tone bleak. "It occurs to me, though, gentlemen, that for the nonce, at least, we are at peace with France. Why could we not use the same peace which worked so well toward Mr. Paine's good to our own advantage?"

"Meaning . . . ?" Lion queried.

"Meaning that my Eugenia would certainly relish the opportunity to visit a Paris modiste now that it is safe to cross the Channel again."

"And my Constance!" added Raptor, tapping his skeletal finger. "Brilliant, Digby! They shall make the crossing together, what?" he added, slowly wavering to his feet. "Come, let us begin making the preparations."

"What? Without me? Without my Hermione?" Lion asserted, rising, too, to gather his black woolen cloak around his affront.

"No, of course not," Fox relented, bounding upward and starting for the door. "But let us make haste to be off, gentlemen. There is no way to know when the Radical subversives will strike."

"Or when the Enforcer shall appear to put a period to everything," Raptor added.

"Lud, Nelson," Lion muttered, worrying at a bruise, "must you mention the man?"

"Here, here!" Wolf added into the general clamor of exit. Following closely behind the others, he added, "I say, Digby, do you suppose the girls would object to my going?"

And then the door slammed open. A slight man stood limned in the doorway, a living, panting plug blocking the way of the Society's headlong exodus.

"Falcon!" the Leader exclaimed after his eyes had adjusted to the increased brightness.

"Please," Falcon uttered in abject misery. "My fellow Black Masks . . . Oh, please, you must help me."

"Dear God, Falcon, what has happened?" Lion cried, taking the stumbling man's arm and assisting him to step into their midst.

"It is Felicity . . . ," he cried as others supported him and tears leaked down his weathered cheeks, "my dearest Felicity."

"What has happened to my sister?" Fox cried, seizing the trembling man's other arm. "Deuce take it, Edward, what has happened to her?"

"She is gone!" Falcon rasped, his eyes beginning to redden with tears. "Dear God, she's been kidnapped!"

To a man, each of the Black Masks again circled the table. At the Leader's signal, each one once more took his proper chair.

"I am certain dear Felicity must only have taken herself off to visit some of your tenants, Falcon," the Leader soothed when all had quieted in the room but the soft sobs of their despairing comrade.

"She has not," Falcon countered, raising his watery gaze from his tear-spotted linen handkerchief. "There was a note, you see."

"A note!" Fox exclaimed. "Tell us, Edward, what did it say?"

"That she was taken against our planned kidnapping of Mr. Paine," he replied miserably. "And it warned me not to allow any of my retainers to participate in the attempt, or else."

"Or else?" Wolf repeated, his painted eyes widening.

"Or else what?" Fox asked, shaking his brother-in-law's shoulder.

"Th-the note didn't say," Falcon wailed, and then he buried his face in his handkerchief again.

"Dear God in heaven, this could happen to any of us," Lion uttered, fear edging into his deep, booming voice. "What are we to do?"

"The spy in your midst must be discovered," Beale suggested calmly.

"What would be the point?" Fox queried agitatedly. "What difference does a deuced spy make if we return home immediately and hole up with our families?"

"I agree," Raptor added vigorously. "The Society is as good as disbanded now. We can do nothing against Mr. Paine under such a heinous threat. We must return to our homes as Fox has said. Until this threat has passed, we must let none of our family out of our sight."

"And what of our cause, gentlemen?" the Leader asked. "What of our defense of George?"

"Let other Loyalists do it!" Lion roared.

"Let the Enforcer!" Fox added, clutching at Falcon's sleeve.

The Leader paused, then took a slow, deliberate breath. "But the Enforcer uses *us*," he reasoned with them. "We are the very troops he would use to combat this threat against us. So what measure of safety do we gain by involving him? And what is to happen to England, gentlemen . . . to the peerage . . . if the Radicals succeed in their plans? Do you wish to see George beheaded as Louis was in France? Do you wish to see your lands made forfeit? . . .

your own wives and children marched to the block?" Slowly the Leader's gaze searched each face in the cold gloom.

"Nay . . . ," Raptor finally uttered in his fragile tremolo, "it must not come to that."

"Then what are we to do?" Lion asked into the room's bleak mood.

"We must stay the course, gentlemen," the Leader wearily replied. "We really have no choice."

"But Felicity . . . !" Falcon cried.

"We shall charge Beale and Wilson to uncover her hiding place," the Leader soothed. "Meanwhile, we must make it look as if we are cooperating with the Radicals. For the nonce, gentlemen, we must end our meetings. If anything of import arises, I shall convey it by messenger or during normal occasions of social intercourse; and when it is time to sail out to intercept Mr. Paine's ship, I shall get word to you."

"What of the danger to our families?" Wolf inserted.

"They can know nothing of our plans, of course," the Leader replied, "but I do think that we must make them aware of the danger to them. They shall have to cooperate with us, shall they not, in remaining secure in our homes until the danger is passed?"

"And the Enforcer?" Fox asked.

"Nothing has changed. If he knows of our plan for Mr. Paine, no doubt he will try to put a period to it. The man is devilishly uppity about acting only upon his own ideas, don't you know. Besides, if he does stop us, even for the most honorable of motives, what is to become of England? No, gentlemen, as beneficial as the Enforcer has been to our success and to our cause, we must still hope that he does not show himself until after the deed is done. This is

the most momentous attempt we have ever undertaken, my
fellow Loyalists. We must rise to the occasion," he exhorted
as he stood to his feet and held out his fisted hand. "We
are the Black Masks!"

Slowly the men gathered about the rude table rose to
join him. Stretching out their hands, they gripped one another's, forming a fisted hub radiating black-clad spokes.

"We are agreed, then," stated the Leader, dropping his
arm.

The circle animated with the nod of each *chapeau-bras*.

"Then let us adjourn, gentlemen," he told them. "Go
and see to the safety of your families until the time."

In moments, the Earl of Walmsley was the lone figure
still standing at the edge of the flickering dome of candlelight. He would not be concerned, he told himself over and
over again as the day lengthened and silence steadily built
a thick pressure in the room to constrict the pulse throbbing
within his throat. She would be safe. After all, she was with
Robert, was she not? And Robert would take care of her.
It was of no moment. Robert was with her. He would not
be concerned.

His hands beginning to tremble, the Leader of the Black
Masks gathered his cloak about him, scratched at a particularly insistent itch on the side of his nose, and, with
aching slowness, sank once again into his chair's scarred,
disinterested embrace.

Eleven

The short winter day had long since given way to darkness by the time the Bainbridge coaches arrived at Spindle Thorn Hall, the home of the Honorable Frederick Litchfield and his wife, Barbara. Since the sixteenth century, the Hall had stood in stately Elizabethan splendor on a picturesque rise above the banks of Loskey Beck not many miles to the north of Hutton-le-Hole. It did so still, though at this advanced hour, it seemed more like a house adrift to Tia . . . like a solitaire floating upon fibers of mist made incandescent by the rising moon, companioned only by the lapping beck and its skirting of bare-branched ash and shrub willow. Watching the mansion's warmly lit windows grow larger with their approach, she considered this, knowing her friend was inside, uneasy as to how she fared.

Perhaps the estate's very remoteness was a possible cause of the Litchfields' difficulties, she reasoned as determination began to build within her blood. And yet Barbara was not alone, she quickly remembered. On the contrary, she had not only her husband, but her old governess, Mrs. Cribbs, still with her for companionship. It could not be denied, however, that isolation was a powerful force for ill in many women's lives and not without its consequence. But was it so in Barbara's? Tia fervently hoped not. With all her romantic heart, she wished that her shy friend's days passed as this one had for her . . . full of exciting new vistas awaiting her discovery, pleasant conversation, and the ease that comes with comfortable acquaintance. She smiled then, recollection taking hold.

Their passing that day had been without consequence. They had reached Castleton in good time and had taken a meal at the Robin Hood and Little John Inn not far past the lovely limestone bridge which had carried them back across the Esk and into the midst of the village's collection of dark stone houses, several topped with blue-tinged slate, others with soft pink pantiles. The inn had boasted a sign which read,

> Kind gentlemen, and yeomen good,
> Call in and drink with Robin Hood;
> If Robin be not at home,
> Step in and drink with Little John.

Tia had laughed at the sentiment delightedly, and that had, of course, evoked many speculations on her part concerning whether or not the famous outlaw had indeed sought refuge in the county, followed by a lengthy avowal from Robert that of a certainty he had done so upon occasions too numerous to count, and that she was a ragmannered hoyden to pish-tosh the notion when everyone in North Yorkshire knew it was so.

Tia, as might be expected, had chortled all the more.

From Castleton, after changing their carriage horses, they had departed again, this time taking a road that turned abruptly southward before it climbed Castleton Rigg, then rode the long, rugged spine overlooking the lush verdancy of Danby Dale for several miles before becoming absorbed into the isolation of Danby High Moor.

They had remarked upon the several huge stone crosses they had come across next, near the intersection of their road and the roads to Westerdale and Rosedale. Not even Robert had known for certain the crosses' origins, but he had relayed to Tia the tidbit that for centuries it had been the custom for travelers to place coins on the top of the stone called Old Ralph for the benefit of fellow travelers less fortunate than themselves.

And once this custom had been made known to her, of course, she would have nothing but that they should leave an offering, too; and they had done so, Robert having been altogether propelled by his cousin from the cozy warmth of the traveling coach into the brisk bite of the moor-chilled wind to receive the necessary boost from Romney, afterward shinnying up the stone's slick, cold, nine-foot height to place a sovereign atop it, then down again, muttering under his breath all the while that he should learn when to keep his deuced mouth shut.

And then moving on . . . on across Blakey Ridge and its spectacular views of Farndale's clustered villages and farms, becks and gills, and the patchwork fields that had conjoined them; and down, as darkness had begun to fall, into little Hutton-le-Hole and the stream that divided it, past sheep allowed to roam freely among the sturdy, cruck-framed, ling-thatched houses to crop the common grasses, and north again until at last Spindle Thorn Hall had come into sight, and both of them, worn and travel-weary, had smiled.

"What on earth do you intend to say to these people, Tia?" the viscount asked as the carriage rolled to a gentle, welcome halt, and he dropped down upon the snow-dusted drive.

"Why, the truth, of course," Tia answered, steadying herself upon his shoulders when he took her waist.

"Just like that?" Robert exclaimed, lifting her down beside him. "You are going to march into the Litchfields' midst, completely unannounced, and proceed to tell them that you are here to mend their marriage?"

"Don't be ridiculous, Robert. Of course I shan't do that," Tia insisted, brushing a collection of wrinkles from her sable-lined traveling cape. "All I intend to tell them at first is that I am looking for the sender of that horrid valentine."

"Wonderful," Robert commented, motioning to his footmen to begin the unloading of their valises. "You realize, of course, that all they shall have to do then is confess or deny it. In seconds we shall be back out here on our duffs."

Tia began to laugh. "What nonsense!" she exclaimed, beginning to stroll down the lengthy walk toward the square front steps, taking care to gather her cloak's orange melton close about her legs so as to keep it from snagging upon the thickly intertwined branches of the walk's encroaching honeysuckle shrubs. "Barbara and I became quite close over the course of the Little Season in which we made one another's acquaintance. I am persuaded she shall be delighted to grant us the hospitality of her home."

"Indeed," Robert commented mostly to himself as he turned back toward the carriage interior to retrieve his silver-headed cane. "Tell me, cousin," he finally called to her, "has it passed beneath your notice yet that it is now quite dark outside?"

"Yes, of course," Tia called back, not turning around. "What of it?"

"Only that it is a long way back to Hutton-le-Hole," he replied, hooking his cane about his elbow before settling his beaver more securely over his Bedford crop.

"Yes, cousin, I believe that it is," Tia replied, almost at the Hall's great polished oak door. "Is that of some significance?"

"It is of great significance to a man who could eat an entire horse right this very moment along with its hooves and tail," Robert growled over his shoulder. "You are taking great risks with my appetite, cousin. Have a care, therefore, how you broach . . ."

Suddenly, several nerves began to tickle across the back of the viscount's neck. He hesitated . . . his words dying away. And then, with the violence of an explosion, every sense in his body began to scream at him that danger was in their midst.

Tia!

As silently as the touch of a snowflake upon the ground, Robert spun back about toward the pathway, his gaze fierce in the blue winter night as it scoured each shade of shadow, then found and riveted upon a dark shape just moving out onto the walk behind Tia from the honeysuckle thicket. Stealthily, the shape crept forward, its posture crouched like a predator ready to spring, its hands stretched outward toward his cousin.

Robert's countermove was blurred by sheer speed. With a single slashing thrust, he swept his cane forward and out to connect with silent precision just behind the attacker's knees. Instantly the form tumbled forward onto the ice-bound flagstones, emitting a slight gasp as his body thudded against the hard surface and his wrists sank into a soft, shallow drift. Shaken, the dark shape shuddered for only a moment, then immediately struggled to rise.

With a detached coldness, Robert stepped out of the carriage's shadow. A man, he observed as he started forward.

A bloody bastard bent on doing harm to Tia. Deuce take it, it was not to be borne!

Seconds later, the viscount seized hold of the man's coat collar, yanking upward with one gloved hand at the same time that the other hand formed a fist, cocked, and aimed for that certain nerve cluster he had learned from John Jackson . . .

And then the man was gone.

Robert blinked. All that remained of the attacker was the empty coat still clutched in his hand. Muttering an oath, he let his balled fist fall back to his side.

"Is anything the matter, cousin?" Tia called back in his direction as she started up the Hall's drifted steps.

Robert looked up from the coat still dangling from his fingertips. He sighed next. And then, smoothing his features, he shook his head.

"Not a thing, my dear," he pleasantly replied, laying the stranger's coat across his arm and stooping to retrieve his cane.

"Well, then, kindly cease your dawdling," Tia chided, still facing the Hall's oak-planked entrance.

The viscount presented his cousin's back a low and courtly bow, acquiescing to her wishes just as a gentleman should, pausing only long enough before starting forward to first motion for a footman to precede him so that he might, if he pleased, make their company's presence known to the master of the house.

"Devil a bit, man, where is your coat?" hissed a dark shape coalescing out of the pitch-black interior of a rude, tumble-down farmhouse not two miles from Spindle Thorn. Suddenly a lucifer flared in the darkness and stuttered against the intrusion of a woven ribbon of wick. Light spread outward, illuminating the speaker . . . the beaver pulled down low over his forehead, the broad, heavy brow . . . the cold, piercing eyes . . . bestubbled cheeks.

"Had to leave it behind," the other replied, convulsively stumbling into the room. "For God's sake, light the fire," he pleaded, reaching for a bottle of porter sitting on a table in the center of the room. "M'ballocks have shrunk all the way up to m'throat."

The other made known his vexation, then bent to hold the lantern wick under the kindling stacked neatly within the crumbling hearth. "You'd best give me your report, then, Billy," he finally said.

"I didn't get her," Billy gasped around swallows of porter.

"I can see that for myself," the other stated.

"Got blind-sided," Billy continued. "Fellow grabbed me coat, he did. Only just got away by wiggling out of it."

"What was in your pockets?" the other asked.

"Nothing! Nothing, I swear it!"

"Who was the man?"

"That viscount."

"Bainbridge," the other stated, placing several logs upon the struggling fire. "He would be with her for protection, of course. Well, it is an annoyance, but not totally unexpected. We shall probably have to take care of him at some point, I suppose." Slowly he rose and seated himself across from Billy.

"So," Billy asked, his cheeks ballooning with his next swig, "what do we do?"

"Try again, I suppose," he answered. "There isn't much time before Paine's ship sails."

"Nor mebbe . . . ," Billy added, finishing the pint as his lids began to droop, "before the Enforcer shows."

"Yes," the other agreed, staring into the fire, his head nodding. "We must get to the girl, and soon. We'll try again tonight."

"Tonight?"

"Yes, tonight, Billy. He is out there somewhere . . . waiting . . . I can feel it. For the sake of the cause, we must have the girl in our possession before the Enforcer appears on the Blackamore again. I tell you, Billy, if I can help it, no bloody Englishman loyal to Mad George shall ever get his hands on the man whose work inspired countless thousands to take back their liberty. Nay, I vow it. No one shall ever touch Thomas Paine!"

Billy's responding belch was loud. In counterpoint to the crackle of the flames, his porter bottle rolled to drop unregarded upon the earthen floor.

"So you can see, can you not, why I must know the sender of this valentine?" Tia concluded several hours later from her place at Spindle Thorn's richly carved mahogany dining room table, her fingers absently learning the texture of the delicate black lace encircling the horrid card.

"Unquestionably, the reception of such a card must have been awkward for you," Mr. Litchfield offered from his position at the head of the long damask-draped table.

"Yes, Tia, how horrible it must have been," Mrs. Litchfield added from opposite him, afterward nodding to a footman to refresh Robert's claret glass.

"I cannot deny it," Tia told them, returning the card to its box, "yet, truly, I have come to think of the actual card as of no moment. Rather, it is a cry for help, I perceive.

Therefore, you have nothing to fear, you see. Revenge is not the purpose of my visit."

"What nonsense," offered the ponderous, pinched woman seated to Mrs. Litchfield's right. "Of course it is. And if it truly is not, then it should be."

"Cribby . . . ," Mrs. Litchfield began.

"Do not think to scold me for my opinion, Barbara. Whatever gentleman sent that beastly thing *should* be punished for his deed."

"And if it was not a man?" Mr. Litchfield asked softly.

"As to that, there is not a particle of doubt," Mrs. Cribbs snapped, casting her benefactor a narrowed glare. "It is just the sort of thing a man would contrive."

"We cannot know that. I am afraid I must agree with Mr. Litchfield, Mrs. Cribbs," Tia told her. "Anyone could have sent the valentine."

"Anyone but the residents of Spindle Thorn, Lady Horatia, as I mentioned when you first arrived," Mr. Litchfield stated. "Neither my wife nor I have sent anything to the Abbey recently."

From Mr. Litchfield's left, Tia sighed. "I accept that, sir," she dejectedly replied.

Mrs. Cribbs took a sip of wine. "Why did you think that either my Barbara or . . . *he* might have?" she questioned with only the merest of acknowledgments cast toward Mr. Litchfield.

"I hardly see that the matter is any of your affair, Mrs. Cribbs," Mr. Litchfield replied levelly, gazing past the centerpiece of forced daffodil blossoms toward his wife's companion.

The elderly woman stiffened. "Anything to do with Barbara is my affair, sir," she snapped.

"Cribby, please . . . ," Mrs. Litchfield began softly from her companion's side.

"I shall speak my mind, dearest," Mrs. Cribbs interrupted, scouring the corner of her down-turned mouth with her serviette. "I have done so since you were in leading strings, and I shall not cease now simply because I am told to do so by this . . . *man!*"

"Then I shall speak frankly as well," Tia replied pleasantly, returning her spoon to the plate beneath her custard dish. "It is true that with a few exceptions, I thought it more likely that the valentine might have been sent from this household than the others of my acquaintances."

"But, I don't understand . . . ?" Mrs. Litchfield softly said.

"Oh, dear, how can I put this delicately?" Tia began, glancing at her plate. "Barbara," she said, looking up, "it is not unknown about our county Society that there are . . . problems . . ."

"Problems?" Mrs. Cribbs snapped in question.

". . . of a marital nature," Tia finished firmly, one curl drooping above the bulge in her jaw as she cast the woman's interference a quelling glance.

"Good God, is nothing safe from conjecture?" Mr. Litchfield uttered tightly, shifting his hard gaze toward his wife, his neck mottling between his collar points.

Beside his host, Robert shifted in his seat. "I assure you, the rumors are not as prevalent as my cousin makes it seem," he scowled. "Tia might, in fact, be the only one who has heard them. Like a hound, her ears seem singularly attuned to the mewl of a tabby."

Tia shot her cousin a fresh glower.

"As I was trying to say, Barbara, I have not come solely to discover the black valentine's sender. I have also come because I am sensible of my role in . . . arranging matters between the two of you. If there truly are problems, I feel that it is only right that I do what I can to help."

"My affairs have become an open book!" Mr. Litchfield rasped, his gaze still locked upon his wife.

"Nothing of the sort," Tia countered, her curl slipping farther with the shake of her head. "Not a word of our conversations shall leave this household, sir."

"You will forgive me if I find no comfort in that, madam," Mr. Litchfield replied.

"Fiddle," Tia countered. "You must have a little faith, sir. Mark my words, I shall have things set right again in a trice."

"What you shall have done, my lady, is to meddle in what is none of your affair!" Mrs. Cribbs interjected, coloring dramatically.

"The room seems to have an echo," Robert observed just before touching his lips to the disk of wine in his claret glass.

"Cribby, dearest, Lord Bainbridge and his cousin are our guests . . . ," Mrs. Litchfield pleaded softly.

"And what am I?" the matron countered, her gaze sweeping toward her charge. "Nothing, I misdoubt. Nay, less than nothing. Only the one who has nursed you and taught you . . . only the one who has ever had your welfare as her sole regard!"

"Deuce take it, Mrs. Cribbs, you will hold your tongue!" Mr. Litchfield admonished. "I shall not tolerate such a scene before my guests."

"Then, of course, I shall no longer burden you with my presence," Mrs. Cribbs responded sharply, suddenly rising to her feet while a footman hurried to arrest the fall of her chair. "I shall be in the drawing room, Barbara," she continued, raising her serviette to the corner of her eye, ". . . alone, of course . . . at my embroidery. No doubt your *husband* shall require you to entertain your guests in the gallery this evening as a consequence of my choice. Therefore, I shall see you when we retire, my darling."

With a flourish, Mrs. Cribbs dropped her damask serviette upon her plate and started toward the door.

"Oh, Cribby, dear, do wait!" Mrs. Litchfield cried, rising as well.

"I shall not stay where I am not welcome," the companion pouted, her eyes pooling with tears.

"Indeed," Mr. Litchfield commented to no one in particular.

Mrs. Litchfield colored prettily. "But you *are* welcome, Cribby," she replied coaxingly, glancing back toward her husband. "I promised you when I was but a little girl that you would always have a home with me."

"A home, perhaps," Mrs. Cribbs countered, "but not your complete trust as I once had . . . not a position of respect in your household."

"But that is nonsense!" Mrs. Litchfield soothed, placing her arm around her companion. "You know how much I value your counsel. And let us hear no more of removing yourself from our company. We shall all spend the evening together as we always do. Come, Tia . . . shall we leave the gentlemen to their port?"

Tia clamped her jaw closed on her imprudent response and swallowed.

"Of course," she answered with ingrained politeness before rising along with her hostess. Before turning away, however, she glanced toward the viscount. "I *will* see you in a short time, will I not, cousin?"

The viscount masked a grin within a candlelit hazel

gleam. "How very humorous you are," he responded, rising beside his host to place his warm lips upon Tia's hand.

"Varlet!" Tia whispered toward his neat Bedford crop.

When he next looked at her, Robert's eyes were dancing with mirth. " 'Service, ma'am," he replied, giving her fingers a squeeze.

Her shoulders just beneath her earlobes, Tia whirled about to stalk after the others. She paused at the doorway, however, only just managing to stop herself from turning back toward her cousin and sticking out her tongue before she continued on.

"Better, Cribby?" asked Mrs. Litchfield as she plumped the cushions protruding out from behind her companion's ample folds of flesh.

"Yes, my darling, I am feeling much more the thing," the woman replied, sipping a Chinese blend. "Though, goodness knows, my nerves have yet to recover. I cannot recall when I have been so overset. Did you hear the way he spoke to me?"

"Dearest, Frederick *is* the master of this house," Barbara replied quietly. "Tia, may I pour you a dish of tea?"

"Yes, thank you."

"Well, master or no master, he is still a man," Mrs. Cribbs spat out like a curse. "Distasteful creatures, all of them . . . fraught with vile habits and foul desires. How right you have been, dearest, to maintain your distance from him."

Distance? Tia thought as Barbara filled her cup.

"I assume that you are not wed, Lady Horatia," Mrs. Cribbs rather baldly stated, next directing her gaze toward Tia.

She shook her head.

"Most intelligent of you," the companion assessed. "And reason enough to extend to you my apology, my dear. Obviously, your lack of a husband is the result of a well-considered choice, given that you are not a particularly unfavored gel, but certainly of advanced age."

Tia's eyes widened above a flush of color.

"Yes," she finally responded, stilling her fingers by gripping her dish of tea. "I have chosen to remain unmarried."

"There, you see, dearest?" Mrs. Cribbs lashed out, her eyes glittering toward Mrs. Litchfield. "Here is another woman with sense enough to know what is best for her sex. You do understand what I feel, do you not?" she again directed toward Tia. "You have experienced it as well, haven't you? Do not bother to deny it. Come, you may speak freely to me, child. Who was the beast, and what did you suffer at his evil hands?"

Blood suddenly began to pound against Tia's ears. Evil? Had her father been evil? And had she suffered? No, but only because of her mother's interference during his bouts of drunkenness . . . and because of Robert, of course . . . the haven she had run to since she was too young to remember otherwise . . . her solace with wide open arms to shoulder her fear and hurt, with healing words that made her whole again, with a handkerchief always in his right waistcoat pocket beneath his watch. Robert . . . her cousin . . . her friend.

"Come, who was it, Lady Horatia?" the companion continued over the thrumming in Tia's head. "Your father, most likely . . . devils all of them! Ah, or was it Bainbridge, my pet?"

No! Tia cried out in her mind. Robert is not my father, she insisted even as fresh memories of the day's carriage trip flooded back into her consciousness to make mice feet of her conclusion.

No, Tia considered, slightly shaking her head. Robert was her comfortable, familiar cousin. Her friend.

"A fine specimen, Bainbridge," Mrs. Cribbs stated, sipping her Chinese blend. "Competent, powerful. What chance would any woman have against such a *man.*"

Her pulse thundering, Tia only just steadied the tremble that would have sent her teacup crashing to the Aubusson.

"W-will you excuse me, please?" she suddenly queried, shakily rising to her feet as a storm of emotions tangled within her. "There is something I must do . . ."

"Oh, Tia, do let me ring for Pearson," Barbara offered. "He shall fetch anything you might need. Dearest, are you quite well?"

"I . . . ," Tia responded, tightening her warm shawl about her shoulders, struggling to gather herself. "I am fine, really. I . . . only wish to retire for a moment before the gentlemen join us."

"Of course," Barbara replied. "Let me ring for Pearson to show you the way."

"No! . . . No, that will not be necessary," Tia responded, starting hesitantly toward the door. "I am certain that I can find the way. Do excuse me, if you please. I do apologize, but . . . I-I must be away."

Only moments later, Tia burst back into the dining room.

"Tia . . . !" her comfortable, familiar cousin exclaimed, looking up from his port at the sudden sound. "Deuce take it, we are still at port and cigars, cousin," he complained. "What in the . . . ?"

"Robert!" Tia whispered, searching his alien, familiar

gaze, hesitating with unaccountable uncertainty, yearning, leaning toward him, her eyes bewitchingly bemused.

Slowly Robert placed his glass of port upon the damask cloth, then rose to his feet.

"Come here, love," he murmured, opening his arms.

Against her own desires, yet knowing that it was necessary, Tia freed one hand from her cousin's warm, wonderful embrace to dig into his right waistcoat pocket for the handkerchief she knew would be there just beneath his watch.

Twelve

"Tia, what is it?" Robert rumbled against her sagging tress, the abrasion of his chin sending it tumbling onto her shoulder.

"I . . . ," Tia began from the depths of his cravat *en cascade*.

"What did you say?" Robert asked, setting her back from him just the tiniest bit.

Tia swallowed, clutched at his lapels, and then lifted her gaze.

"I said . . ."

Yet, unaccountably, she could not.

It was happening again. Peering up into her cousin's face, suddenly every thought splintered into a thousand shards. Yet nothing about Robert had changed. Tia could see that very well for herself. His face was just as it always had been . . . beloved, comfortingly familiar. Yet now, at the same time, it was an alien thing, rugged, strangely compelling in its sinuous shadows and planes, mesmerizing in the fierce intensity of its eyes' woodland green.

Unable to draw her gaze away, Tia avidly rode his nose up to his hairline, back and forth across it, then down again to touch upon the corner of each jaw, framing the sinewy curves of his chin and cheeks.

"Are you quite all right, Lady Horatia?" Mr. Litchfield asked, glancing toward the viscount for confirmation.

"Tia?"

With an effort, Tia broke off her fascination with a wonderful silver fleck she had just discovered at one iris's edge.

"I . . . yes. Yes, of course I am," she answered, reluctantly gathering herself. "Th-there were merely several questions I needed answered," she added, drawing in a deep, stabilizing breath.

"Which obviously were so important they could not wait until I and our host had finished our cigars," Robert teased in spite of a steady gaze intense with concern.

"Fiddle," Tia tartly replied, grasping at the goading prick of her cousin's voice like a rescue craft, quickly using it to clear the last vestiges of each unsettling perception from her mind. "What is so sacred about this time that you gentlemen always chafe so at being disturbed? And who says that you have a right to separate yourselves from us females? Is it any wonder, I ask you, that Barbara feels she has the same right?"

Beside her, Robert's brows shot up to his hairline. Appalled silence settled over the room.

"Exactly what right are you referring to?" Mr. Litchfield asked quietly after an interminable time.

"Why . . . ," Tia began awkwardly, "why, the right to maintain a distance from you, as I am certain you are aware."

"Barbara told you this?" he rasped, his face drawing into rigid lines.

"No, as a matter of fact, Mrs. Cribbs was the one who mentioned it, but—"

"Damn!" Mr. Litchfield exploded, launching his serviette onto the plate of chocolates and rocketing to his feet. "Damn that woman's eyes!"

"Oh, dear, Mr. Litchfield . . . ," Tia breathed, altogether horrified by her host's violent reaction. "Truly, I did not mean for my impulsive words to overset you. I do say things without thinking, you know. Yet even though I acknowledge the fault, still there are times when I forget myself. Goodness, Robert can tell you—"

"Hush, Tia," the viscount commanded her. "Let it go."

For the next few moments, Mr. Litchfield scrubbed at his jaw, then turned back toward Tia, again the proper host. "Do accept my apologies, Lady Horatia. My outburst was, of course, unconscionable. And you are correct. I *am* sensible of my wife's feelings, for all that it matters," he finally responded quietly. "It is that woman . . . !"

"Mrs. Cribbs?"

"Tia, let it go," Robert interjected.

"How can I, cousin, when I am intimately involved?" Tia returned as Robert's eyes widened and then slowly closed over the innocent double entendre. "And it is for precisely this very reason that I came, after all. I tell you, I am duty bound to do what I can to help, and I am persuaded that the place to begin is with an explanation of . . ."

"Tia, for God's sake!"

". . . An explanation of what Mrs. Cribbs meant when she said that Barbara was right to maintain a distance from her husband."

The viscount's eyes rolled up to support his brows.

Mr. Litchfield, however, and quite surprisingly, took on the aspect of a man resigned to whatever might poleax him next. Motioning for them all to be seated again, he passed the plate of chocolates to Tia for her selection, then folded his hands before him and began.

"The meaning is just what it seems," he stated softly, his blue gaze growing matte. "My wife, you see, has never . . . that is, we do not . . ."

"Do go on, sir," Tia gently urged. "Do not be afraid. She has never what?"

"Oh, for the love of . . . ," Robert muttered, seizing a delicate *glacéed* plum.

"Yes, Robert?"

"Deuce take it, what our host is trying to convey to you, my innocent, is that he and his wife have never shared the same bed."

"But why is that a problem?" Tia asked, staring between the two gentlemen. "Most husbands and wives of my acquaintance have separate beds."

"Granted," Robert responded. "But they do not always sleep in them, Tia."

"They do not? But I have never seen . . ."

"Of course you haven't," Robert replied patiently. "When have you ever had the opportunity? Only consider it, Tia. Your father died when you were very young, as did your Aunt Elizabeth. And unless there has been something very interesting going on all these years between the countess and Cousin Brumley, you, my dear, have completely missed out on that particular childish pleasure of walking in on one's parents while in the throes of . . . bed-sharing."

"I . . . see," Tia responded thoughtfully. "Is this a comfortable arrangement, then, Robert? One to which most women do not object? I must say that I can see how a woman might perhaps prefer to avoid such an occurrence if she were not accustomed to it."

"Trust me . . . it is a very comfortable arrangement, Tia," Robert informed her, his gaze growing warm as it washed over hers, "as well as a wife's marital duty and a husband's right."

"Then the solution seems simple," Tia said, turning again toward Mr. Litchfield. "You merely must make this duty known to Barbara. I am certain that once she understands it she will wish to comply."

"I am afraid that it is not as simple as it seems, my dear," Mr. Litchfield replied.

"But why?" Tia asked, noting with some concern that her host had colored quite radiantly over the past several moments.

"Because Barbara knows already and is deathly afraid of the concept. And I am afraid that if I push her too hard to overcome her fear, I shall only succeed in driving her away."

"Afraid? Of sharing a bed with you? Dear me, that does rather complicate things, does it not?" Tia commented. "Of course, Barbara has always been a timid thing. I confess I have at times wondered why."

"That would be Mrs. Cribbs's doing, I'd wager," Robert said, swallowing the last of his *glacéed* plum.

Mr. Litchfield nodded. "Barbara has been under that woman's influence since she was in leading strings," he told them. "As sweet . . . as gentle and docile as my wife is . . . she has never been a match for her companion."

"Rather like a whisper in a gale," Tia agreed as Mr. Litchfield nodded his acknowledgment. "Do go on, sir."

"Why not? I can see no harm in it." Their host shrugged. And then his gaze grew distant. "Were you aware, Lady Horatia, when you introduced Barbara and me, that she had already rejected four other suitors?"

"No! . . . I was not, sir. But, why?" Tia asked, setting aside the remainder of her chocolate.

In response, Mr. Litchfield released a deep sigh. Propping his elbows upon the damask, he dropped his chin disconsolately onto his fists. "Because of her fear," he answered in a rough voice.

"Yet she did agree to become your wife," Tia pointed out.

After glancing up at Tia, Mr. Litchfield straightened and flattened his palms upon the table. "My dear, the only reason my suit was successful was because her widowed mother had reached the point of despair where her daughter was concerned," he told her as his voice strengthened with anger. "Barbara, I discovered, agreed to marry me because her mother had threatened to cut her off without a groat if she did not."

"How awful for you!" Tia commiserated. "And for Barbara, too, of course. How horrid to become caught between the threats of her mother and the teachings of her trusted governess!"

"Yes," Mr. Litchfield said, relaxing back against his chair. "Utterly beyond the pale."

"Poor Barbara found herself in what, to her, must have been an untenable situation," Tia reasoned, shaking her head as segments of her own discussions with the countess flickered through her mind. "Why, as I see it, Mr. Litchfield, what choice did she have but to be disingenuous with you? Yet I wonder if she truly was."

"What do you mean, Tia?" Robert asked, sipping from his port glass.

"I mean that in spite of your belief to the contrary, Mr. Litchfield, I am persuaded that there are cracks in the mortar of Barbara's resolve. I believe that she cares a great deal for you."

Mr. Litchfield released a mirthless snort. "I am afraid you will have a difficult time convincing me of that."

"Then pay attention, sir," Tia confidently replied. "Ever since our arrival, I have been observing Barbara. Do you know that she looks at you when you are not aware of it? . . . that her cheeks color when you come near?"

"Do they indeed?" Mr. Litchfield commented, trying to keep his voice from betraying a sudden nudge of hope.

"They do," Tia affirmed with a nod. "Your wife may be frightened of you, sir, but she also cares. Another woman can tell these things."

"And you, of course, have so much experience," Robert murmured from beside her.

For the sake of maintaining her point, Tia sacrificed the crow she itched to pluck.

"I believe that beneath her fear, she wishes this 'bed-sharing.' "

"Yes . . . well . . . I appreciate your observations, my lady, but I fail to see how such intelligence helps," replied Mr. Litchfield, reddening slightly. "My wife shall not alter her thinking because of it. After three years of marriage, the whole idea of . . . a closeness to me . . . still frightens her to death."

"Thanks to Mrs. Cribbs," Tia added softly.

"Exactly so," affirmed Mr. Litchfield, his smile sad and soft. "To her credit, I suppose, the witch has done her job well."

"She feeds Barbara's fear," Tia concluded after several moments had passed.

"Continually."

"Oh, why do you not just throw her in Loskey Beck!" Tia exclaimed.

"Because she is dear to my wife," Mr. Litchfield explained, cheering slightly, "and because Barbara has made promises to her."

"And so . . ."

Again Mr. Litchfield colored.

"The deuce!" Robert inserted into the awkwardness. "And so, my impertinent baggage, as a result of Mrs. Cribbs's interference, there has never been a wedding night!"

"Ah . . ."

"Worse," Mr. Litchfield added. "Most likely there never will be."

"Rubbish," responded Tia tartly. "Do you care for Barbara?"

"I love her," stated Mr. Litchfield firmly.

"And I am convinced she loves you as well," Tia responded. "I am persuaded that all she needs is a chance," she added, suddenly settling into thought.

Just as suddenly she looked up again.

"A question, sir. Am I correct in assuming that this lack of a wedding night is what is wrong in your marriage?"

"It is," Mr. Litchfield affirmed.

"And would you venture a guess that all would be well between you and Barbara if you could do this 'bed-sharing' with her?"

"That would be two questions, Tia," Robert noted, peering into his port glass.

"Yes, but they are all of a piece, Robert," Tia explained. "Mr. Litchfield?"

"In my opinion, it would," Mr. Litchfield again agreed, this time his eyes taking on just the tiniest hint of gleam.

"Very well, another question, then, if you please, sir," Tia announced. "You speak of her joining you in your bed," she said. "Could it not be the other way around? What if

Barbara has been waiting all these months for you to share hers?"

"I hardly think that likely," Mr. Litchfield replied.

"Why?"

"Because Barbara already shares her bed," Mr. Litchfield sighed.

"With Mrs. Cribbs," Tia concluded, beginning to tap the tablecloth with one fingertip.

"Indeed."

"Well, I suppose that does put a different complexion on things. Although I do with some frequency share my bed with one of my friends and do not suffer for it. I imagine, however, that including yourself into their twosome might be a bit awkward given Mrs. Cribbs's animosity."

"I think so," Mr. Litchfield replied, choking on a bit of cigar smoke.

Beside her, Robert, too, began to cough.

"Tia, this whole bumblebroth is a bit more complicated than you understand . . . ," he gasped when he could breathe again. "Which is precisely why you should not be meddling in any of it. Contrary to your beliefs, you simply do not have the experience—"

"But I do have the duty," Tia countered, casting her cousin a quelling glance, afterward tucking her chin into her fists and narrowing her eyes in concentration. "Just give me a little time, Robert. I promise you, in the twentieth part of a moment, I shall come up with a plan."

Without a ready argument, the viscount had no choice but to subside.

Mr. Litchfield, on the other hand, for some unaccountable reason found that his spirits had amazingly revived. He lifted a sideways grin at the woman sitting so still beside him, totally absorbed in thought, then winked at Bainbridge, feeling more hopeful than he had in months.

For the first time in three long years, he completely relaxed. On the spot, the master of Spindle Thorn Hall forgave his guest for totally oversetting the quiet sanctuary of his and the viscount's after-dinner port and cigars.

The minutes ticked by.

"What about Barbara waiting to retire until Mrs. Cribbs has fallen asleep?" Tia suddenly asked.

"The deuced woman never retires before us," Mr. Litchfield responded. "What's more, before she joins Barbara, she looks in upon me as well to make sure that I, too, am settled down for the night."

"Devil a bit, man," Robert uttered in sympathy.

"You have the right of it." Mr. Litchfield nodded.

Again Tia returned to her scheming. The evening lengthened; one candle in the sconce nearest Robert sputtered and then went out.

And then Tia once more glanced between the two gentlemen.

"Well, sirs," she began levelly, "I have it at last. Now, as I see it, there is no way around the fact that nothing shall be accomplished unless first, Mrs. Cribbs is somehow separated from Barbara when it is time for everyone to retire, and, second, a liaison between Barbara and Mr. Litchfield is effected."

"Very astute of you, cousin," Robert offered.

Tia considered leveling her cousin with a scowl, but did not, deciding that there were more important things upon which to expend her efforts. Steadfastly, she resisted the impulse.

"Ordinarily, this would not be a difficult objective to accomplish," she continued, folding her fan. "However, in this instance, I doubt we shall be able to count on either woman's cooperation."

"I think that is a safe assumption," Mr. Litchfield quietly concurred.

"Then we shall have to resort to a dual subterfuge," Tia concluded. "We shall have to both maneuver Barbara into the same chamber as Mr. Litchfield, and, at the same time, deflect Mrs. Cribbs from her appointed rounds."

"And how do you propose we go about this, cousin?" Robert casually inquired.

"I am about to tell you. Listen carefully. It is a bit complicated," Tia commanded like the best of His Majesty's officers.

"What does that signify?" Robert wheedled. "Complications have ever been merely the whetstones upon which to sharpen your meddlesome little teeth, have they not? Do go on, my dear. I have every confidence in your machinations. I can hardly wait."

This time Tia did glower. "Have a chocolate-covered caramel, won't you, cousin? And do let it melt in your mouth," she sweetly replied, "for a long, long time."

With a nod, Robert grinned his admiration of his cousin's parry and counterthrust.

"Now, if I might continue . . . ?" she asked, waiting for her cohorts' consent. "First, it must be said that the liaison cannot take place in the master bedroom."

"Why not?" Mr. Litchfield asked, resting upon his forearms.

"Obviously, because Mrs. Cribbs checks on your presence in your own bed each night," Tia responded. "But there is another reason. If Barbara is as frightened of you as you say, she would never willingly go to your room knowing that you would most likely be occupying it at the time."

"There can be no denying it," acceded Mr. Litchfield, reaching for the port bottle and pouring a measure for each of them.

"For once I shall have to agree with you, too, cousin," Robert stated, looping an arm over the back of his chair. "The meeting will have to take place in neutral territory."

"I am relieved that you see it that way, Robert," Tia replied with a nod that allowed another strand of hair to escape. "Then you shan't mind if Barbara and Mr. Litchfield meet in your room, shall you?"

"My room!" Robert exclaimed, sitting bolt upright. "Why my room, devil take it?"

"Well, because you shan't be using it, for one thing," Tia told him with a bright smile.

"The deuce I won't," he grumbled in reply. After their gazes had dueled sufficiently, he asked, "All right, why won't I be using my room?"

"Because you shall be taking Mr. Litchfield's place in his bed so that Mrs. Cribbs will see your form beneath the covers and think that you are him," Tia told him in a tone that was far too pert, one finger poking him in the chest.

The viscount skewered his cousin with his glare. "Tia," he finally said, his head sinking into his hand, "what haven't you told us yet?"

"It shall all become clear if you will just give me your attention," Tia replied, moistening her throat with a bit of her wine. "After all, we haven't much time if we are to carry out my plan tonight."

"Tonight?" both gentlemen said at once.

"Tonight. Now here is what must happen. Mr. Litchfield, at the proper time you and Barbara must go to your beds, sir, just as has been your habit. Once there, you must put out the candles and wait until Mrs. Cribbs has looked in upon you and confirmed that you are indeed abed."

"And then?" Mr. Litchfield asked, a bit nonplussed by the whole concept of the subterfuge.

"Robert will have been watching, of course. When he sees that Mrs. Cribbs has gone to your room, he will position himself so as to waylay her when she is on her way to join Barbara."

"And the reason I am doing this . . . ?" Robert queried, turning his head to peer out at her from between his fingers.

"Do use your imagination, cousin," Tia chided. "You are doing this so that you might redirect her back down the stairs."

"And how am I to do that?" the viscount rasped. "The woman is a man-hater!"

"What a perfect test for your charms!"

"Tia . . ."

"Oh, very well, Robert, ask Mrs. Cribbs for an explanation for her obvious animosity toward Mr. Litchfield, if you like. You are a peer, after all. Tell her that you are anxious about Mrs. Litchfield's undeniably unhappy union. Impress her with the fact that you only have Mrs. Litchfield's welfare at heart, and that, as a gentleman, it is your duty to protect the gentler sex."

"I shall do nothing of the sort!"

"Then make up your own tale," Tia commanded. "Just make sure that it is good enough to coax her back down the stairs and out of the way again."

"What shall happen once Mrs. Cribbs is below stairs?" Mr. Litchfield inquired.

"Ah, now we are coming to the most important part of the plan," Tia told him with a conspiratorial grin. "As soon as Robert has Mrs. Cribbs safely occupied, you shall go immediately to Robert's room. Meanwhile, I shall go to Barbara and tell her that all is not well with Robert. As the lady of the house, she will, of course, be distraught that one of her guests is uncomfortable. She will hasten at once to Robert's room, and there she will find . . ."—and at this point Tia gestured triumphantly toward her host—*"you, sir."*

Into the pause, Mr. Litchfield blinked.

"Lud, it just might work," he murmured, fingering the stem of his glass.

"Until Mrs. Cribbs tires of my 'charms' and returns to Mrs. Litchfield's room," Robert stated like a splash of cold water over their stratagem.

Mr. Litchfield's shoulders slumped. "And discovers that Barbara has gone," he added, his tone again flat.

"Ah, but she shall not," Tia informed them brightly, "because by that time I shall have put into place the rest of my plan."

"Good Lord," Robert muttered.

"What is the rest of your plan?" Mr. Litchfield asked a bit helplessly.

"Just this," Tia told them with growing excitement. "When Mrs. Cribbs returns to Barbara's bed, she shall discover that all is as it should be."

"Oh?" Robert said.

"Yes, indeed, gentlemen." Tia grinned. "You see, I shall have taken Barbara's place! Of course, as soon as Mrs. Cribbs has left your company, Robert, you must make all haste to regain Mr. Litchfield's bed just in case she decides to check in upon him again, but that should be no problem as long as there is another way up to the third story."

"The servants' stairs," Mr. Litchfield supplied.

"Of course, the servants' stairs!" Tia cried, clasping her gloved hands. "Well then, there you have it. Mr. and Mrs. Litchfield shall be together so that they might at last share a bed as husbands and wives ought so my cousin says, and Mrs. Cribbs shall be none the wiser as Robert and I shall have taken the others' places in their assorted beds. Do you not think it the most brilliant of plans?"

"I would, had I a liking for dissolute house parties," Robert remarked.

"Fiddle, it shall not be like that at all," Tia told him, her excitement fading. "Very well, cousin, owing to your sensibilities, I shall make sure to lock the adjoining door between our chambers."

"That would only be proper, of course," Robert agreed gravely.

That said, he reached over and tucked three dangling strands of hair behind Tia's ears.

Thirteen

It was the coat that nagged at him, Robert decided later that evening as he awaited Mrs. Cribbs's return from the necessary after her check on Mr. Litchfield and before she sought Barbara's bed. Panting a bit as his heart settled after his rather wild dash to the shadowed recess of the linen closet adjacent to Mrs. Litchfield's bedchamber—a sprint, mind you, with which he would never have had to debase himself if it had not been for the looby-headed scheme his cousin had devised requiring him to become a proxy husband—he drew himself deeper into the darkness, making sure that he was not visible from the corridor.

And still the discrepancy gnawed.

The coat had not been of the quality that he might have expected in the garment of an impoverished ruffian. On the contrary, it had been surprisingly well constructed . . . not up to London standards, of course, but certainly adequate, and it had boasted an excellent quality of wool. And that was what ate at his thoughts, the viscount assessed. The coat was no poor man's garment . . . that much was disturbingly obvious; more, it was tellingly Yorkshire in its twist and weave. A local man's, then. But whose? And why had the blackguard dared to accost his cousin in plain sight of his armed retainers?

And why, deuce take it, the viscount nearly groaned

aloud as he raked long fingers through his dark brown hair,
was he suddenly developing a distinct dread that the whole
bumblebroth smacked of Brumley's fine, fumbling hand?

Perplexed, Robert scrubbed his jaw.

Even more vexing, why the devil had Dex chosen to take
himself off to Sunderland now?

The ludicrous question soon had Robert chuckling softly
at his own arrogance. He knew why, of course. And it was
not as if he really needed his friend, after all. He was alert
to the danger now. Not even hell's minions would be able
to threaten Tia after this day's debacle. But one never knew
when one might need an extra hand, he allowed, considering his cousin's penchant for meddling her way into a deuce
of a lot of trouble.

On the heels of that disgruntlement, in the distance, footsteps began to murmur against the Axminster runner extending the length of the corridor.

In response, Robert peeled his shoulder away from the
alcove door to peer in the sound's direction. As he watched,
a globe of candlelight bloomed just beyond Mr. Litchfield's
empty chamber where the corridor abruptly turned to disappear into the Hall's east wing, then began to waver forward in advance of Mrs. Cribbs's voluminous wrapper and
crossly grooved face.

A quick rehearsal of Tia's advised ploy flickered
through his thoughts, vexing him further. He ground a layer
of enamel off his teeth. And then, like the polished gentleman that he was, with the companion bearing down upon
him, he martialed a courtly smile.

"My dear Mrs. Cribbs," he began quietly, stepping out
in front of her, "I wonder if I might—"

"Egad, sir!" Mrs. Cribbs gasped toward the looming
shadow she quickly discerned to be the viscount, her candle

wobbling precariously in its dish. "Do not even think to ravage me, my lord!" she cried, clutching at her lapels and backing away from him. "I assure you, I am well acquainted with how to defend myself."

"Let me assure *you*, madam," Robert soothed with upraised palms, "nothing even remotely resembling such an urge comprises my intentions. I merely wish a word with you."

"Indeed. Well, as far as I am concerned, sir," she replied, attempting to circumnavigate him, "we have already exchanged all that I ever intend to speak."

"Unfortunate," Robert responded evenly, "and very unwise, madam."

"Rubbish!" Mrs. Cribbs spat out. And then she paused in her efforts to pass him by. "Very well, why?" she demanded, glowering up at him.

"Because it is my belief that Mrs. Litchfield shall undeniably be the worse for it."

"Barbara?" Mrs. Cribbs responded, curious in spite of her revulsion toward the compelling man. "How so, sir?"

"My dear lady, surely you cannot believe that your obvious animosity toward Mr. Litchfield has escaped my notice?" Robert asked, relaxing as he sensed his acquisition of the upper hand.

"I have no idea what you are talking about," Mrs. Cribbs declared, squaring her massive shoulders.

"Come now," Robert soothed, "of course you do. And you must not mistake my intent, Mrs. Cribbs. I have only the greatest of sympathy toward Mrs. Litchfield. After all, I am a gentleman. I cannot help but feel obligated where the well-being of my peers is concerned . . . especially those who have, shall we say, unwisely bound themselves somewhat beneath their station. Let me be frank, my dear.

It is hard to ignore the signs that matters between our host and his wife are . . . strained."

"Indeed. Then I shall be equally frank, sir," Mrs. Cribbs replied icily. "Such matters are none of your affair."

"Then am I mistaken, madam?" Robert softly asked. "You need no help? No one to confide in? . . . no stronger arm upon which to depend?"

"I . . . no. No, I do not, sir."

After a brief pause, Robert bowed. "Then I shall accept your word, of course," he replied, straightening again with a slow smile. "Obviously, I only imagined Mrs. Litchfield's unhappiness . . . her possible abuse . . ."

Mrs. Cribbs bit into the wrinkled flesh of her lower lip. Suddenly she gasped, "If you only knew . . . !"

Candlelight wobbled about the corridor.

"Knew what, madam?" Robert gently asked.

"The horror of it!"

"Of what, madam?"

"Of . . . of what that *man* expects my Barbara to do! What you all do," she accused.

"You are referring, of course, to a husband's rights," Robert stated in a soft rumble.

Across from the candle flame, Mrs. Cribbs's lips pinched into a tight, ribbed circle. "Of a certainty, sir, and it is despicable . . . disgusting! He expects her to do . . . horrible things . . . unconscionable acts . . . exactly as Mr. Cribbs demanded before he callously abandoned me. Unspeakable things! I warned Barbara . . . I warned her! She has suffered terribly under the anguish of resisting her husband's constant attentions!"

Muscle slowly rolled at the corner of the viscount's jaw.

"My congratulations, madam," he finally uttered through tightly clenched teeth. "You have indeed made clear to me the extent of Mrs. Litchfield's misery." After several deep breaths, he again schooled his expression, then efficiently ensnared the companion's elbow and turned her toward the staircase. "Yet I am persuaded that there is a great deal more that I should know about Mrs. Litchfield's situation. Shall we go where we might speak privately? Come, let us retire to the library."

For a moment the bubble of candlelight rocked with Mrs. Cribbs's hesitation; then slowly, silently it began to accompany her compliance, sliding along the papered walls and down into the stairwell alongside the viscount, its remnant in the corridor softening, fading, and finally gone.

Only the twentieth part of a moment later, just after the corridor again grew dark, soft footsteps halted just outside Mrs. Litchfield's door. The door opened only a few seconds after the rather insistent scratching began, spilling a narrow slice of candlelight over the caller's shapely form.

"Yes? Oh, Tia," Mrs. Litchfield said, widening the aperture when she saw her friend standing there. "Is anything wrong?"

"I am afraid so, Barbara," Tia replied, her slight smile convincingly worried. "It is my cousin, I fear. He is moaning so."

"Moaning!" Mrs. Litchfield exclaimed, beginning to belt her wrapper as she stepped into the hall. "Heaven forfend! Have you any idea what his lordship's ailment might be?"

"Acute dyspepsia would be my guess," Tia responded, hurrying along after her hostess.

"Then I shall leave a note for Mrs. Cribbs to prepare an infusion of agrimony," Mrs. Litchfield stated, abruptly turning back toward her room.

"Oh, no, Barbara!" Tia exclaimed, seizing her arm. "Er,

that is . . . would it not be better to examine my cousin first and make your own assessment? What if I am mistaken?"

To Tia's great relief, Mrs. Litchfield nodded. "Yes, that would be more sensible, would it not?" she replied, starting off again for Robert's room. "Goodness, how distressing! . . . that such a thing might result from a meal at my table!"

"Now, do not overset yourself," Tia soothed, her voice bouncing in her haste to keep pace as the two rounded the corner and entered the west wing corridor. "Certainly it is but a common malady and easily treated. Why, only listen! . . . even now Robert must be improving. I cannot hear a single moan, can you? Here," she urged, opening the chamber door, "let me hold the door for you. Robert is right over there on the bed. Do hurry inside."

Mrs. Litchfield did not hesitate to comply.

Not the twentieth part of a moment later, Tia closed the door firmly behind her and quite smugly dusted off her hands.

"Well, that went off quite nicely, I think," she said aloud, quickly turning about and hurrying away down the corridor. "Now for the next stage of my plan."

As soon as she had gone, two crouched figures separated themselves from the deepest of the shadows and hesitantly began to hurry after.

Within Robert's chamber, Mrs. Litchfield stopped dead in her tracks.

No one was in the bed. Puzzled, she hastily glanced about, then focused upon the sick bed once more. It was not her imagination. It was true. The coverlet had not even been mussed.

Whatever was the meaning of this? she wondered as her eyes again skipped over the room, this time noting that the drapes had been drawn against the winter chill; afterward that an animated fire danced within its frame of ancient stone.

A brandy decanter, half full, stood on the small, round table beside the adjacent high-backed settle, she next noticed. A glass lay beside it . . . not quite empty of the warm amber liquid still shifting slightly within its bowl.

Shifting slightly? she repeated as her heart stopped. But that meant . . . that meant that someone had just taken a sip of it!

Within seconds of that realization, Mr. Litchfield slowly rose from the shadowed depths of the settle's warmth.

"Frederick . . . !" Mrs. Litchfield gasped, her voice airy with alarm, her gaze wild, riveted to his movements as he straightened to his full height.

In response, Mr. Litchfield slowly turned to face her. "Hello, Barbara," he whispered, casting her a smile of such tenderness that in spite of her terror, it warmed her to the tips of her toes. He moved again then, casually, so as not to alarm her, lifting a forearm to rest it upon the rough wood of the mantel, schooling his gaze so as not to give the slightest hint of his desire.

Across the room, unaccountably, Mrs. Litchfield's body thrilled at her husband's avid stare.

And then he moved again . . . easily, unhurriedly, slipping out of his coat, waistcoat, and cravat as she regarded him with startled eyes, before depositing them upon the settle. With the utmost of care, he next removed several of his shirt studs and placed them upon the mantel, revealing with the lazy motion an astonishing mass of crisply curling hair.

Mrs. Litchfield's breath stuttered around the constriction in her throat; instantly, her gaze soared to the safety of his Brutus cut. Unconsciously she compared its color and texture to what had been revealed in the open vee of his shirt. His hair was uncharacteristically rumpled, as a little boy's would have been if he had been nervously tunneling his fingers through it. Had he? she wondered, the thought helping her to relax somewhat. Beneath a pretty blush, now quite curious, her regard intensified.

Her husband shifted again then to pour another measure of brandy into his glass. Lifting it into his other hand, he let the dark liquid swirl lazily around and around.

Mrs. Litchfield watched, fascinated for reasons she could not begin to understand. And yet she did. He was beautiful, she suddenly realized . . . utterly beautiful to her. Yet still a man . . . and she must be wary of that fact. Mrs. Cribbs had warned her, had she not?

"Won't you sit down, my dear?" Mr. Litchfield softly asked.

"No . . . I—"

"Barbara, do you not know by now that I shall never harm you?" he abruptly, softly, interrupted, imprisoning his wife's gaze with the fervency of his own.

"I . . ."

"Think, my dear! We have been married for three years. If ill had ever been my intent toward you, would I not have acted upon it before now?"

"I-I suppose . . ."

"Then for God's sake, Barbara, believe me! There is no need to be afraid of me, my love," he said softly. "Trust me not to harm you."

"I . . . ," she whispered, her limbs tensed for flight, her pulse suddenly beginning to pound as an overwhelming desire to run into his arms began to war with her need to make her escape. "I-I should not be here. I must get away."

"If that is your wish, you may, of course," he granted in that same soft tone. "I will not stop you." He smiled then. "But it would make me very happy if you would stay."

Horrifyingly, Mrs. Litchfield felt her feet begin to move. How they had started, she did not know. She felt her body sway with the motion, felt her skirts brush softly against her legs. She was mindlessly afraid. She waited for the door, the pathway to her escape, to bump against her back, but, incredibly, it did not.

She was moving toward her husband instead.

What would Cribby say? she thought, her eyes rounding with desperate dismay. She would . . . she . . . oh, who *was* Cribby anyway?

"Wh-what will you do to me?" she stammered as she came to a quivering halt before him.

"Nothing that the two of us do not decide upon together," he said without a moment's hesitation. "I would hope that you might wish to sit before the fire with me and talk for a while. There is so much that I wish to know about you, but there has never been the opportunity . . ."

"Yes. I know," she confessed.

"And I would wish to kiss you, Barbara," he said honestly. When her eyes flew to his face in alarm, he added, "But only if you agree."

"I have never been kissed before," she told him barely above a whisper. "Not . . . not really."

"Have you not?" her husband questioned with a grin. "It is most pleasant."

"Cribby says . . ."

"Just what *does* Mrs. Cribbs say?" asked Mr. Litchfield in gentle command.

Mrs. Litchfield's gaze dropped to her fisted hands. "Th-that men are lustful b-beasts," she began in the monotone of a litany. "Th-that the wedding duty is awful . . . that there is horrible pain." She was almost light-headed now. Her body began to tremble violently.

"Barbara, may I hold you?" whispered Mr. Litchfield, in agony himself over her obvious distress, cursing the day she ever came under the aegis of her damnable companion. "Please, my love, let me show you that you will come to no harm with me," he coaxed. "Let me take away your fear."

Mrs. Litchfield's eyes lifted to his and were instantly awash with tears. "Frederick," she sobbed quietly, wanting so much to be in his arms, yet so very afraid.

Mr. Litchfield smiled and slowly set his glass on the table near the settle. Then, with love radiating from his eyes like a warm flame, he opened his arms. "I am here, my love," he declared from the depths of his heart. "I shall always be here. Trust me, Barbara. Come to me."

In no more than a pulse beat, he was crushing his wife within the warm circle of his comforting strength.

Fourteen

Knowing that she did not have much time before Mrs. Cribbs's return, Tia quickly stuffed her hair into a hastily donned nightcap, then clambered up over the needlepoint bed stool to snuggle herself down, dinner gown and all, between the sheets of Barbara's bed, her lips curving into a satisfied smile. Everything was happening just as she had known it would, she thought, smugly burying her hands beneath her head. Mrs. Litchfield was even now safely ensconced in Robert's room, and her husband's patient arms . . . Mrs. Cribbs had been successfully waylaid and dealt with . . . mercy, all that was left now was to get a good night's sleep, or as good a one as could be had when still wearing one's diamond and ruby earrings.

Let Robert just try to cut up stiff with her for this scheme! she vowed, peering over toward the window to make sure she had left it open just a crack the way she liked to even in the wintertime. All was just as it should be. Yes, she considered, widening her smile, everything was going perfectly according to plan.

An insistent breeze suddenly penetrated the chamber, snuffing out Tia's bedside candle and ruffling the lace fringe of her nightcap as if the pressure inside the room had changed, sucking in a blast of cold air. Shivering slightly in the darkness, once more she glanced toward the window, frowning after a moment. Odd, she thought, pulling her hostess's down-filled coverlet up almost over her head.

And then her smile returned. Goodness, how easy it was in the excitement of the evening's adventure to let her fancy run away with her! Much better to turn her thoughts toward the pleasures that lay ahead . . . lovely dreams, a pleasant rest, and warmth! . . . right *there* where some thoughtful maid had slid the warming pan and let it rest for a few extra seconds for the benefit of her feet! Ah, exquisite! And right *there* where her nether region nestled so comfortably into the pillowlike softness of the mattress. Mmm, the bliss of it! Slowly, heavy with contentment, Tia's lids began to sag.

And then, quite in the most contrary manner, the portion of the coverlet just over her face began to press itself most firmly against her nose and eyes; more, one of its corners was now trying to force itself inside her mouth! Startled, Tia choked on the impediment and began to struggle, pushing with all her strength upon the fabric from the inside with one arm while lashing out wildly with the other.

To her amazement, her fist connected solidly with muscle, then ineffectually rebounded to strike next against a construction of rough wool that smelled of cold, fresh air.

And then, frighteningly, both hands became ensnared within a thick-fingered fist and pinned behind her back at her wrists. In the dark, warm, port-laden breath filtered down beneath the coverlet's warmth. Weakened by the resulting spate of coughing, she was painfully wrenched upward even as she was wrapped about by the coverlet, putting an efficient period to her heated objections, effectively trapping her struggles.

In the next moment, however, just as suddenly as the skirmish had begun, it ended. In quite the most rag-mannered way, Tia dropped back down upon the bed, rudely landing for all the world like the slap of a side of beef upon a butcher's marble.

"The deuce!" Tia fumed as her head popped out from the coverlet cocoon, her nightcap charmingly askew.

"Ah, ah, ah," chided her cousin from across the room in the act of closing the window, "such language, cousin. Not at all the thing, you know. And do light a candle, Tia, will you?"

"Robert!" Tia exclaimed, finding and then striking a lucifer. "Oh, I might have known it was you!" she complained, touching the flame to the wick. "Really, cousin, it was all well and good to sneak up on me like that when we were children, but I *am* three and twenty now, and you with eight more years in your dish. And, for heaven's sake, cousin, you shall make ducks and drakes of everything! This is Mrs. Litchfield's chamber. You are in the wrong room."

"I am well aware of that," Robert replied, his attention still centered upon the ground below Tia's window. "I could not resist the impulse, however. Old habits die hard, I suppose."

After a moment, he pulled the drapes tightly together and turned toward his cousin with an appealing grin.

One look later, the grin had instantaneously disappeared.

"Tia, for God's sake . . . ," he choked, all thoughts of his fear upon hearing the sounds of Tia's struggle as he passed by the chamber earlier, of his rage as he opened the door to see what was toward, of his cold calculation as he disposed of the villains out the window, forgotten. "Deuce take it," he growled as his gaze transformed in its intensity, then raked over the length of Tia's innocent sprawl.

Inhaling sharply, he spun forcefully away, afterward tunneling every one of his fingers through his thick, dark hair before sliding them down to press behind his skull.

"What?" Tia asked, stretching out across the coverlet to push the candle to a safer position upon the bedside table.

"What? At least have some propriety!" he finally said, his voice husky, his memory still burning with the sight of her burnished legs, his hands still tingling with their imagined feel. "Get back under that coverlet. It is hardly acceptable for you to be lolling about with your skirts above your ears."

"Lolling about?" Tia objected, sitting bolt upright. "May I remind you that I was quite properly ensconced beneath this coverlet until you started your ridiculous romp? And as for my skirt, what lies beneath is nothing you have not seen a hundred times before."

"Yes, when we were children!" the viscount rasped, again whirling around to face her, struggling to hold his voice to a mere whisper.

"Fiddle," Tia countered dismissively. "What can that possibly signify? Now will you please do as you promised and cross over to Mr. Litchfield's room? Do you realize how long you have been here? Goodness, I am persuaded that Mrs. Cribbs shall be walking in here at any moment."

"Just as soon as you cover up those . . . as soon as you adjust your gown," Robert insisted, scraping a hand across his eyes. "And while we are on the subject, what the deuce are you covering up with your nightcap?" he asked with a scowl, wagging a finger in her head's direction.

"Hair?" Tia suggested, climbing down from the bed and beginning to straighten the coverlet over the bed again.

"No," he answered, again waggling his finger, "that. Whatever it is you have all over your head. You never had *that* under your cap when we were children."

"No, I did not," Tia sniffed, bending over to smooth the fine linen. "These are a fairly recent addition to my toilette."

"Well, what the deuce are they?" Robert growled again, his gaze helplessly riveted to the enticing sway of the feminine curves pointed directly toward him.

"Merely a few curling rags, if you must know," Tia told him, reaching up to jerk her nightcap down almost below her eyebrows. "But only a few. I did not have time to affix more."

"Well, take them out," the viscount commanded, venting his frustration upon the hapless scraps of material.

"Take them out?" Tia replied, whirling around. "Whyever?"

"Because I shan't have it, that's why," he steamed. "Because you look like a bloody rag-and-bone man's cart."

"Oh? Well, you look like an accident with an electricity machine," Tia retorted, gesturing toward his own mill-tousled coif before spinning back around. Launched by the twirl, several rags flew out from under her cap to lay like witnesses for the prosecution upon the coverlet. Groaning, Tia quickly scooped them up and stuffed them in her pocket. "And, for your information, I have to wear them else Nancy can do nothing with my hair."

"She can do nothing with it anyway!" Robert returned, forcing his gaze upward, away from the sensual swing of silk about her slim waist and hips and around the sweet curve of her legs. "It never remains as she arranges it. Deuce take it, you should let it hang as it was meant to, Tia," he ordered, suddenly finding that he had crossed the distance to the bed and was standing quite close beside her; worse, that his voice had deepened and grown revealingly rough.

"You mean lank as a horse's tail?" she laughed, fluffing one of the pillows.

"No, I do not. I mean straight . . . and long," he told her, his eyes flickering over each plane of her face, each drooping strand, ". . . and as silky between my fingers as the water rippling in a cold, moorland beck. You have beautiful hair, Tia, just as it is. Let it hang free. It was not made to be bound."

A soft smile played at the corners of Tia's mouth as she recalled their argument in the inglenook the previous evening.

"Nor was I, Robert."

A slow nod was the viscount's acknowledgment of his cousin's remembrance.

"Touché," he complimented, bowing. "Very nice, Tia. A very nice thrust and parry. I see I shall need a change of tactics."

"Indeed! What shall it be, then?" she asked playfully.

"Diplomacy, I think," Robert responded. "We shall work toward a state of compromise."

"What compromise?" Tia repeated with a soft chuckle.

"Why, yours, of course," Robert replied in light tones, though his gaze had become very dark.

"I-I am not exactly certain what you mean . . . ," Tia remarked after her smile had faded somewhat.

"You will. But for now, put yourself back under the coverlet, Tia, else I—"

"Hush!" Tia said quite suddenly, cutting off the remainder of the viscount's threat. "Oh, Robert, did you hear that?" she whispered, crowding close to him.

Removing her fingers, the viscount listened. Out in the corridor, not too far away by the sound of them, familiar footsteps began an insistent rhythm toward the chamber.

"Oh, dear heaven, Mrs. Cribbs!" Tia hissed toward her cousin's ear before glancing wildly about. Unexpectedly, she then began to shove him toward the entrance to Mr. Litchfield's dressing room. "Quickly, Robert, you must leave immediately! Go through the adjoining door."

"Tia, wait," the viscount said, resisting her efforts.

"Why?" Tia exclaimed.

"You locked it, remember? What is the woman to think when she hears you rattling the key to get it open?"

Tia stopped stockstill.

"Lud, she will think that Mr. and Mrs. Litchfield have been together in here!" she soon wailed. "Oh, goodness, Robert, we cannot allow that to happen. She will go directly to Mr. Litchfield's room to check on him . . . er, on you, that is. And you are not even there! It shall ruin everything! Oh, fiddle, we are well and truly caught, thanks to your not being where you are supposed to be like I instructed you. And we dare not make the slightest noise! Here," she said, now tugging him back in the opposite direction toward the bed, "get in quickly."

"What?" Robert asked, again applying resistance.

"Get in, I said," Tia hissed, finally abandoning all pretense at gentility by putting her shoulder to the viscount's nether portions and levering him onto the stool. "Into the bed! Oh, will you cease being so stubborn, Robert! Where else can we both hide?" she reasoned, driving him against the high mattress. "All we shall have to do is just stay close together," she reasoned, blowing out the candle before shoving him beneath the coverlet and springing in after. "And remain in the dark, of course."

"Tia, for the love of . . . ," Robert growled when one of her knees dug into his abdomen. "For God's sake, cousin, we shall never get away with—"

"Yes we will!" Tia insisted in a whisper. "What other choice do we have, after all? Oh, dear, I should be in the middle, should I not? Hold still, Robert, while I climb over you," she commanded, rocking the mattress as she scrambled across his broad chest, turning the coverlet into writhing mass. "Oh, dear . . . do hush, cousin, the door is opening! Now just lie still. No, do not pull away from me. We must lie very close to one another. We shall make too big a shape else. Yes, just like that. Oh, really, Robert, do be quiet! Whyever are you groaning so?"

In response, the viscount pulled the coverlet up over both their heads. Mrs. Cribbs entered just as the fabric settled.

"Well, dearest, I misdoubt I shall ever spend a more bedeviled evening," blatted the companion as she entered Mrs. Litchfield's room and began her accustomed toilette.

Beneath the coverlet, the cousins twitched. To steady her, of course, Robert slipped his arm about Tia's waist.

"I am completely overset," Mrs. Cribbs continued, plopping onto the bed and bending to yank at her half boots while Robert and Tia soared upward on the mattress's pillow-soft swell, then helplessly rode the rebound back toward the companion's soft, massive hips.

"To have suffered that young woman's insults, and then to be accosted in the hall by the viscount . . . Well, that, at least, might come to some good. His lordship was very interested in your welfare, my pet."

"Was he? . . ." Tia responded in as close an approximation to Mrs. Litchfield's soft voice as she could manage, desperately clutching at the mattress with her fingernails while Robert bobbed and rolled against her nether portions and desperately clutched at her.

"Oh, he was indeed! He could sense your discomfort immediately, my dear," Mrs. Cribbs continued, standing again to remove her clothes. "Told me so himself," she added as Tia rolled back in the other direction toward Robert, the two of them mere flotsam on the mattress's quilted wave.

"I see . . . ," Tia remarked, reaching for her roiling stomach and seizing Robert's instead.

"Abuse, that is what he called it," Mrs. Cribbs cried vehemently as she settled a chaste muslin night rail over her large frame. "Said it was his duty to see to your welfare. Of course, he is a *man,*" she continued, crossing once again to the bed and throwing back the covers on her side.

Across from her, Tia and Robert braced.

"However, I am inclined to think that he could be manipulated into demanding that your husband allow us to live separately from him if we were to play our cards right."

Upon that summation, Mrs. Cribbs took to her bed with authority, collapsing with a satisfied sigh back upon her pillow before slinging her heavy legs beneath the fine muslin sheets.

Robert and Tia rose upward upon new swells of their muslin sea. To their credit, they did not cry out in abject dismay. What they did do was the best they could, flailing about for anything that might cross their palms which was substantial, seizing upon the least of each other's bodily protrusions upon which to hang. It was inevitable, however, that they would be pitched to the edge of the bed by so massive a displacement of goose down. It was also inevitable that they would be caught in the compelling wash that immediately sucked them back again. After all, there existed nothing in nature with enough power to stop that primal tide. And so the two manfully rode their feathered ship of the line; at once almost nose to nose with the companion, in the next few seconds, flung to safety again on the opposite side.

"Well, we shall see what tomorrow brings, my dearest," Mrs. Cribbs sighed as her body relaxed and eased toward slumber.

Suddenly she rolled to her side and threw her heavy arm over both Tia and Robert.

"Sleep now, my pet," she murmured just before sleep overtook her. "I have a feeling that tomorrow all our problems shall be solved."

In the deep silence of Mrs. Litchfield's room, an eternity passed.

Then, with the first of the rumbles emanating from the companion's nose, Tia dared to move.

"Robert?" she mouthed from beneath the coverlet in the barest of whispers, pressing her back more closely against him. *"Robert!"*

"What, deuce take it?" Robert breathed into her nightcap, swallowing as he slowly eased a hand up between Tia's breasts to cup her lower shoulder, his whisper a thready rasp.

"Are you falling asleep?"

"No, as a matter of fact."

"Good, then take yourself off to Mr. Litchfield's room!" Tia ordered firmly, twisting toward him even more.

"And how do you suggest I do that?" Robert sighed, snuggling her closer with his forearm, spooning himself more tightly around Tia's back. "I am just as trapped under Mrs. Cribbs's arm as you are."

"But you cannot stay! As you have explained it, we would be 'bed-sharing' then, would we not?"

"In a manner of speaking," Robert responded, smiling

against her cap in spite of a discomfort that was quickly migrating into the realm of pain.

"But, cousin, we are not married," Tia pointed out.

"Which merely demonstrates how effective my new tactic of diplomacy is," Robert told her. "Mere minutes have passed since that decision, my dear, and already you are quite unquestionably compromised."

Several taut moments then crawled by.

"Fiddle," Tia finally argued. "You are my cousin. We have shared a room on countless occasions throughout our lives."

"True," Robert replied with a hint of laughter in his voice. "Unfortunately, *cousin,* if we should happen to be caught now, at our advanced ages and on this particular occasion, I fear the *ton* shall see it otherwise."

Successive waves of embarrassment, anxiety, and outrage next washed over Tia.

"Touché, cousin," she finally whispered as she settled into a heartfelt fume.

"Damned right." Robert grinned, nesting his nose into the sigh of curling rags. "Go to sleep, cousin."

Oddly comforted, Tia complied.

Morning crept into Mrs. Litchfield's bedchamber on a slow diffusion of sunlight filtering through several pairs of drawn slubbed-silk draperies. Consciousness came a bit more precipitately to Viscount Bainbridge. He awoke to the repeated blows of a chamber pot about various portions of his head.

"Beast! . . . Beast! . . . Beast!" Mrs. Cribbs shrieked with each stroke of the fine Sèvres porcelain. "Get away from my Barbara! How dare you attempt your perversity in our very bed! Get away, you disgusting *man!*"

"Damnation!" Robert roared, as within only a few moments the woman had his full attention. "Madam, you are a menace!" he shouted, easily wresting the chamber pot from her grasp and flinging it away with a resounding crash. "Have done, I say!" he demanded, surging upward upon the rolling mattress like Neptune emerging from the depths of his kingdom.

"Goodness, Mrs. Cribbs," commented Tia when the coverlet slid away to expose her, too. "Do have a care. Whatever can you be thinking to bash my cousin about the head like that?" she added, sitting up and beginning to brush hopeless wrinkles from her dinner gown.

"You!" Mrs. Cribbs exclaimed, staggering backward as the true identities of her bedmates finally penetrated into her enraged brain. "But you are not . . . !" she gasped, staring at the viscount. "A-and you are not . . . !" she cried, her gaze next slewing toward Tia. "Dear God in heaven, what have you done to my Barbara? Barbara!" she called out loudly, turning toward the door. "Barbara!" she repeated even more urgently as she then stumbled out into the hall.

"Shall we go after her, do you think?" Robert asked when the room had quieted, glancing at his cousin.

"Absolutely not," Tia sniffed, scrambling off the bed. "Everyone should know then that I have been compromised."

"They shall know anyway, cousin," Robert countered, tugging his cravat loose as he unlocked the adjoining door. "After all, Mrs. Cribbs was witness to it all."

"Barbara!" echoed the distant cry.

At the sound, Tia grinned.

Several heads appeared in the stairwell leading up to the servants' quarters . . . Nancy, Romney, and a few of the more curious Spindle Thorn staff.

"At the moment, the woman is fit for Bedlam, Robert," she stated with satisfaction.

On a deep sigh, the viscount nodded. "Therefore, no one will believe a word she says."

"Just so."

From far away, *"Barbara!"* rang out in tones of shock and disbelief.

"Must have located her," Robert commented, opening the door.

"What will happen, do you think?" Tia asked, strangely blue-deviled at the prospect of Robert's leaving.

"If I were to guess, I should say that we have just gained the dubious honor of being the last persons with whom Mrs. Cribbs shall ever share a bed."

Tia smiled. "Then they shall be all right, Robert?" she queried softly, her eyes suspiciously moist.

"Believe me, it galls me to admit it, Tia, but thanks in great part to your interference, they have every chance. Now send for Nancy," he added, letting his gaze once more travel the length of her before turning toward the door. "It is time we left."

A few hours later, the cousins were again on the road, this time traveling toward Viscount Epworth's principal seat near Osmotherly, a sprawling brown sandstone farmstead named Blackamore Grange; more, perhaps at last toward the point of origin of the black valentine.

Fifteen

"Hand me a towel, Romney, will you?" Robert asked from the depths of the copper hip bath warming before the fire in his room at Blackamore Grange, his other hand noisily splashing the soap suds from his eyes.

Suddenly the chamber door swung wide.

"Never mind, Romney, I shall get it," Tia replied brightly, breezing into the room. Without pause, she plucked the towel from a nearby chair and started forward.

"Tia, the deuce!" Robert sputtered along with a noble attempt to cover himself. "Romney, my robe!"

Tia stopped abruptly and stared. An instant later, when it finally occurred to her that a scratch at the door might have been in good taste, she belatedly slapped a hand over her eyes.

"I am at my bath, cousin," the viscount complained in distinct syllables, rising behind the curtain Romney had hastily made of the robe, then slipping it on. "At least I was. What the devil do you think you are about barging into my room? No, do not answer that yet. First, have the decency to turn around!"

Tia did so without the slightest delay.

A masking of her mortification was called for. She used the only weapon at hand: bravado.

"La, Robert, you act as if I had never seen you in the

altogether before," she tossed back at him, her chin elevating loftily.

"Tia, I was only twelve when the countess forbade me giving you any more swimming lessons in Rigg Mill Beck. I *have* changed a bit since then," her cousin growled, concentrating on holding still while Romney belted his robe, placed slippers on his feet, and affixed a poet-style cravat over the expanse of his bare chest. He glanced scathingly then toward her back. And then his jaw dropped.

"Good Lord, cousin, where is your wrapper?" he sputtered, waggling a finger toward Tia as light from the fire played over the hint of her feminine curves with tantalizing, capering shadows. "You have come calling in your night rail! . . . and with Romney here! . . . and, deuce take it, once again your head looks like a laundry bag!"

Tia glanced down at the fine soft wool of her gown, then up toward the lengthy overhang of her nightcap. Moments later, she threw up her hands.

"I have already explained about the rags," she told him, whirling around to face him again. "And I have no idea if you have changed or not."

"No?" the viscount replied, one brow cocked.

"Well . . . no," Tia confessed, taking a sudden interest in her toes. "Everything happened so fast I had no time before you rang a peel over me to take a peek."

Robert's gaze wrinkled with a rueful smile. "Pity," he murmured after a nod that signaled Romney to summon footmen to remove the bath. "Two steps forward . . . one step back."

"What? Oh, never mind," Tia said dismissively as she started forward. "La, cousin, of late you have been saying the most incomprehensible things. But none of that signifies."

"Indeed. I am cut to the quick."

Tia cast him a reproachful glance. "Kindly pay attention, if you please. What *does* signify is the urgency of our task."

"Your task," Robert corrected, delicately replacing two soft, runaway strands back beneath the ribbon of her nightcap.

Tia blinked. "Whichever. Now, to my way of thinking, our first step is to compare what we each might have learned during our after-dinner discussions with Ambrose and Elizabeth. Once we each know what the other knows, I am persuaded it shall be a simple matter to formulate our plan of attack."

"Tia," her cousin rumbled, finding much of interest to look at just below her shoulders, "may I remind you that it is the small hours of the morning . . . and that you have come to a gentleman's bedchamber . . . alone . . . and in a most improper state of *déshabillé.*"

Hesitating slightly, Tia's glance flickered toward Robert's.

"I am aware of that, Robert. Of course I am," she unsteadily replied, quickly looking away again to pour herself a suddenly necessary glass of Oloroso sherry. "But you *are* my cousin, after all. Besides, our hosts would most likely learn that we are secretly meeting if I had come at a more prudent time."

The viscount's lips pursed. "Tia, if anyone were to find out . . ."

"Cousin, sometimes s-social risks must be assumed in the pursuit of the nobler cause," she stammered, edging around him to warm her noticeably icy fingers before the flames. "Although I do admit to completely forgetting what I was wearing when the notion came to me to seek you out," she added, her voice shrinking to a mumble.

"Tia . . ."

"Oh, Robert, will you not sit down! Goodness, I cannot be expected to converse with you properly when you are . . . staring at me so."

"Is that what I was doing? My apologies," the viscount replied, his eyes glittering as he suavely scooped up his empty brandy snifter and, with a bow, offered one of the two fireside chairs to his cousin. "Very well, far be it from me to alter a direction I cannot help but benefit from. Let us by all means set aside the matter of your impropriety for the 'nobler cause.' Tell me what you have learned from your old school friend."

Across from him, Tia again peered at him in confusion, then seated herself and slipped her clasped hands down to nest between her knees. "It is that bed-sharing thing again, it seems." She shrugged and sighed.

"I see," Robert commented, his fingers unobtrusively edging across his mouth.

"Elizabeth is very unhappy, Robert," Tia continued, her shoulders hunching, "and angry. At Ambrose, of course, but I fear mostly with me."

"Why you?" Robert asked.

"She blames me because I promised her that marriage to one of your best bows would be wonderful above all things," she confessed.

Refreshing his brandy, Robert softly chuckled. "Tia, you cannot make such promises," he chided.

"Well, I know that *now*," Tia groused. "At the time, however . . . well, I suppose I was . . . swept away. And, in my defense, Ambrose did seem the most eligible of *partis* on those occasions you brought him home with you from Cambridge."

After a long sip, Robert rubbed his eyes. "Tia . . ."

"But, do you know, cousin, Elizabeth has quite opened my eyes. Why, the man is a scoundrel! Not only does he avoid bed-sharing with Elizabeth except on the rarest of occasions, but he keeps a mistress on the side!"

"Does he?"

"Elizabeth told me so herself," Tia insisted, "as well as the sordid fact that he refuses to give the tart up! I tell you, Robert, it was the most dismal of conversations. By its conclusion I was quite willing to march into the dining room and give the reprobate a taste of my fives."

"My congratulations on your restraint," Robert replied. "One interruption of my after-dinner port was sufficient, I believe. I don't suppose Elizabeth gave you a clue as to why Ambrose is engaging in this rather unsavory behavior."

Tia shook her head. "We are both counting on you. What did you learn of the matter?"

"Why, nothing."

"Nothing? But what did you talk about for all those hours?" she asked, her mouth remaining charmingly ajar.

"Friends . . . matters of Parliament . . . how we were faring on the 'Change."

"Robert!" Tia cried, jumping to her feet. "You were supposed to discover what was failing in his marriage! . . . why he might have sent the black valentine!"

"On the contrary, Tia," Robert replied evenly, "that is *your* quest. *I* refuse to meddle in another's private affairs. But you may rest at ease on one count at least. I did determine that Ambrose was not the sender of the ill wish."

"Fiddle," Tia responded, slumping back into her chair. "Neither was Elizabeth."

"Excellent. Then I shall make plans to leave in the morning," Robert said, setting down his glass.

"No, you shan't!" Tia exclaimed, again bounding to her slippered feet to restrain his arm. "There is still my duty to the marriage, cousin. I tell you, I shall not budge from his place until I have brought about an improvement."

"Tia . . ."

"Not another word, Robert," Tia interrupted, beginning to pace. "Now let me see . . . how can we make Ambrose take more notice of his wife . . . ?"

"Tia, once again you are poking your pretty nose into affairs which—"

"I have it!" Tia exclaimed, snapping her fingers. "You shall make him jealous."

"*I?*" Robert bellowed, his demeanor completely astounded.

"Well, of course you," Tia sensibly replied. "Who else is there, cousin? And I am not asking you to sweep her off her feet. Just pay a bit of attention to her in Ambrose's presence."

"Tia, this is a very dangerous game you are playing."

"Why?"

"Because you are meddling in other people's lives, and because it never works, that's why!"

"Then you shall certainly wish to employ the greatest restraint in your attentions, shall you not, cousin?" she stated, tapping a fingernail upon her chin. "You must demonstrate prudence . . . subtlety . . . finesse."

"Tia, you are going to lose me a very good friend," Robert fumed with fists planted upon his hips, "not to mention make things much worse between Ambrose and Elizabeth."

"Nevertheless, you will do it, won't you, Robert?" Tia asked, her eyes fluttering up at him.

"No, Tia, I *shan't*," he replied, scowling down at her, his eyes now flecked with immutable brass.

"Yes, you will," she countered sweetly, smiling as she reached up to straighten his cravat and pat his chest, "if, that is, you ever intend to get free of Blackamore Grange in time for the opening of Parliament."

Beaten, the Viscount of Bainbridge nodded his acquiescence.

It was Ambrose's suggestion of a ride to view St. Mary's Priory that resulted in Tia's machination being set into motion the following morning just after the breaking of their fast. Unfortunately, as it happened, it was also the ride that later resulted in one of Viscount Epworth's expertly fitted leather riding gloves being set into motion squarely aside his friend Bainbridge's head.

"You and I shall meet at dawn, sir!" Epworth declared in an ominous hiss, pointing his riding whip at Robert's sprawl. "You, however," he roared, wheeling about toward Elizabeth, "I shall never wish to meet again!" That said, he began to stalk toward his tethered stallion.

"Ambrose! Whyever . . . ?" Elizabeth stammered in confusion, trailing after.

"Why? You have no clue, wife?" he railed, casting aside her restraining hands. "It does not seem just the slightest bit rag-mannered to you to cuckold me right under my nose, and with a *friend?*"

"Ambrose!" Elizabeth gasped, clutching at the lace bunched beneath her throat.

"Save your tears, Elizabeth. They no longer move me. Do not forget, my dear, that I, too, have other outlets available to me."

"Ambrose!" Elizabeth reprised.

"Actually, that gives me an idea," the viscount said, pausing with his foot in one stirrup. "Since you obviously feel free to taunt me with your *cicisbeo*," he explained, snarling in Robert's direction, "why should I not have the same privilege?"

"What do you mean?" his wife asked, reaching toward him again.

"I mean that as soon as the duel is concluded, I shall bring Tess into our home, my dear," he answered, mounting and turning his stallion about. "She, at least, has no disgust of me."

Nearby, Tia extended her hand toward Robert. Fiddle . . . disgust again, she thought, helping her cousin to his feet. This bed-sharing must indeed not be at all the thing.

"Elizabeth, dearest . . . ," she attempted next as the viscount galloped away.

"Don't you 'Elizabeth, dearest' me!" cried the viscountess, spinning away from her and bursting into tears. "This is all your doing, Tia Hilton. I just know it is!"

"But, Elizabeth! . . ."

"Tia . . . ," Robert tried to interject.

"I merely wanted to tell Elizabeth that I have only recently had valuable experience with a woman who felt as she does, cousin . . ."

"And how do you know how I feel?" Elizabeth sobbed, her tears making wet ovals on the blue velvet jacket of her riding habit.

"Why, Ambrose just told us, dear," Tia soothed, trying to take her friend's arm only to have it shaken away. "You have a disgust of your wedding duty."

"I do not!" Elizabeth wailed.

"You do not?"

"No!" Elizabeth quite improperly shouted in a watery voice. "I like it above all things! Wh-when Ambrose holds me . . . when he touches me . . . I can hardly remain still as is proper for a lady."

"You like it," Tia parroted, confusion furrowing her brows.

"Yes, I like it!" Elizabeth snapped as she mounted her horse and yanked upon the ribbons. "B-but he never comes to me anymore. I wait and I wait, but he goes to *her* instead," she spat into the bright, wind-washed air. "And now, owing to you, Tia Hilton, I shall likely never experience my husband's touch again!"

Several clods of dirt sprang backward to bounce against Tia's riding skirt as Elizabeth's gelding dug his hooves into the soft snowmelt, then thundered off after the stallion.

Nearby, one small snow bunting chipped into the soft sigh of the wind.

"Cheer up, Tia," Robert said, busying himself with brushing snow off his brown Melton tails. "Your plan did work, after all. The man was certainly jealous."

Tia's responding glower fairly blistered the intervening air.

"This is all your fault, you know," she grumbled, thrusting his riding crop against his chest.

"Mine?" Robert gasped, finding his beaver in a patch of scrub heather where it had been knocked during the challenge.

"Yes, yours!" Tia asserted, stalking over to her horse and mounting. "You were only supposed to pay Elizabeth a bit of attention, cousin, not make love to her!"

"And that is all I did," he insisted, swinging up into his own saddle. "I talked to her. I held her umbrella. I fixed a plate of food for her from the willow hamper."

"You *looked* at her!" Tia accused, starting forward toward Osmotherly.

"I looked at her?" Robert repeated, perplexed. "Perhaps you haven't noticed, cousin, but that is quite acceptable when carrying on a conversation."

"Not the way you were looking at her," Tia growled, picking up her mare's pace.

"And how was that?" Robert asked, coming up to her side.

"Like . . . like . . . ," she sputtered, "like the way you looked when you entered my ballroom three nights ago!"

Very slowly, the viscount cast his cousin a sideways glance, afterward falling back slightly behind her so that she could not see how very smug his demeanor had become.

"Like that, eh?" he commented, vigorously battling a hallelujah that threatened to erupt. "Just out of curiosity, cousin . . . at whom was I looking at the time?"

"Well . . . me," she curtly replied as a delicate flush crept up above her jabot to stain her chin and cheeks.

A star exploded within Robert's heart. One of them; perhaps two. He had no idea of the actual count. But with a suddenness that astounded him, he was restored; energized. Easily he captured a low-hanging Scots pine branch and lifted it out of his cousin's path. Even more easily, he hung on to it, drawing it after him as he trotted along until, with a flick of his wrist, he released it to spring back into place, effortlessly unseating the two battered attackers he had spotted earlier galloping up behind them in yet another go at whatever the deuce it was they were trying to attempt.

So this is joy, he thought as the two grunted at the impact, wheezed, then dropped like stones upon the brittle path.

Not bad, he concluded smugly, touching his crop to his mount's shoulder, then swiftly catching up with his cousin again.

Sixteen

Tia was just rinsing the last of the lavender-scented soap bubbles from her breasts later that afternoon when the door to her chamber burst open and Robert strode blithely in, dressed to the nines in a cutaway of dark green velvet, immaculate white silk waistcoat and inexpressibles, and an expertly tied Belcher cravat.

The viscount's woodland eyes sparkled with purpose. It was the same look, Tia thought with chagrin in the twentieth part of a moment before it registered in her brain that she was wearing nothing but a hip bath, that he used to affect when he was attempting to flagellate her with French and mathematics. Immutable. Implacable. It did not bode well for her afternoon.

"Robert, for heaven's sake!" Tia quickly gasped, sloshing water as she ducked behind the tub's rolled edge.

"Mr. Robert, sir!" Nancy chided, whisking the coverlet from the bed, then swirling it about her mistress.

"Why, whatever is the matter?" the viscount innocently asked, deftly snagging Tia's gold silk wrapper from the chair where it reposed, then strolling forward to drape it over the coverlet enclosure. "Never say that you object to my presence! After all, we *are* cousins, are we not?"

"Well, yes . . . but—"

"Then there you have it," he abruptly interrupted, crossing purposefully to the clothes press. "Now, what shall you be needing, I wonder, *cousin* dear?" he asked, digging through the press's contents. "One of these?" he suggested, wafting a lacy petticoat into the air. "Or perhaps one of these?" he again asked, tossing a delicately constructed chemise over his arm.

"Robert!"

"Mr. Robert!" Nancy exclaimed, seizing the items and concealing them within her apron pocket.

"Why, Nancy, why so overset?" the viscount asked, next finding a pair of sheer olive stockings. "We *are* cousins, are we not?" he added, casting a smug grin toward Tia. "Besides, I have matters of great importance to discuss. Oh, but do go on with your toilette, cousin," he generously offered after Nancy had whisked the stockings, too, from his hand. Shrugging, he strolled then to the fire's blazing warmth and settled himself comfortably in a nearby chair. "Pay no attention whatsoever to me," he said, enjoying his cousin's discomposure, stretching out his legs toward the tub and clasping his hands behind his head. "While you dress I shall tell you about the very lowering apology I just made to Epworth."

"To Ambrose!" Tia exclaimed, all her vexation forgotten as she hurriedly dried off. "He spoke with you? But you are set to duel at dawn!"

"No longer," Robert responded, his gaze dropping to the most interesting shapes that had begun contouring the thick fabric. "Once I explained your chuckle-headed scheme to cure each of North Yorkshire's troubled marriages and how you blackmailed me into abetting your plan to make him jealous, he quite willingly called it off."

"You told him?" Tia cried, her damp, tousled head popping up over the coverlet's edge. "What did he say?" she asked, reaching for her wrapper.

"Actually, he was rather amused . . . after he got over his urge to shake you till your teeth rattled in their sockets.

"You may be excused, Nancy," he added with a lordly nod.

"Now, sir . . ."

"Now, Nancy . . . ," the viscount countered, turning his palms up, "we *are* cousins!"

The maid glanced toward her mistress.

"It is perfectly all right, Nancy," Tia reassured her, stepping out from behind the coverlet to adjust her wrapper's sash. "His lordship is quite correct. Leave the door ajar when you go, will you? I shall summon you when I am ready to dress."

After a moue of pique, Nancy smoothed the coverlet back across the bed, then left to seek a cup of tea in the sanity of the servants' quarters.

"Well, I am pleased that you have been released from Ambrose's challenge, cousin, but what of Elizabeth?" Tia asked, crossing to take the other chair adjacent to the fire, her hair long and slightly tangled from her bath, the silkiness of her wrapper innocently, enticingly, accentuating her womanliness. "Will Ambrose also forgive her?"

Robert drew in a very deep breath.

"For her alleged unfaithfulness, yes," he answered, reaching over to comb the fall of her hair for a moment with his fingers. "As for the other, cousin, it would not at all have been the thing for me, as a gentleman, to raise such a personal issue . . ."

"The other? What other?" Tia asked, leaning toward him, her wrapper gaping open just enough to expose shadow, slope, the suggestion of one well-formed breast. "The problem between them?"

Robert's jaw clenched.

"Problems, Tia," he said, adjusting his bite to chew at his inner cheek. "There are two of them."

"Two . . . ," Tia repeated, clasping her hands in her lap, unknowingly throwing both smoothly rounded globes into prominence against the conforming silk. "How have you come to know this when I haven't a clue?"

"By calling into play my far superior experience, my finely honed powers of observation, my skill at sorting and analyzing the minutiae of information . . ."

"La, Robert, I am just trying to help two friends, not conquer the Continent," she interrupted, the shake of her hands migrating up into her shoulders . . . and down again to echo across her torso. "What is the first of them?"

"It is Elizabeth's," the viscount answered after swallowing twice. "It is the difficulty she has in her duty to her husband."

"But, Robert, she said that she *likes* that," Tia countered, settling back into her chair and crossing one delicately tapered leg. "If you recall, she said so quite emphatically this afternoon."

"Yes, I heard her," he agreed, quite suddenly shooting to his feet and scrubbing at his freshly shaved face.

Still seated, Tia shook her head. "Then I cannot understand the problem."

"Tia, we are dealing here with matters of perception," Robert told her, now rubbing away at his forehead. "It is much as it was with Barbara Litchfield. Just as she was taught to fear her duty to her husband, so Elizabeth, and I am persuaded Ambrose as well, have been taught things that are interfering with their happiness."

"What things?" Tia questioned, her wrapper parting to expose the side of her slim, crossed calf.

Helpless to stop it, Robert's gaze rode the entire length of the smooth, tapering shape. It was then that he first began to suspect that the lesson to be learned that day was not to be Tia's. He gritted his teeth with chagrin; and being a man, of course, he fought the deuced development with a vengeance.

"My first clue came while Elizabeth was cutting up stiff with you this afternoon after Ambrose had left," he told her, averting his gaze toward the ormolu clock on the mantel above her while dragging in another deep breath. "During her scold she said that when Ambrose was with her it was very difficult for her to remain still as was proper for a lady."

"I remember," Tia replied, reaching up to push a lock of hair out of her eyes, giving Robert yet another teasing glimpse of silk and shadow, of feminine roundness. "How is that significant?"

The viscount's eyes closed above an indrawn breath.

"Because a man likes his wife to . . . participate in the bed-sharing, Tia," he told her on a huge exhalation, turning away and beginning to pace. "Unfortunately, the women of our class are almost never told this."

"And rightly so, I should think," Tia chuckled, closing her wrapper's gape. "Even we women have no need of being instructed in how to participate in sleep, Robert."

"Tia, that is not what I meant," Robert told her with an exasperated massage of his forehead. "Deuce take it, there is much more to the whole matter than that!"

"Oh?"

"Yes!" Robert informed her, striding back and forth before his cousin, each lap eating up an even greater distance.

"And, unfortunately, it is often difficult for a mother to discuss the subject with her daughter comfortably. As a consequence, the only instruction many women receive is that if they lie still, let their husbands do what they will, and try very hard to imagine themselves in some other pleasant place while their duty is being performed, it will all be over quickly."

"In other words," Tia concluded, slowly rising to her feet with her understanding, "it never occurs to them to participate."

"Just so," Robert agreed, abruptly halting when Tia wandered into his path. "Obviously, Elizabeth has taken her mother's instruction to heart."

"So it seems. And Ambrose?" she asked, looking up at him with huge hazel eyes.

Aside his hips, Robert's fingers twitched.

"My clue as to his thinking came just after he called me out. He claimed that his mistress, at least, did not hold him in disgust, if you recall. It is difficult to avoid the conclusion, therefore, that he believes Elizabeth does."

"But why would he make such an assumption?"

"Most likely because before his wedding, *he* was taught by his father to expect *that*."

"Oh, dear," Tia assessed, staring beseechingly up into her cousin's eyes. "Whatever are we to do, Robert?"

The viscount swallowed twice. With Tia's warm, lovely eyes pleading upward from just below his chin, fine rents began to appear in his willpower's fabric. He shuddered, clenched, drew in a cloud of lavender. The tiny tears burgeoned into jagged holes. . . .

The decision was made even as the plan suddenly formed within his mind. It was quick; it was easy. And the repercussions would be enormous. Yet he would do it. He had to. It was the only solution it was beginning to appear would ever effect his cousin's eventual capitulation. He wondered if, afterward, she would ever speak to him again, then dismissed the notion.

Smiling slightly, he wondered instead why the deuce he had ever waited.

"We are not going to do anything," he finally answered, his eyes now gleaming green and amber with reflected candlelight. *"You* are."

"I?" she repeated, furrowing her brows.

"Exactly so. You meddled us into the middle of this, Tia," he stated in a reasonable tone. "Therefore, you shall get us out."

"Well, how am I supposed to do that?" she cried, fully exposing the lovely valley between her breasts as she threw up her hands. "Elizabeth is fit for Bedlam over the impending arrival of Tess the Tart, Robert, and Ambrose refuses to seek Elizabeth out. What do you suggest *I* do? . . . ask Tess to teach Elizabeth how to participate?"

"Don't be ridiculous, Tia. That would be most improper," Robert replied, focusing his gaze upon her widening pupils. "You are not to even speak to such a person. Besides, in her state of mind Elizabeth most likely would jump to the conclusion that Ambrose only wishes for her, too, to act the courtesan. No, you shall have to do it."

"I?"

"Assuredly," he responded, taking no small pleasure in the steady shift of the whip hand. "Only consider, Tia. We know Ambrose will not go to his wife as things now stand. He is certain he shall only be rejected again. No, of a certainty, it is Elizabeth who must approach Ambrose."

"But *I* cannot . . ."

"You shall have to, cousin; and not only that, but you

shall have to persuade her that when she does go to him, she must be prepared to enthusiastically participate in her duty to her husband. Remember, his mistress arrives on the morrow. Elizabeth shall only have this one chance to convince Ambrose that she truly wishes his attentions before it is too late. It is imperative that she make sure Ambrose wakes in the morning with no doubt in his mind as to her willingness to share in what he attempts."

"Then . . . fiddle, Robert, I shall *have* to enlist Tess!"

"Nothing of the sort. Would you insult Elizabeth? Absent an older female relative, such a discussion may only properly be presided over by a lady," he boldly prevaricated, "and you are the only one available."

"What nonsense! I am not married, cousin!" she cried, closing the distance between them, clutching at his black velvet lapels. "I have no idea what to advise her."

Tia had no idea that with those words, her cousin's neatly laid trap had sprung.

Robert, however, had. Seizing Tia's shoulders in a powerful grasp, he suddenly swung his woodland gaze to spear into hers.

Well, now . . . as to that . . . ," he murmured, impaling the twin shadows of her eyes. "That is, indeed, a problem."

Tia felt pinioned to the air behind her. Trembling, completely overpowered, she slowly released his lapels.

Slowly, very slowly, the viscount lifted one finger to trace the delicate curve of her lower lip; his gaze sweeping repeatedly over the cherished contours of her face. Then, with the utmost care, he trailed his touch across her flame-gilded cheek, at last ensnaring it within the soft golden aura the fire had made of her tangled hair.

"I suppose, then, that you shall just have to find someone . . . of rank, of course, as that would only be proper . . . to explain it to you first."

"Someone of rank? But . . . that only leaves . . . *you*, cousin," Tia gasped.

Very slowly, Robert smiled.

"Yes it does, doesn't it?" he answered, tunneling each of his fingers into her hair, gently drawing her face upward toward his.

"Robert?" Tia breathed.

"Hold still, Tia," he murmured huskily. "I promise you. This won't hurt a bit."

Seventeen

"Oh . . . g-goodness! Wh-what are you doing, cousin?" Tia gasped when the full length of Robert's body came into contact with hers.

"Beginning your instruction," he replied, initiating a disconcerting nibbling just at the base of her neck. "The first step, you see, is for the man to interest the woman in her duty just as much as he is."

"Oh-h . . . I see," Tia sighed when Robert's lips began a gentle, slow ascent. "Oh, my! And h-how is a woman to know if she has become interested?" she shakily inquired.

"Her body will tell her," Robert instructed, beginning to lave the soft, silky lobe of her ear. "Her heart will begin to pound . . . her breathing will quicken," he whispered, kissing the shell-like curve. "She shall wish to draw closer to the man . . . and still closer . . ."

Within the viscount's arms, Tia arched, unable to restrain the motion.

"Robert . . . ," she gasped, her moss green eyes huge with wonder, "I-I do believe that I have begun to . . . participate! Oh-h-h!"

"Excellent," he replied, smiling slightly as he leisurely slid his hands down the length of her back. "Then we are ready for the next step."

"What is that?" she sighed, unknowingly slipping her arms around his neck.

"The man begins to touch the woman," Robert murmured, beginning to caress her temple with his lips.

"T-touch? But . . . but that c-cannot be proper!" Tia breathed, pushing slightly away from him.

"True, but are we not setting all that aside for the 'nobler cause'? Besides, how else am I to instruct you so that you might properly teach Elizabeth?" he countered in a low rumble, drawing her back against him as he shifted his attentions once again to her ear, easily diverting her objection to his exploration of the curve of her hip.

"C-could you not simply tell me?" she sighed, relaxing against his chest.

"No, Tia," Robert responded softly, stroking the smooth blue silk. "This is something you must experience in order to fully understand."

"I . . . oh, Robert, how very odd that feels! Oh, goodness!" Tia told him, suddenly, inexplicably, growing weak in the knees. "Very well . . . ah-h! Wh-what is the object of this step?"

"To prepare the woman's body for the bed-sharing," he murmured softly, shifting his hands at last to begin a slow, caressing shaping of the warm rounds of her *derrière*.

"Oh-h-h!" Tia sighed, helpless now to stand on her own, struggling to hold at least one thought in her head. "And h-how shall a woman know if she is p-prepared?" she asked, raggedly gasping her question into the shoulder of his cutaway.

"She'll be wet," he growled low against the tangle of her hair.

Somewhere, within his embrace, Tia found the presence of mind to assess the state of her preparedness.

"Why, Robert . . . so I am!" she suddenly exclaimed in wonder as gooseflesh pebbled her skin.

All around her, the viscount's powerful arms clenched.

"Tia . . . ," he rasped low and deep, shuddering as he buried his face into her hair and slid one hand between them. "Tia," he whispered, gently parting the silk of her wrapper and finding her treasured warmth. "Tia!" he breathed, unable to get enough of her, hoping it would never end.

And then his fingers began an exquisite caress.

The sensations poured over her . . . chills, warm honey, exultation, mindlessness. In wave after wave they inundated her; building, always building toward something . . . just out of reach . . . somewhere. If only she knew what . . . if only she knew where. . . .

"Robert, what is happening to me?" she cried, frightened now, burying her face into the strength of his neck, seeking shelter in the familiarity of his scent.

"I am, Tia," he told her, his fingers relentlessly moving, pushing her ever closer to what awaited at the end. "Don't be afraid. Never be afraid in my arms."

"But . . . oh, Robert, you must not touch me so!"

"No," he whispered, pressing her even more tightly against him. "Yet this is a lesson you must learn, cousin, and from me. Only from me. No one else . . . ever. I swear it. Reach for it, Tia. It is yours . . . take it."

Trusting him, Tia did. In moments, the sensations focused, tightened, curled into a spiral that began to rise within the deepest part of her. Tia gasped at the strange new feelings, clinging to her cousin's shoulders, pressing closer to his warmth . . . closer still. His fingers moved again. And then it happened. Suddenly, beneath his touch, her body rocked with an exquisite melody of tiny convulsions.

"Robert! . . ." she cried out as the tide washed over her and her legs gave way in the face of it.

"Robert . . . ," she whispered when, spent, her cousin gently lifted her into his arms and carried her to the bed.

"Rest now, Tia," he told her as he settled her upon the soft down, his face, his voice, oddly taut. "The lesson is over. In a few moments you shall be yourself again." Tucking the coverlet about her, he turned then and slowly started for the door.

"Robert . . . ?" Tia asked in a small worried voice, gripping the coverlet, her hair a silken tangle, her eyes huge against the stark white pillowcase. "Am I now a fallen woman?"

His back still toward her, the viscount paused. A slight smile flickered over the tension rigidly sustained within the thin line of his mouth.

"No, cousin, you are still a maid."

"And . . . is that all there is to . . . b-bed-sharing?"

"No," he said, advancing to the door, "But I have shown you enough for you to speak knowledgeably with Elizabeth. By the way, your participation in the lesson was more than satisfactory."

"Th-thank you. But . . . wait, Robert! Where are you going?" Tia asked, summoning the strength to sit up, her hair tumbling about her shoulders in ramrod ribbons of disarray.

"For a walk," he answered.

"But it is snowing outside!" Tia warned.

"All the better."

"But, cousin . . . !"

The viscount placed one hand upon the door frame, then

turned back slightly. Even in profile, Tia could not help but notice the restlessness of his mobile jaw, the tension in his drawn brows.

"Robert . . . ?"

"Do not be concerned, cousin. I shall return before dinner is served."

"But, Robert . . . !"

"Let it lay, Tia," he ground out, his fingers clawing wood. "For God's sake, this time just let it lay."

Tia had much to ponder once the viscount had abandoned her room.

Eighteen

How had it happened, Tia wondered for the thousandth time since she had awakened the following morning, that things had come to this pass? How had matters changed between herself and her cousin so quickly? . . . become so awkward? Worse, how had it happened that she had allowed it? She had always dismissed the advances of gentlemen . . . viewed them as of no particular moment save on Valentine's Day; and, on her mother's counsel, had chosen the safety and contentment of the single life. Her feet were firmly set upon her course, were they not? Why, then, did she now, suddenly, feel so at sea over the concept?

Because the man who had just tossed her whole life top over tails was Robert. Her cousin. Her dearest friend.

Again Tia's glance flitted perversely toward him and clung as the coachman cracked his whip and the two Bainbridge carriages lurched into motion, rumbling away from Blackamore Grange on a route that would take them northeast across the rolling hills bordering the moors toward Clifftop, the estate of the Earl and Countess of Clyde, just inland from the pleasant seaside village of Redcar. He was still sitting just as he had been when he had waved his last goodbye to Ambrose and Elizabeth, the varlet! . . . as if nothing had happened; contained . . . smug . . . vexingly self-assured.

The same, and yet . . .

How would she ever be able to look upon her dear, familiar cousin again without remembering what had passed between them? . . . the low huskiness of his voice . . . the softness of his lips upon her skin . . . the caress of his hands . . . how good it had felt to be surrounded by his warmth . . . buoyed by his tender strength?

Or pinioned by the altogether predatory bearing of his gaze, either, she acknowledged when, suddenly, that same autumn gaze slewed toward her. Her own eyes widening, she swallowed thickly; a tremble frolicked over her.

"Tia . . ."

Instantly, Tia's glance skittered toward one of the dangling straps.

Sighing, shaking his head, masking the motions behind a York tan glove, Robert smiled, then returned his attention to an inspection of a passing packhorse train carrying goods up from the lowlands to the high moors on an ancient flagstone trod.

What was she to do? Tia continued to consider, now that, in the space of a few short moments, her whole assurance in her choices, her knowledge of her place in the scheme of things, her security in the immutability of her surroundings, had irrevocably crumbled? Her cousin, the one person in the whole world upon whom she had staked her complete trust, had changed. No longer was he Robert, her childhood protector . . . her comfortable friend. In the course of one lesson he had taught her the truth. Somehow, when she had not been looking, he had transformed into . . . a man. More, after what had just happened between them, very likely he would soon be transformed into her husband. Tia swallowed back the threatening tremor that accompanied a sudden image of her father and bit at her lower lip.

"Tia, you shall have to talk to me sometime," Robert attempted again after the carriage had rolled over the bridge spanning Carr Beck.

Across from him, Tia pushed her hands more deeply into her sable muff.

"Come now. You haven't said anything about your conversation with Elizabeth after I left your room last night," Robert noted, seeking a safe subject upon which to begin. "At least speak to me of that."

Tia's glance flickered toward her cousin, then down into her lap again. "It went well, I believe," she replied at last, snuggling more deeply down within the sable lining of her orange Melton traveling cape. "You saw them as well as I in the dining room this morning, Robert. They could hardly take their eyes from one another."

"While ours can barely stand to meet," Robert observed, his gaze suddenly seeming to bleed.

"I cannot help that," Tia told him softly, staring out at the hills rolling away from the moorland riggs and into the horizon.

The road turned slightly then, and the village of Swainby came into sight. Robert eased out the breath he had been holding and once again looked out the window, watching as the muted sandstone cottages passed by.

"I shan't apologize, you know," he told her when the village had been left behind.

"I-I have not asked you to," Tia replied, intent upon the study of her gloved hands. "Did you see the belated valentine Ambrose gave Elizabeth? It was a parure of rubies he had been waiting to give her since their wedding trip."

"I saw them. Tia—"

"And how lovely that the two of them are to be spending

the weeks before coming up to Town for the Season on a second wedding trip to the spa at Cheltenham."

For a time, Robert did not respond while he collected his patience. Inhaling, he tried again.

"Tia, we cannot avoid discussing what happened between us last night," he finally said, his gaze firm, yet at the same time, very warm.

"Yes, we can," she responded softly, still avoiding his eyes.

"Tia . . ."

"You were merely teaching me what I needed to know in order to help my friend, Robert," she stated, twisting her fingers together.

"I went far beyond the bounds of propriety and you know it," Robert countered in a firmer tone.

"Well, then, of course I see why you would not wish to apologize," Tia quickly remarked, afterward wondering for a bit where in the world that tease had sprung from. Oddly, the thought heartened her. Within her cocoon of sable, she slightly relaxed.

"No, I do not," her cousin replied with no hesitation. "For . . . reasons of my own."

"Ah, well. It does not signify. You said yourself that my virtue was still intact."

"Barely," Robert countered as the carriage approached a small outcropping of rocks skirting both the road and the bed of a shallow, frozen beck.

" 'Barely' is still adequate, is it not?" Tia supposed, reaching for a strap when the coach tipped slightly downward and stumbled over several deep ruts.

"Not if wind of the liaison makes its way to the ears of the *ton*," Robert stated flatly, "not to mention the intelligence that we spent the night together in Mrs. Cribbs's bed.

You are not to be concerned, however. When we arrive back at the Abbey, Tia, I shall seek out Cousin Brumley at once and offer . . ."

In the instant that Tia understood the direction of her cousin's thoughts, her eyes grew huge.

"Nonsense!" she blurted out to cover his conclusion. "There is no possible way for word of last evening to get out."

"Tia, anyone in the house could speak of it. All it takes is a word in the wrong ear . . ."

"Which shall never happen," she countered more emphatically as the shadow of the outcropping suddenly shuttered away the wan sunshine. "Nancy will never speak of it, nor will Romney, and they are the only ones who could!"

Robert scrubbed his brow. "Tia, I am a gentleman. It is my duty to offer for—"

"No!"

"What do you mean, 'no!' Deuce take it, Tia, look at me!" Robert commanded, reaching for her arms. "I do not consider the duty a hardship . . ."

"No, I say!" Tia replied, struggling against his restraining hands.

"Damn it, Tia, listen to what I am saying!"

"No!" Tia cried, wriggling free of his restraint, clamping her hands over her ears. "I shan't speak of this any longer." Suddenly she thumped her fist upon the carriage roof. "Stop the carriage!" she cried up to the viscount's coachman. "I want to get out!"

"Tia!" Robert shouted when she threw open the door and jumped to the ground even before the carriage had rolled to a complete stop. "Come back here!" he ordered, swinging his body toward the door. "Tia!"

Desperation was the last thing he remembered before a

thick cudgel descended to smash into his forehead, crumpling him like a jilt's letter upon the frozen ground.

At the very moment Robert fell, miles away on the outskirts of Whitby, with the utmost secrecy as their bywords, the Black Mask Society massed.

"Devilishly good idea, Digby, to use the viewing of my newest litter of pups as an excuse to gather," Lord Fullerton whispered, casting his proud gaze toward a long row of enclosures as several of the Black Masks wandered about taking the measure of the earl's extensive kennels.

"Fox," the other hissed. "I cannot conceive why you will not use my secret name!"

"Because *here* you are not," Fullerton argued smugly, rearranging a bit of the corpulence being uncomfortably restrained beneath corset and velvet riding habit.

"I am if I wish to be," Digby huffily replied.

"Now, now . . . Fullerton has the right of it, Digby," Walmsley refereed *sotto voce*. "Try to keep in mind that we wish this meeting to seem nothing more than a social occasion regularly enjoyed by our ranks," he added while his watchful gaze slid side to side, "not an official gathering of the What's-its-name."

"I know that," Digby responded with a bit of a pout. "However, I cannot see the harm. We are surrounded by heavily armed retainers, after all. And I have not been called 'Fox' for days."

"Nevertheless, we must take pains to protect our anonymity," Walmsley replied. "There is the chance, after all, that Beale and Wilson were mistaken. Now where is Walpole?"

"Taking the measure of my best bitch, I believe," Fullerton responded with pride. "Means to breed her with his black when she comes in season again. I shall make a pretty penny on that stud, I vow! Why, the last time she whelped, I realized—"

"Gentlemen, the business at hand . . . ?" Walmsley reminded them, signaling one of the milling servants for a bracing tot of the Scots' brew which was even then being poured from his silver flask.

Whalebone creaked with the force of Fullerton's sigh. "Very well, Brumley, what do you have to tell us?"

Once again, Walmsley's gaze shifted. Leaning closer, he whispered, "The ship has sailed." That done, he took his silver cup from the servant and downed its contents in a single gulp.

"Oh, I say!" Digby breathed, huddling closer to the other two. "Then it shall be today?"

"This very afternoon," Walmsley replied in a low murmur.

"What is this afternoon?" bellowed Walpole in his ancient warble, approaching at a rickety pace, then easing his bent frame into their midst.

"Sh-h-h!" the other three steamed at his wispy, beaver-warmed head.

"Good God, Walpole, why not tell the town crier that Paine is on his way!" Lord Fullerton exclaimed, snapping affronted fingers behind his back for a cup of Armagnac.

" 'Tis the time, then?" Walpole asked in a low tremolo, poking his beaver-clad head into the center of the circle. "When does the bounder arrive?"

"This afternoon!" Digby repeated impatiently. "Now, do go on, Brumley, if you please. Give us the details."

"Very well," Walmsley responded, shrinking the circle even more tightly. "Here is the plan. As there is no way of knowing precisely when Mr. Paine's ship shall approach the harbor at Whitby, I have thought to post Wardle in the eastern tower of the Abbey to watch for sign of sail. When he spies the ship, he will ring the bell. As soon as you hear it, hie to Turnbull's in the Upper Harbor with every man you can arm, then make for the collier."

"Collier?" Walpole questioned.

"Yes, you remember, Nelson," Brumley explained. "I suggested at our last meeting that we hire a collier upon which to sally forth when the time came."

"Ah, yes. And did you?" quavered Walpole, now struggling to uncork his beaver from the press of lordly shoulders.

"Just said that I did."

"No, you did not. You merely intimated it. It was not so stated with certainty."

"Oh, for heaven's sake, Walpole!" Digby cried. "The man hired the collier! Now get on with it."

After a pause, Walmsley scratched his nose. "Very well. Now, where was I? Oh, yes . . . as Turnbull is renting us a ship he has newly repaired, make for the Whitehall yard. *And* I have hired a crew."

"A crew? But is that not a bit risky?" Digby warned. "What is to keep one of them from telling someone what's toward?"

"Nothing, ordinarily," Walmsley acknowledged. "However, I recognized some of the men as Robert's . . . idle now that he's off about the moors with my niece and glad of the chance for a bit of adventure, I'd wager. Nay, gentlemen, I am persuaded that we have nothing to be concerned about there. Robert will have trained them well on his own ships, don't you know. If he trusts them, why, then, I shall as well. For now, however, the matter of greatest importance, gentlemen, is to begin making ready, and to await the ringing of the bell."

"Done," Fullerton stated with a definitive nod of his head.

"Excellent," Walmsley replied with a smile. "Now, Digby, do tell us what you know of your dear brother-in-law and his poor Felicity."

"Ah, as to that, I have the best of tidings," Digby replied with a wide grin, clapping Fullerton upon the back. "Only last evening she was returned."

"Huzza, sir!" Walpole exclaimed in a high-pitched tremble. "What an agreeable happenstance! But how did such a joyous conclusion to poor Edward's torment come about?"

"There is no explanation, it seems," Digby answered, shrugging and shaking his head. "The blackguards merely, and most rag-manneredly, to my way of thinking, dumped her out of their conveyance at the foot of her drive, then left her to make her way alone and unaided the entire six yards up to the entrance."

"The devils!" Fullerton exploded.

"I was sent for at once, of course," Digby continued after nodding his agreement. "I fear my poor sister was beyond distraction by the time I arrived, however. Kept going on and on about the abuses heaped upon her by her captors . . . how her requests for her dinner wine to be served at no less than sixty-two degrees were met with the most appalling of rude noises . . . how not one soul would listen to her understandable objections as to why she should not be expected to perform her own toilette each morning . . . and worse! how she was given nothing of that Radcliffe woman's to read . . ."

"Horrible. Truly horrible," Walpole quavered in sympathy.

"The gel was in the hands of beasts," Digby agreed. "And then, suddenly, she was free."

"Who can explain it?" Fullerton asked with a shrug.

"What is the need?" Walpole added, throwing up his hands. "With the return of Felicity, the Radicals' counterplan is foiled, is it not? Indeed, we are all of us back together again . . . *and* safely ensconced within our own sturdy walls!" he added, clasping his palms.

And then a thought occurred. As one, all eyes slewed toward Walmsley.

Suddenly quite mortified, Walpole's thick brows wobbled. "Rather . . . that is . . . ," he stammered, averting his gaze to run a bony finger back and forth beneath his nose. "Oh, dear me . . ."

"Quite naturally, what Nelson meant was . . . ," Digby offered by way of assistance before turning his intellect toward dislodging a small clot of excrement from his boot heel.

"Here now! The gel is with Robert, is she not?" Fullerton declared, barging into the awkwardness with a thump of his cane.

Instantly, "So she is!" and "She is indeed, I vow!" rumbled in relief about the circle.

"So she is," Walmsley agreed with a quiet nod, his eyes colorless in the mid-morning light. "Well, then, let us repair to our homes, gentlemen. The morning wanes. We must be ready for Wardle's signal."

Nineteen

"Robert! Oh, let me go, you . . . you insufferable black-guard!" Tia cried, swinging a foot backward in an attempt to kick her captor in the shin. "Robert!"

"This struggle is useless, milady," stated the man so rudely pinning Tia's arms behind her.

"Nevertheless, it shall con . . . *tinue!*" Tia gritted out as she next tried to swing her reticule. "You villain!" she cried, again reaching toward her cousin. "What have you done?"

"Taken advantage of the opportunity you presented me with, my dear," the man said, sidestepping the drawstring bag while fastening an elbow about Tia's neck. "Billy and I had thought that we would have to stop your carriages at gunpoint. Imagine our delight when you did the job for us, and then proceeded to run straight into my arms.

"Billy," he called to his partner, "have the occupants of the second carriage disarm. Remind them, of course, that I shall blow a sizeable hole in our lovely captive should any of them raise an objection."

"Scoundrel!" Tia pronounced, attempting to butt her head backward into the man's heavy jaw. "At least let me go to my cousin, sir! He is bleeding!" And then it occurred to her. Every struggle stopped. "H-he might be dead!"

"Hardly that," the man countered blithely. "Yet definitely unable to save you from your fate as he did upon those other occasions, my dear."

"What other occasions?" Tia asked, stiffening, struggling to whirl around.

"The previous ones," her captor informed her a bit less smugly, tightening his hold.

"You have tried to capture me before?" Tia questioned at a most improper volume. "When?"

"Once outside of Spindle Thorn Hall," he responded reluctantly, "but that debacle was strictly Billy's fault."

"You never!" Tia exclaimed, her eyes growing round.

"We did," the man admitted. "Madam, you have been a deuce of a lot of trouble. We almost had you the second time, though . . . had you nicely bound in your coverlet and ready to carry off. It would have worked, too, if it had not been for his lordship over there. Bastard threw us out the window."

"Then it was you . . . ," Tia summarized, pointing back toward her captor. "And he . . . ," she finished, pointing toward her cousin.

"All right, all right," the man ground into her ear, "so he unseated us at Blackamore Grange as well."

Sudden tears blurred Tia's vision. "Oh, Robert! . . ." she breathed in watery tones, again reaching toward him as a freshet of love swelled within her throat. "Oh, dearest, I had no idea . . ."

"He cannot help you now, madam," the man stated quite heartlessly, drawing her tightly against himself again. "I have managed to put quite a nice period to that at last.

"It worked just as I said it would, did it not, Billy?" he then called again to his partner as the other went about collecting weapons of several different sorts and dropping them into a canvas bag. "I told you that in order to get to her, we would have to dispose of her protector, did I not?"

"You did," Billy called, dragging the bag over to the lead carriage's boot.

"And I was correct," he directed toward Tia's drooping coiffure. "Now, milady, if you will kindly reboard the carriage . . ."

"I shall not, you cur!" Tia declared, stamping down upon the captor's instep. "I am staying with my cousin!"

"Ouch! Devil a bit!" the man cried, shoving Tia away from him, yet still keeping her arms captive behind. "Get into the carriage, madam," he commanded, forcing her to walk forward, "or the sizeable hole I blow shall be in *him!*"

Gasping with offense, for the third time since the day of her Valentine's ball, Tia did exactly as she was bid.

Moments later, the one called Billy took the ribbons and, with a startling cry, set Robert's horses galloping down the road toward Guisborough. Across from Tia, a stranger now occupied the place that had once been her cousin's.

"You shall pay for this," Tia promised the man in low tones.

"Perhaps," he benignly replied. "But not until good use has been made of you."

"What use?" Tia demanded to know. "Why have you done this to my cousin and me?"

The man considered Tia's question for a moment and then shrugged. "I suppose it does no harm to tell you. All this was necessary in order to take you hostage, milady," he told her.

"Hostage? To what end? And how is it that you know who I am?"

"Dear me, so many questions!" the man laughed. "Let me see if I might answer them."

"How very civil of you," Tia snapped.

Still smiling, the man ignored her sarcasm. "First, I know you because the whole county knows that you are Brumley Hilton's niece, and I am *well* acquainted with him, madam," he told her, adjusting his arms more comfortably across his chest. "For several years, you see, I have been a spy for the Radical movement planted in the midst of your local Loyalists."

"Indeed. How delightful for you," Tia replied loftily, staring at the man in distaste. "I fail to see, however, what such tidings can have to do with my family."

"Can it be that you do not know?" the man asked, his gaze narrowing above a growing smile. "But this is delicious!" he cried, swiping a gloved hand across his mouth.

"What is?" Tia demanded.

"The fact, my dear lady," he chortled, "that you apparently have no idea that your precious uncle happens to be the leader of the Loyalists."

Stunned, Tia sank back into the squabs. "Uncle Brumley?" she suddenly cried, beginning to chuckle. "A Black Mask? Surely not!"

"I assure you, he is," the man replied, a bit vexed by the lady's unexpected levity.

Suddenly, Tia's thoughts began to race. Memories flooded back to her . . . of her uncle's endless meetings, his disappearances over the course of several days, of how very good he had become in the past several years at never quite answering her questions. Yet . . . Uncle Brumley? . . . a Black Mask? Ridiculous! But there was that rash. . . . Reluctantly, Tia yielded to the probability.

"It appears, then, that you have taken me hostage in order to get your hands on my uncle," she concluded when words could again form in her brain.

"Not at all, my dear," the man replied. "I could have, of course, had I wished to. I was, after all, within snatching distance of each of the Black Masks dozens of times. It is interesting that you suggest the idea, though. I, too, have always been persuaded that taking Walmsley hostage would have been the better plan. However, this particular directive came from London, and one cannot just arbitrarily disregard an edict from the movement's highest ranks, can one?"

"What edict?" Tia asked, her hazel stare directed fully toward him.

"Why, the edict directing me to capture members of the Black Masks' families to use as hostages," he told her, smiling solicitously, steadily returning her regard, "with you as the first choice, obviously."

"Because my uncle is the leader," Tia concluded, chewing her inner cheek.

"Just so," her captor replied.

"But again, sir, toward what end?" Tia asked, her brows drawing together.

"Toward the averting of the Black Masks' intention to do likewise to Mr. Thomas Paine," he responded triumphantly, settling his arms back across his chest again.

Each of Tia's lungs deflated.

She quickly recovered, however. "When is this to happen?" she cried, knocking several strands of hair to her shoulders as she rubbed her forehead.

"Today. That is why we must carry you quickly to our headquarters in Staithes. We must arrive in time to have a message delivered to Walmsley telling him of your fate."

"But this is outrageous!" Tia cried. "Uncle cannot mean to do such a notorious thing. The whole scandal broth is beyond anything."

"Yet true."

"You are telling me that you, sir, have for years served as a double agent in the midst of the Black Masks, all the while devoted to the Radical cause?" she reprised, staring at the man as if he had just sprouted an extra nose.

"I am."

"And that my uncle has plotted with the Black Mask Society to kidnap one of the most brilliant essayists of our time?"

"Correct again."

"And that the Freedom Brigade has devised a counter-strategy to prevent the kidnapping of Mr. Paine by doing the same to someone of importance to the Loyalists? . . . in this instance, me?"

"That is the case, yes."

Tia's brows soared. "Well, you simply cannot. How shall I ever be able to get to my cousin Estelle's estate in Redcar?"

"You shall not, of course, madam," the man replied. "You are a prisoner."

Tia's lips pursed. "One more question, then," she said, holding up a finger. And then her volume soared. "If you persist in this idiocy, how under heaven shall I be able to discover the origin of the black valentine?"

"I have no idea what you are talking about, madam," her captor responded, covering a yawn.

"I am talking about the purpose of my quest, Mr. . . . . er, what is your name, if I might ask?"

"That would be two questions, milady," the other pointed out.

"Nevertheless . . ."

"Wilson," her captor responded, "and, quest or no, madam, we are not taking you to Redcar."

Upon hearing that pronouncement, Tia took a few moments to fume.

"Well, Mr. Wilson . . . fiddle!" was all that she finally said.

There was only one thing to be done, Tia thought several minutes later after her captor had ceased his rag-mannered chuckling and occupied himself with the more proper pursuit of looking out the carriage window. Somehow she must make her escape, find Robert again, and return them both to the Abbey in time to prevent her uncle from doing something quite beyond the pale. The leader of the Black Masks! she considered with a slight shake of her head . . . and intent upon kidnapping a man such as Thomas Paine! No, there was no question about it. Somehow she must find the means to free herself and put a stop to the endeavor. Such goings-on were really not at all the thing. Someone could get hurt, after all. Wiggling more comfortably into the squabs, Tia settled into watchfulness, holding herself alert for her best opportunity.

It came not long after the coach had left Guisborough behind. After several hours of rattling over the frozen countryside at a grueling pace, the carriage quite unexpectedly changed direction, veering off toward what a wooden sign informed Tia was the direction of the little town of Tockett's Mill and, if she judged correctly, the expectation of an inn, a warming cup of tea for her, fresh horses for the carriage, and for her captors, undoubtedly two warm, foamy pints.

At the coach's sudden sway, therefore, she reached up to clutch at the nearest leather strap, hanging on tightly when Billy whistled piercingly, then began to straighten the tired team's direction, chopping them at a relentless pace down the new path, heading straight for an arched limestone bridge spanning the warmer, freely flowing waters of Howl Beck. The horses hit the incline of the bridge at a dead run. Up and over it they went, trailing the rocking carriage behind, throwing Tia and her captor into a moment of weightlessness before each landed roughly once more upon the squabs; then pounding on across the narrow expanse before lunging down the opposite side.

It was then that each of them saw the series of jolting ruts just where the path resumed. It was also then that it occurred to Billy that it was too late to do anything about what would surely happen. And happen it did. Beneath his gaping jaw, the carriage followed the team to its fate, bouncing off the bridge to slam into the frozen mire; at times shimmying, wobbling erratically, at times completely airborne.

In revenge, an iron rim screeched, warped, then skewed on one of the carriage's huge rear wheels.

"Whoa!" Billy called out, bringing the team to a sudden, jarring halt when the rim began to twist upon its wooden support.

Within the carriage, Tia and Wilson soared, tangled, and fell upon the floor.

"What the deuce! . . ." Wilson demanded, helping Tia back up to her seat while the creak of wood and leather diminished into silence.

"We be losing a rim," Billy called down.

"Damme!" Wilson muttered, throwing the door wide and swinging down to the ground.

"I feel it only my duty to inform you, sir, that if you have harmed even the smallest particle of my cousin's traveling coach, I shall inform the magistrate," Tia called after his disappearing beaver, rubbing at the top of her sable hat where it had come into rather abrupt contact with the carriage roof, and, naturally, releasing several more strands of hair from their tentative place.

"Cease your ridiculous threats, madam, and kindly get down," Wilson tersely replied, returning to the open doorway after inspecting the rim.

"I shall not, sir!" she replied, pressing more firmly back into the squabs.

The idea came to her, than, that if she could just remain within the carriage, she might slip away when they were otherwise occupied. She smiled.

"Go right ahead and shoot me if you like," she bravely jibed.

"What? . . . you, milady?" Wilson responded with a cold smile. "And lose my trump card? Nonsense. I have no qualms whatsoever, however, about shooting the viscount's bloods."

Glowering, Tia quickly accepted the offer of the blackguard's arm.

And, within moments, found her wrists efficiently secured by a leather thong quickly tied to the topmost segment of the adjacent front wheel's iron rim.

Appalled, Tia's eyes grew round. "How dare you, sir!" she cried when her captor then turned to stroll away with his partner in the direction of the beck.

Curiosity, of course, soon overcame her pique. Completely forgetting to demand an answer, and craning her neck, she peered ahead. In the near distance, a shrouding of low-hanging mist clung to the beck's bank. Within, the suggestion of snagged branches held captive against the bridge appeared and disappeared at the whim of the gentle wind.

"Release me at once!" she at last remembered to insist, straining to hear her captor's mumblings.

Completely ignoring her, the two finished their conversation, then, bending beneath several tendrils of fog, freed a number of large, twisted portions of ash and oak from the snag and began to drag them back toward the carriage boot.

"I shall have you both up before the beak!"

"Do not be absurd, Lady Horatia," Wilson wheezed as he and Billy drew up to the carriage again. Taking only a moment, he then selected the larger of the logs and positioned it beneath the rear axle. "You are my prisoner," he grunted, heaving upward on the log while Billy levered a slightly smaller piece of wood beneath the original.

"Prisoner or no, I have never before been treated so shabbily," Tia huffed above the sounds of Billy's groans and rasps as he pushed down upon the second log with all his strength.

The carriage rose slightly, then a bit more. Startled, Tia paused in her harangue to watch. Again the carriage inched upward. When the crooked rim began to slowly circle upon the suspended rear wheel, Wilson left Billy to hold the lever steady, then quickly pulled out the pins holding the wheel in place and took it in his hands.

"My apologies," he offered, wiping his brow on his coat sleeve. "But then my guess is that you have also never been a hostage," he added, straining as he wiggled the wheel free from the axle. "I assure you, madam, your treatment is quite *de rigueur.*"

"Got a hammer in the box up front, I'll wager," Billy commented, quickly propping another log under the axle and hurrying to help his partner lay the wheel flat upon the ground.

"Get it, then," Wilson ordered after several gasps. "There, you see, milady? We shall be on our way in no time. This rim shall be right and tight in a trice."

"Aye. Have to soak it, though," Billy reminded him, rooting around in the box just beneath the coachman's seat, then jumping down again with a large mallet in his hand.

"Soak it all you like," Tia told them with a sweet smile. "Hours even. It shall only give Robert the time he needs to come to my aid."

"It pains me to disabuse you, madam," Wilson responded, "but after the blow I gave him, I misdoubt your cousin will be ambulatory until the morrow. You must begin to reconcile yourself to the fact, my dear, that no help shall be forthcoming.

"Now, have at it, Billy," he commanded his companion. "After the rim is affixed, we shall soak it in the river. And do have a bit of patience, milady," he called to her when the ringing blows of metal against metal began to reverberate within the still silence of the glade. "It shall not be long now."

"Perceptive," came a low, brittle sigh like the skate of fingertips upon dew-touched glass, somehow seeming to come from all around them.

Startled, Tia glanced wildly about. A telltale movement stirred the stagnant fog at the river's edge. Without conscious thought, her gaze swung to the motion; held.

Then, suddenly, she saw him . . . a phantom, she was certain, coalescing even as her breath stalled in her lungs, to stride toward them out of the vapor like a specter born of the diaphanous, his cloak swirling away from his muscular form, every part of him clad in black except for the portion of his face left bare by his conforming half mask;

his every movement, his very presence, a definition of power and menace.

And she was completely captivated.

Billy's hammer suddenly fell from his fingers to clatter noisily against the iron rim.

"God save us!" he gasped, huddling against his partner, staring at the relentless, rolling approach of muscle, the clench of fingers into sinewy fists. "We be dead, Wilson," he uttered dreadfully. "It be the Enforcer!"

Nearby, raptly staring, Tia softened like butter on a toasted bun.

Twenty

"Well, well . . . Wilson. We meet again," the Enforcer hissed, settling into a predatory stillness before them, his voice like the rustle of parchment in the wind, "and in such interesting company."

Still bound to the wheel, another curl sliding from beneath her sable brim to bounce upon her breast, Tia could only gape. It was inexplicable. She had never met the man before in her life, yet she could not put a period to her rag-mannered perusal. He was a stranger, yet each word he uttered seem to caress the most hidden, sensitive places on her skin.

Like hands, she thought, remembering . . . like Robert's hands.

Nearby, under the Enforcer's raptorial gaze, Wilson swallowed, then visibly stiffened.

"S-so it seems, sir . . . ," the captor admitted, mustering a thread of courage, "though not, I regret, under the most f-felicitous of occasions."

"What will you do to us?" Billy breathed, his eyes bulging like a man just hanged.

At the question, the Enforcer's gaze slowly shifted between the two conspirators. "Advise you to quit the country," he replied in a fierce hiss, tossing his cape behind his shoulders to reveal his coiled whip. "It would be wise.

After all, you have lost your usefulness to the Freedom Brigade. There is nothing here for you now but swift retribution."

"From those paltry Masks?" Wilson asked, a slight smile forming.

"No," the Enforcer stated, fingering the bound leather handle of his whip, "from me."

Beside the front wheel, wholly unable to control her impulse, Tia sent her gaze skating over each new glimpse of the Enforcer's frame. She squeezed her eyes tight then, almost overwhelmed by a fresh upswelling of awakened sensibilities; a series of exquisitely remembered sensations . . . weakness . . . warm chills . . . soft demands. Meadow pipits began to frolic within her abdomen.

A slight tremble agitated Wilson's lower lip. "I am sworn, sir," he countered, knowing he had nothing else to lose by his honesty. "I have given my word to protect the great Thomas Paine."

Suddenly, imperceptibly to any save someone who was staring at the man as if he were Apollo incarnate, Tia realized with no small measure of chagrin, the Enforcer gathered himself into stillness. As she watched, his gaze narrowed slowly.

"Have you?" he responded at last, still holding his restless energy admirably impassive, Tia thought, though she, of course, could easily detect the slight twitch of muscle just aside one corner of his heavenly lips.

"It is true," Wilson replied, gathering more courage from the justness of his cause, "I was taking her ladyship to Staithes, of course, so that a message of her capture might be sent to Walmsley in time to stop the Black Masks from their attempt upon Mr. Paine."

"A reasonable move," the Enforcer allowed.

"I wonder . . . ," Wilson responded. "At this point, why is it even necessary? All I really need do is assure that she remains on the moors this one last day, do I not?" he questioned. "Walmsley need not even know that we have her. All that really is required is that he be uncertain where she is, would you not agree? As long as there is any doubt, he shall never be able to bring himself to defy our directive and proceed with his kidnapping plans. And he shall not know, shall he?" he concluded with a noble flare of his broad nostrils. "The day has waned in all this talking. You shall never be able to return the lady to the Abbey by the time Paine's ship is scheduled to pass on its way to Sunderland."

Cloaked in stillness, the Enforcer listened like a coiled spring.

"Unless I cut across the Blackamore," he at last offered, his voice the murmur of a swollen stream.

"On what, sir?" Wilson asked, increasingly pleased with his growing advantage. "One of these carriage hacks? . . . and with Billy and me in pursuit?"

Under fierce, narrowed eyes, the Enforcer smiled.

"Fortunately, that shall not be necessary. I shall leave as I arrived, gentlemen . . . on my own stallion," he told them, his low chuckle a rustling, like flame consuming autumn leaves. "Unfortunately . . . for you, of course . . . I shall not be best pleased traveling with the two of you nipping at my heels."

Wilson's eyes enlarged. "H-how shall you stop us?" he questioned, nervously narrowing the gap between him and his cohort in crime.

"Like this," the Enforcer told them; and then, before Tia's astonished eyes, the coil released.

In a single blurred motion, the Enforcer bent and easily

lifted the huge carriage wheel into his hands. Then, like a whip suddenly unfurled and cracked, he raised the wheel high up in the air and brought it crashing down over the captors' huddled shapes . . . crushing their hats, popping their shirt studs into the mire of snowmelt, scraping their noses, neatly pinning each pair of their arms between the wheel's surviving spokes.

"You must admit, I did advise you to quit the country of your own free will, did I not?" he continued, easily toppling the wheel up on its iron rim. "I see that I gave you too much credit, however."

"Devil a bit, sir, what can you be about?" Wilson gasped, kicking wildly atop his comrade.

"You have obviously chosen to ignore the wisdom of my suggestion," the Enforcer sighed like the passing of wood smoke on an autumn eve, immediately afterward giving the wheel a mighty shove. "Pity. I had hoped that you would not need to be convinced. Do have a pleasant trip, however, gentlemen," he hissed as Tia watched the wheel bounce down the length of the embankment, Wilson and Billy rolling one on top of the other, over and over, until, with a great splash, the whole plunged into the dark, frigid flow of the beck. "I hear Denmark is quite pleasant this time of year. Oh, and one more bit of advice," he called out as the wheel caught the current and the captors began to grow distant. "Hang on tightly to the rim, won't you? Howl Beck is particularly swift. In no time at all you shall arrive at the coast."

The first bend in the beck was not far downstream. Tia watched the wheel approach it, bump against its grassy bank and hesitate, then spin free, the two men still inside, still struggling within the spokes as they rode their liquid steed. Moments later, several mounded tumuli rising above a more distant stretch of the embankment blocked any further view of their craft.

It was then, when they had gone, that Tia realized she was now very much alone with the closest thing North Yorkshire had to a legend . . . worse, a powerfully magnetic, wholly mystifying, very dangerous man. The realization brought her pounding heart perilously close to popping out of her throat. Slowly, very slowly, she began to move toward the opposite side of the wheel.

The Enforcer, however, in a slow, fluid movement, shifted into her path. Afterward, for several moments, he stood silent, regarding her from beneath his hat's wide brim, his focus unwavering, his muscles tensed, expectant, like a cat cornering a terrified tidbit.

"Are you all right, Lady Horatia?" he asked at last, his voice as deep as the passing of time.

"I . . . yes," she responded, unable to help staring up into his face, so very near now and, oddly, seeming to get closer by the moment; still awestruck over her reaction to him and the power she had just seen him so easily wield.

"I am relieved to hear it," he whispered, lowering his shadowed eyes as he slipped a knife from his belt and deftly severed the cords bound about her wrists.

He paused then, studying her once again, Tia realized as she observed a dance of golden slivers deep within the shadows beneath his hat. Enthralled, she did the same, her eyes slowly widening as her body, too, began to echo the taut restraint contained in his. It was just as it had been before with Robert, only greater . . . far more powerful. And for the first time, Tia comprehended. It was desire . . . sweet, compelling desire. Slowly, her lips separated.

The Enforcer stretched out his hands and began to gently

rub the marks encircling her wrists, his gaze never leaving
her, never giving hers respite.

"You are very beautiful," he told her with rumbling
huskiness, raising one finger to trace the line of her cheek,
his lips closing the distance between them even farther,
and his warm breath beginning to insidiously invade her
being.

Tia's eyes grew huge as she swallowed a sudden gasp.
She knew that she should cry out . . . flee . . . anything! . . .
to escape the exquisite sensations rapidly building within
her, feelings she had only the night before learned that she
even possessed . . . yet she could not. Lost in the Enforcer's
compelling gaze, a silent insistence persuasively enveloped
her, eroding her will, dissolving her restraint. Unable to do
anything save yield, she trembled, then steadied herself on
the sweep of his black silk cape.

The command came again . . . this time firm fingers
aside her cheek, drawing her nearer as if she had no
strength. Helpless, she quickened deep within . . . so very
deep. Soft breaths gusted in an erratic rhythm against the
Enforcer's mask.

"I . . . ," she stammered, placing a hand against his solid
chest.

"You make a man forget that he is a gentleman . . . ,"
he murmured, slipping a powerful arm around her waist
and easily pulling her tightly against his full length, "forget . . . everything . . ." He slowly, predatorily, lowered his
head.

On a soft sigh then, quite suddenly he claimed her awaiting mouth.

Warm. So very, very warm, Tia thought with that portion
of her brain that could still function. Warm and soft . . .
surrounding her, carrying her cocooned within compelling

strength, taking her where she had never been before; coaxing her, teaching her, tempting her, demanding her response.

And she gave it . . . pressing into his power, wanting nothing more; granting him entrance, clinging as their moans blended . . . willingly accepting his mastery over her.

And he had been waiting for the yielding, it seemed. At the moment he felt it, he ended his tender assault. Kissing her once again, he smiled into her eyes, then accepted her sigh into his open mouth.

"We must go," he finally whispered against her lips.

"Wh-what?" Tia asked, still helplessly boneless in his embrace.

At her question, the Enforcer laughed, sounding like a chuckling beck.

"As much as I would delight in continuing with this, milady, I am afraid that we have a rather pressing kidnapping to attend in Whitby this afternoon. Can you stand?"

"I . . . yes," Tia responded, her cheeks blossoming with embarrassment.

"Then put your feet on the ground," the Enforcer suggested with a slight smile.

Suddenly, quite close by, a pistol cocked.

"Yes, do, Lady Horatia," came a sudden, sharp command from just beyond the carriage team's lead gelding.

Instantly, Tia spun around.

"You, sir, however . . . ," the voice continued, "put your God-cursed hands above your head!"

Reluctantly, the Enforcer released Tia. Then, touching his hat brim in admiration, he complied.

Beside him, Tia mortified all the way down to her half boots.

Twenty-one

"Mr. Clark!" Tia exclaimed, immediately putting a proper distance between herself and the Enforcer. "Good heavens, how you startled me! However did you come to be here?"

"One might ask you the same question, milady," Dex replied acidly, ducking into the open from beneath the shield of the gelding's thickly muscled neck, all the while keeping his pistol pointed directly at the Enforcer's chest. "Where is Bainbridge?"

"I-I cannot say for certain," Tia answered, shaking her head. "We were just outside of Swainby when I last saw him. He had been knocked unconscious, you see . . ."

"The deuce! And you just left him? . . . to ride off with this Black Mask devil?" he ground out, gesturing toward the Enforcer's jaw with his pistol barrel.

"Of course not!" Tia replied, planting her fists upon her hips. "I would never have willingly left him behind. As it happens, I was carried off by two of *your* Radicals, if you must know. They were the ones who struck him."

"Then how did you come to be with this . . . this . . . ?" he asked at quite an improper volume. Suddenly his gaze slewed to the man standing slightly behind. "Who the devil are you anyway?"

"I am called the Enforcer," the other replied, sweeping into a low bow.

"Dear God!" Dex cried out while steadying his aim. "So you do exist, you blackguard! And you, milady . . . you were embracing him! . . . when Bainbridge has loved you to distraction since you were both in leading strings!"

Across from him, Tia gasped. All around her, the world settled, stilled.

"He has?" she breathed, tilting her head to the side.

And in that moment, everything fell into place. Images came to her . . . words she had not understood . . . glances she had surprised. . . . kindnesses she had mistaken . . . the myriad thoughtful gestures.

He loves me. He loves me, she repeated a thousand times over and over in her mind.

Behind her, the Enforcer shifted. She turned to him then, gazing once more up into his shadowed eyes. Robert loves me, she pondered one more time, trying to touch the reality of it, wishing with all her heart that she might succeed; and failing . . . dear God in heaven, failing! . . .

Because in one breathtaking moment, everything had changed. And, for the first time, she understood the whole of it. Robert loved her . . . and she loved him, too, with all her heart . . . and had always done so. It was true. Yet quite without meaning for it to happen, she had *fallen* in love as well, she realized, tears pricking at her lids. She had fallen in love with him—with the Enforcer!—against all of her choices, every ounce of sense in her head; and nothing— not one of the countess's warnings, not one of her fears, not one of her carefully considered decisions—mattered anymore in the face of it, not even a whit.

And it broke her heart. As comfortingly familiar . . . as wondrous . . . as glorious as it had been in her dear cousin's arms, as much as she truly loved him for all he had been to her, all that he now was, how was she ever to forget this man . . . this Enforcer? How was she ever to forget her inexplicable desire for him . . . the taste of his wondrous kiss?

"My apologies, milady," Dex continued somewhat uncomfortably. "I fear that in the heat of the moment I spoke to you of matters which by rights are Bainbridge's to declare."

"Your apology is accepted," Tia said softly, turning toward him again after taking brisk swipes at her tears. "We shall speak no more of the matter."

"No, indeed . . . not once my friend's honor has been restored. Stand aside, if you please, milady," Dex ordered, shouldering his pistol. "And you, sir, draw your weapon. It is my intention to teach your felonious, libertine heart a lesson."

"No!" Tia cried, stepping firmly in front of the Enforcer just as a piercing whistle sounded behind her.

"I am afraid I really must agree," the Enforcer said, quickly withdrawing two of his fingers from his lips. Even before Tia's skirts had again settled about her ankles, hoof-beats began to pound toward them from the direction of the beck. "Rather urgent business awaits me in Whitby," he told them, capturing the ribbons of a pure black stallion that suddenly thundered forward out of the gathering mist. "Unfortunately, I cannot wait for something so tedious as a duel."

"Stand your ground!" Dex commanded, trying to find a clear shot.

"Mr. Clark, no!" Tia cried, swinging her reticule against the pistol barrel.

Instantly, the glade rang with the sound of gunfire. Less

than the twentieth part of a moment later, several chips of
limestone exploded from the side of the bridge.

Spinning toward it, Tia clapped both hands to her horrified cheeks.

The Enforcer, however, used the timely distraction to
swing up onto his stallion's back.

"My thanks, milady," he said, touching the brim of his
hat. "Till we meet again."

"And shall we, sir?" Tia asked, a desperation to know
easily overriding any sense of proper restraint.

Above her, one corner of the Enforcer's mouth curled.
"Absolutely. Count on it," he told her huskily. Then, digging his heels into his horse's flanks, after a rumble of
hoofbeats, he was enveloped by the distant trees.

"This is not the end of it, you blackguard!" Dex called,
shaking his fist at the other's retreat. "We shall finish this
should I ever see you again!"

Tears sprang into Tia's eyes. She understood it all now,
she realized as she listened to the stallion's hoofbeats fade
into the distant, empty vastness. Everything . . . the bond
that can so suddenly form between and man and a
woman . . . the feelings that so quickly arise . . . the crushing ache of knowing you shall very likely soon bring pain
to the one person who deserved it least in all the world.
Robert had done her no favor teaching her of what lay
between a man and a woman. Yet there could be no going
back. She knew now, and with the knowledge could come
love . . . or loss. Either one . . . or both.

Never in her life had Tia felt so alone.

"Lady Horatia, why the deuce did you stop me?" Dex
began sternly when, around them, the glade had grown
quiet again. "Surely you must realize how this whole scandal broth shall appear to Bainbridge . . ."

"Oh, Dex," Tia whispered, dabbing at her tears with gloved fingertips, "please do not scold."

Immediately Dex's features softened.

"Then tell me what I am to do, if not to scold?" he asked more moderately. "My lady . . ."

"Tia," her ladyship sniffed.

"Very well . . . Tia," Dex corrected, "you were in the man's embrace!"

"I know. I-I felt the need to thank him, of course . . ."

"Thank him!" Dex exclaimed, jabbing his pistol barrel into the waist of his buff inexpressibles. "Tia, that was no kiss of gratitude!"

"Nevertheless, he did rescue me from the Radicals, Dex," Tia defended, pleased to discover that a few threads of her spirit remained yet unsinged by her embarrassment. "And it was necessary that he return to Whitby as soon as possible. The Black Masks do have that horrid kidnapping going on."

"Yes . . . of Thomas Paine," Dex murmured, beginning to pace.

"You know of that?" Tia asked, looking at him.

"Yes. I learned of it from my father's acquaintances within the Radical movement."

"Then you know that I was the object of their repeated attempts. It was during the last that Robert was wounded. The carriage made it only this far and then was disabled."

"And that is when the Enforcer came upon you," Dex stated.

"Yes," Tia told him. "I am persuaded that he must have been on his way to Whitby to aid the Black Masks when he arrived at the bridge. You can see, can you not, why I could not let you harm him?"

"Of course. Because he had saved you," Dex gently supplied. "But perhaps might it also have been because of the harm that might yet befall your uncle?"

Tia's face fell along with her very proper posture and her sigh. "Oh, dear," she replied softly, holding herself about her waist. "So you know about that, too."

"Yes. The Radicals know each of the Black Masks, Tia."

"La," Tia sighed again, "Loyalists . . . Radicals . . . kidnappings . . . How did such a bumblebroth begin?"

"It was a combination of things," Dex told her. "The two groups vying for advantage in the county . . . the timing of Mr. Paine's release . . . and the fuse to it all lit by the explosion at the Penfield mine."

"The mine?" Tia questioned. "But whatever can that have to do with any of this?"

Nearby, Dex stopped his pacing and stood silent for a moment, biting at his inner cheek, looking at Tia. At last he spoke.

"The mine was destroyed by the Black Masks."

Tia's eyes rounded. "H-how do you know?"

"It was the Sinnington Mill all over again," Dex replied with a soft smile. "There were black tatters everywhere."

Blinking, Tia bit at her lower lip. "And Uncle Brumley was in command?"

Dex nodded. "He is their leader, Tia. There can be little doubt."

"No, I don't suppose there can," Tia agreed, taking an interest in the grooves still visible in the snow where the carriage wheel had once lain. "Do you hate him very much, Mr. Clark?"

"Oddly, no," Dex told her with an easy grin. "Do not ask me to explain it, however. I should be blazing mad. But having met his lordship, I find it devilishly difficult to work up the necessary indignation."

"He does have that effect on one," Tia agreed.

"Yes, he does, does he not?" Dex laughed. "And, too, there is the consideration of the physical evidence."

"What evidence?" Tia asked, adjusting her reticule.

"The evidence our own powder monkey found about the site of the explosion. It is his opinion that it was never the Masks' intention to blow up anything but the office building."

"Indeed!" Tia exclaimed, taking heart.

"Not the way it looks. In their usual fashion, however, they made a mull of the exercise. You cannot imagine the number of barrels they must have located about the perimeter of the office, Tia . . . and, obviously unknown to them, the whole collection sitting right above a series of fractures in the coal seam! It's little wonder everything collapsed."

"Yet still, Dex, your family is ruined," Tia pointed out, laying a glove upon his arm.

"Happily, no," Dex told her with a shake of his head. "I cannot credit it, but somehow just before I left, enough money was mysteriously deposited in my father's bank account to effect the mine's restoration."

"But that is wonderful, Dex!" Tia cried, seizing his arm. "Who, do you think?"

"I cannot say for certain, but I have an idea, and believe me, he shall be my friend for life."

Just like Robert, Tia thought as a tender sadness suddenly squeezed her heart.

"And so shall I be if you will just take me back to the Abbey," she spoke aloud, willing away a freshet of tears.

"What? Are you, too, set upon donning the black mask?" Dex teased, leading her toward his curricle.

"No, indeed," Tia softly smiled, stepping up to the seat. "I am set upon stopping the kidnapping."

"As am I," Dex concurred, settling beside her and taking the ribbons into his hands. "As a matter of fact, I was on my way to Whitby to do just that when I came upon you and that . . . that *rakehell*. We have little time before Paine's ship nears, however. If we are going to arrive in time, we must go directly, and go now."

"Without Robert," Tia completed with resignation.

"I am afraid so. However, knowing Rob as I do, I am persuaded he would not want us to delay if the earl were in danger."

"No, he would not," Tia conceded soberly.

"He is a loyal man, Tia . . . ," Dex told her, glancing in her direction as he snapped a long carriage whip above his matched mares, *"and* worthy."

Yes, all that . . . and the man I have loved and trusted all my life, above all others. But he is not the Enforcer, Tia thought, hanging on to the edge of the tufted seat as the curricle started forward.

Twenty-two

The bell in the eastern tower was tolling like a somber scold when Dex's mud-spattered bays came to a halt just before the crossbarred entrance to Whinstone Abbey later that afternoon. For Tia, as she accepted Dex's hand and bounded down onto the freshly swept walk, it was all of a piece, of course. Why should a bell that had been silent for several centuries not be adding its voice to the incredible events of the past few days? It was quite the most reasonable of occurrences, she thought, preceding Dex up the age-warped rows of sandstone steps and knocking solidly upon the door . . . every bit as reasonable as the fact that her cousin had been rendered senseless, she had been taken hostage by two jackanapes intent upon preventing her uncle from doing the same to Thomas Paine, and, even more reasonably, the fact that she, a confirmed spinster, had somehow managed to find herself hopelessly in love with two gentlemen.

As icing on the raspberry tart, Miss Tutweiler was now, it seemed, an Abbey footman.

"Miss Tutweiler!" Dex beamed after the latch had suddenly been released and Margaret had wrestled the heavy door aside to stand a bit breathlessly before them.

"Margaret! Whatever . . . ?"

"Oh, Tia!" Miss Tutweiler cried airily, rushing forward

to draw her into a smothering embrace. "And Mr. Clark!" she added, stretching out her hand. "Thank goodness you have finally arrived!"

"What has happened?" Dex asked, taking her hand and drawing her around to face him.

"It is his lordship, sir . . . But then, the countess . . . Oh, everything is at sixes and sevens!" Margaret replied on a vast exhalation, touching a handkerchief to the tip of her nose.

"Uncle Brumley? Mama?" Tia demanded, seizing her other hand. "Margaret, why is the bell ringing? And whyever have you answered the door?"

"It seemed the most sensible thing to do," Margaret answered, squeezing Tia's fingers. "Why, I could never have expected the countess . . ."

"Dearest, what about the countess?" Tia questioned worriedly, spinning Miss Tutweiler about to face her again.

Suddenly the creak and rumble of an arriving carriage sounded just outside. As one, the three turned to see the second of the Bainbridge traveling coaches swing into the drive and start forward at a gallop down its pebbled length. Moments later, Viscount Bainbridge, impeccably clad in buff inexpressibles, claret superfine, and a fine, large abrasion, lithely stepped down.

Immediately, he found Tia with his wonderful woodland eyes. For only a moment, he paused, looking at her. Then, grinning up at her with a warmth Tia was persuaded would banish what was left of winter, he threw open his arms.

Feeling as if her very own heart had just come home safe and sound, Tia burst into tears.

"Oh, Robert!" she cried, running into his familiar, comforting embrace as her eyes puddled and overflowed. "Oh, my dear, are you well?" she asked, searching his eyes, stroking his cheek, gingerly probing the angry, swollen laceration just above his temple.

"Yes, *are* you all right, Rob?" Dex asked, descending the steps to seize his friend's shoulder.

"I am," he replied, withdrawing the handkerchief from his right waistcoat pocket just in time to catch a new overflowing of Tia's tears. "But more importantly," he continued, carefully inspecting every sparkle of her worried eyes, "Tia, love . . . are you?"

And there was the heart of the matter, was it not? Tia thought as the implications of the innocent question caused a slight furrow in her brow.

"Yes. I . . . I am unharmed," she answered, averting her gaze to pat at his Waterfall. "But, come, dear," she quickly recovered, beginning to escort him up the stairs. "You will wish to have a glass of brandy, will you not? . . . and the apothecary, of course. Dex, I would be most grateful if you would ask one of my cousin's footmen to go for Mr. Knoles."

"No, stay as you are, Dex," the viscount countered, holding up a staying hand as his gaze sharpened noticeably above his cousin's bustle. "I have no need to be bled. All I have need of is the truth, Tia."

"The truth?" she responded, pausing in her progress.

"Just so. You forget how well I know you, cousin," Robert replied, his gaze beginning to uncomfortably pierce. "You are hiding something."

At that, Tia fidgeted, then drew in a deep breath. "Nothing of the sort. That was the truth, Robert. I did not lie to you. I never have."

"Then tell me what happened when you were with the kidnappers," he softly demanded, stepping aside so that the others might enter the Abbey vestibule before him.

"Nothing, Robert. Truly," she responded above the steady toll of the tower bell. "I was told by my captors that I was to be taken to the Freedom Brigade headquarters in Staithes and used as a hostage to prevent Uncle Brumley from leading the Black Masks in an attempt upon Thomas Paine. It did not happen, however, because the carriage wheel broke near Tockett's Mill."

"I see," he replied, his eyes narrowing. "Was that when you made your escape?"

"No . . . I . . . ," Tia began haltingly.

"It was rather that Lady Horatia was rescued, Rob," Dex broke in evenly.

"Indeed. By whom?"

"By the Enforcer," Dex told him.

One corner of the viscount's mouth twitched. "And . . . ?" he asked, turning toward Tia again.

"And he, in turn, was driven off by me," Dex confirmed. "We have just this moment arrived back at the Abbey from that encounter."

"I let them in," Margaret added quickly between two of the bell's reverberant peals. "There was no one else here to do it, you see."

Slowly, the viscount nodded.

"Yes . . . I am quite confident that I do see," he replied, drawing in a deep, quiet breath before gently tucking a strand of hair behind his cousin's ear.

"Well, I do not!" the countess suddenly cried from the drawing room doorway just off the landing above.

"Mama!" Tia cried, quickly covering the distance between them. "Dearest, are you well?"

"Hardly, Horatia," she answered, loftily pushing aside her daughter's arms to complete her descent of the stairs. "I am undone. I cannot hear myself think with that constant clanging, yet there is no one to command that it end. Where has everyone gone?"

With the proper sobriety, Dex made a pretty leg. "You will have a great deal to discuss, I misdoubt. If you will excuse me, milady," he requested upon rising, "it would be my privilege to seek out the bell tower and do what I can to put a period to the annoyance. In no time you shall feel more the thing."

"Yes, well . . . ," the countess began, her countenance growing a bit more benign, "you have my gratitude, of course, Mr. Clark. But do hurry . . . ," she sighed, placing fingertips aside her temple. "My head is pounding . . ."

"Mama, perhaps you should sit down," Tia stated, taking the countess's arm as Dex bounded off in the direction of the insistent, penetrating ringing. "Margaret, would you bring a glass of sherry from the drawing room?"

"Yes, of course," Margaret whispered in reply, dutifully gliding away.

"Now, Mama," Tia began when, aside from several footmen unloading trunks from the carriage and shouldering them up the stairs, the three were alone, "you must not overset yourself. I am persuaded that there is a reasonable explanation for everything."

"And so am I," Robert concluded, crossing his arms over his chest. "Obviously, cousin, today is the day the Black Masks shall make their attempt for Paine."

Startled, Tia's gaze flew to his. "Yes," she finally replied, staring at her cousin in surprise.

"What can that signify?" the countess asked testily. "The bell has been ringing since mid-afternoon, and everyone has disappeared. That is all that should be of consequence to us. Thank goodness Miss Tutweiler arrived as she has done each day to see if you had returned, Horatia.

We have since done what we could to give comfort to one another."

As the countess finished, Margaret again joined them, extending the restorative she had brought into the circle. "Here you are, milady," she softly breathed.

"Ah, thank you, child," the countess murmured, patting Margaret's hand beneath a weak smile before taking a sip. "Such a comfort in your absence, Horatia. But nothing shall comfort me in this . . . ," she sighed, raising her fingers from the spot they had been rubbing aside her temple to waft them in the direction of the tower.

At the instant of the lady's gesture, suddenly, and mercifully, the tolling stopped. To Tia's way of thinking, even the air around them seemed to rest more lightly upon their heads. Smiling with relief, she drew in a deep breath.

"Ah! There, you see, Mama!" she cried, kneeling before the countess. "Mr. Clark has met with success."

"So it seems. And you will again convey my deepest gratitude, will you not, dearest?" Sophie replied, rising rather unsteadily to her feet.

"Of course," Tia told her.

"Milady, are you not well?" Margaret breathed in concern, taking the countess's arm.

"I fear I have the headache, Miss Tutweiler," the lady replied, giving Margaret a weak smile. "But never worry, my dear," she continued, starting across the vestibule. "I shall seek a bit of laudanum and my bed. Of a certainty, I shall be well again soon. Goodness, it would not be at all the thing if I could not preside over our evening repast!" That said, the countess slowly mounted the stairs, the others watching her progress until even the Greek key design bordering her hem had disappeared.

Moments later, Dex descended with Wardle at his heels.

"Behold for whom the bell was tolling." He grinned, gesturing toward the dusty, web-covered man.

"Wardle?" Tia exclaimed, her eyes widening.

Stepping into the vestibule, the butler brushed at his shoulders and tugged a bit of order into his tails. "If you could just speak up a bit, miss . . . ," he shouted when he at last realized that he had been addressed.

Tia bit back a laugh. "Never mind, dear," she cried quite loudly into his ear, nudging him toward the servants' domain. "Do go take a dish of tea."

"Why, miss, how could you know that he is coming by the sea?" Wardle bellowed with a nod of his head. "It was supposed to be a secret. That is why I was ringing the bell, you see," he continued, turning to walk with slow dignity toward the hall. "I was to do so when I spotted sail."

Instantly, Tia looked between Dex and Robert.

"And the bell has been ringing for several hours! Dear heaven, Dex, we have come too late," Tia breathed.

"Perhaps not," Dex uttered, all trace of levity gone. "You two stay here," he commanded the women.

"Indeed not," Tia replied, tucking a stray strand of hair beneath her sable hat as she started toward the door. "I returned to put a period to this scandal broth and I shall. You cannot deny that if anyone shall be able to dissuade Uncle Brumley from this course, it is I."

"Lady Horatia, a woman cannot—"

"Of course, she can," Tia replied, opening the door and striding briskly toward the Bainbridge carriage.

Dex threw up his hands. "Very well, then, Miss Tutweiler, you shall remain—"

"No, I shan't," Margaret stated with surprising strength, slipping into a warm, wool pelisse. "If Tia is going to whatever is happening, so am I."

"Margaret, it is not seemly . . ."

"No, Dexter."

"No!"

"No," Margaret stated, tying a bonnet beneath her chin. "I have said 'no' correctly, have I not, sir?" she called back to him as she, too, started for the door. "Yes, I am certain that I have said my 'no' just as you taught me only days ago."

Still in the vestibule, Dex glanced toward his friend.

"Is it always like this with women?" he asked, displacing his beaver so that he might scratch at his head.

"Always," Robert answered with a wise nod.

"Well, hell," Dex said, starting for the door. "Come on, then, Rob. I shall tell you what you need to know on the way to town."

Only moments later, the Bainbridge traveling chaise was thundering toward the bluff overlooking Whitby harbor.

Twenty-three

"There! Look there . . . just to the south," Dex cried, pointing toward the sea as he spurted out of the chaise's confines at the top of the Church stairs like ale from a newly broached keg. "A sail!"

"A brig by the look of her . . . ," Robert assessed after his own hurried descent, shading his eyes against the sting of the salt-laden air, "square sails on the foremast . . . fore-and-aft on the mainmast. And she's her royals up," he stated, now pointing toward the ship as well. "She's running before the wind."

"And Uncle Brumley with the tide, so it seems," added Tia, motioning toward the harbor after taking her cousin's hand and stepping down to the narrow carriage track. "La, Robert," she continued, crossing to the first of the one hundred and ninety-nine steps, "either that is the entire contingent of Loyalists standing about on that collier just clearing the swing bridge, or the draper reduced the price of black worsted while we were off about our quest."

"*Your* quest," Robert chuckled, quickly joining her, "and it appears that you have the right of it. Stay here with Miss Tutweiler, Tia. Dex and I shall have to chop it if we are to catch up to the collier before she clears the Upper Harbor."

"Not a bit of it," Tia replied, hooking her fingers on his elbow.

"Tia . . ."

"I am going, too, cousin."

"Tia, deuce take it . . ."

"He *is* my uncle, Robert," she insisted, slipping around him to begin her headlong race down toward the water.

"Tia, damnation!" Robert cried, throwing up his hands as he hurried to follow after.

Beside the carriage, Dex's brow arched. "Pity," he lamented, turning to stare at the cousins after clasping Margaret about the waist and lifting her to the ground. "Some females simply cannot be controlled, can they? I am persuaded that you, however, have the good sense to stay with the carriage."

"No."

"What?" Dex queried, neatly stacking the bones of his spine.

"No," Margaret repeated, brushing past him to bound after her friend.

"Lud, why did I ever teach her that word?" Dex muttered, quickly catching up to her and, for safety's sake, of course, commandeering her forearm.

Tia was the first to reach Church Street at the foot of the stairs.

"Oh, cousin, look!" she exclaimed, running out onto the quay. "We shall never make it in time! The collier has almost cleared the last of the pilings."

Coming up beside her, the viscount quickly cast his gaze about. "Then we'd best hurry, hadn't we? I suggest we borrow that coble down there," he said, pressing her onto a nearby ladder. "Our Whitby fishing boats are maneuverable and fast, cousin. In this wind, no doubt we shall soon overtake her."

"I cannot see how," Tia complained, throwing her hem

over her arm as she gingerly stepped into the dipping bow
and pulled herself onto the nearest of the plank seats.
"Look at the collier now, Robert. It has already passed into
the open sea!"

"I am aware of that, cousin," he responded, helping Margaret, too, to descend into the small boat upon her breath-
less arrival. "But colliers are coal transports, if you
recall . . . built stubby of hull, flat-bottomed, and bluff-
bowed. In other words, they are cumbersome and slow.
This sleek little coble, however, can cut through the waves
like a spoon through trifle. Dex, climb aboard and cast off
the line, will you?"

"Right," his friend replied, bounding out onto the quay
to lithely unhook fore and aft mooring lines from their companion stanchions, then hurriedly boarding.

The viscount waited a few moments for Dex to settle
while the coble drifted out into the sluggish current circling
the harbor, then, with practiced movements, loosened the
reef-points securing the sail. Next, with a few tugs on the
halyard, he sent the sturdy linen canvas climbing to the top
of the mast. It took only a quick swing of the coble's small
boom wide to port just after that and the heavy sail suddenly
snapped, cupped its width, and gorged itself with the cold,
blustering wind. In response, the little boat shot forward,
cutting a path with its narrow bow straight toward the
mouth of the harbor, and from there, out toward the open
water.

"We shall never make it!" Tia cried out as her orange
Melton traveling cape dampened with bow-tossed spray
and the harbor's outer pilings swiftly passed by.

"We shall," Robert called ahead to her, his voice all but
lost in the slap of waves against the coble's skimming hull

and the steady creak of the taut, straining lines. "Trust me, Tia. Everything shall be all right."

In spite of herself, and as she had always done ever since they were children, even to her own unraveling at Blackamore Grange, Tia did. Without hesitation. And with it came peace. Taking a deep breath, she settled herself more comfortably upon the coble's rough plank.

"Ah, the sea!" the Leader sighed from the deck of the collier, *Lady Beatrice,* when the harbor had been left well behind them, his black-clad nose facing into the wind. "Is there anything like it, my friends? And look at the French brigantine run, Captain Romney," he called back in the direction of the leader of his hired crew. "Beautiful! Why, at this rate, I am persuaded we shall have Paine inside half an hour!"

"Aye, sir, if not before," the taciturn man replied from aside the wheel on the quarter deck, his odd, one-eyed squint assessing the display of fast approaching sails.

"A happy thought!" the earl exclaimed, gripping the gunwales with a pair of fifteenth century studded gauntlets.

"Aye." The captain readily nodded again.

Just then, unremarked by any of the gathered Black Masks, the first mate turned from his intent perusal of the receding harbor mouth and silently nodded toward the captain. Immediately after, he descended the short rise of steps onto the main deck and gestured toward several nearby hands. In response, they in turn unobtrusively slipped up the shrouds and quietly shortened sail. Afterward, imperceptibly but steadily, the collier slowed.

"And a commendable pace, of a certainty," commented Raptor, his strained, quavering voice sounding like pebbles rolling about in a pewter tin, both wizened hands clinging for dear life to the several lines fastened about the foremast. "However, once we reach the brigantine, has anyone given any thought as to how we are to prevent her from merely passing us by?"

At the question, a good deal of the preparations taking place on the deck faded into a restless, and rather clanking, murmur.

It was Wolf who came up with the first suggestion. "Why do we not simply command our Captain Romney to pull to a stop in their path?" he offered, returning again to his tying of the perfect emerald silk Oriental over the burnished fourteenth century breastplate he had borrowed from Bainbridge Castle's former armory.

"No, no, that will never do," the Leader replied, trying vainly to shake his head and scratch the side of his neck while affixing the haute piece of his own borrowed breastplate above his shoulder. "There is drift to be considered, don't you know . . . momentum . . . things like that. But you do have a point, Raptor," he continued, again casting his gaze toward the oncoming brig. "How *are* we to stop the ship? She'll have fourteen guns, don't you know."

Suddenly Lion appeared in the low doorway leading below deck to first sag against the door's frame, then, pushing off again, to trundle unsteadily into their midst.

"We sh'll belay the aft tops'l," he cried out, shoving a fifteenth century basinet helm back upon his broad forehead while hoisting a brightly polished silver cup high into the brisk, biting wind.

"Good God, Harry, have a care!" Fox scolded in vexation when the other caught a toe on a ventilation grate and careened into his mail shirt. Spinning about, he scowled, then resettled his black *chapeau-bras* over a well-oiled mail coif. "And what on earth are you braying about?"

"Belaying the aft tops'l, of course," Lion informed him, making a wide, tottering arc around the capstan, ". . . or hois' the sprits'l, p'rhaps . . . ," he continued, demonstrating with his cup and, as a result, sloshing a pungent liquid upon the deck. "Either one'd do, I suppose."

"Sweet sugar sticks!" Wolf remarked, three fingers drifting up to cover his mouth hole. "I do believe our Harry is boskey."

"And jib the mizsenm'st," his lordship added with an appraising stare up into the rigging after another moment's thought, afterward taking a hefty swig.

"Oh, dear," the Leader sighed, his mouth hole narrowing into a flaccid line of bewilderment.

"Harry, you nodcock, you are four sheets to the wind!" Fox exclaimed, clenching both teeth and fists.

"And with battle imminent!" the Leader gasped in dismay. "Gracious, what could you have been thinking, Lion?"

"You realize that you are fit for Bedlam, do you not, sir?" Fox ground out, and then he threw up his hands. "No, I have changed my mind. Heaven help me, I believe that I am. Confound it, Fullerton, you shall ruin everything . . . again! What the deuce are you drinking?"

"Pusser's rum," his lordship informed them, looking down the considerable extent of his nose, and, overbalanced, weaving over to collapse against one of Raptor's tightly knotted fists. "Exactly as is allotted to all His Majesty's seamen. Brought a cask of it on when I boarded, don't y' know. After all, what's good for the goose is good for the gander," he justified, poking Fox in the mail shirt while drawing in another sip. "No reason to my way of thinking why our ship sh'dn't have the same as Horatio Nelson's."

"Perhaps because navy seamen are only allowed two ounces! . . . ," Raptor complained, releasing his grip on the lines just long enough to push his fellow Loyalist farther on around the mast, "not the bumper you seem to have imbibed!"

"Pusser's, eh?" Wolf said to himself, thoughtfully tapping his chin. "I've heard of it. Believe I shall have some of that," he decided, wandering toward the door leading to the crew's quarters below deck.

"Wolf . . . gentlemen, please," the Leader pleaded, at last motioning in frustration to one of his patiently awaiting footmen to complete the attachment of the hammered steel shoulder piece to his ancient breastplate. "Paine's ship shall be upon us in moments. Only look," he ordered, gesturing toward the fast-closing distance. "Her captain is coming on deck to determine our intentions even as I speak. We must attend to the task at hand. What are we to do, my fellow Loyalists? How are we to stop the brig?"

It was at that exact moment that the coble bumped the collier just to starboard. It was also at that exact moment that the solution for how to stop the brig was born within Lion's rum-induced fog.

"We sh'll sire a fot across her brow!" he shouted, his features hardening with determination as he unsteadily began to stagger toward the collier's thrusting bowsprit, all the while digging down into his clothing, fumbling about, and finally drawing a dueling pistol out from under his shirt of heavy mail.

"Whatever!" cried the Leader, torn between the disaster rapidly developing above decks and the curiosity taking place below.

"Fullerton, what the deuce are you about?" Fox asked in horror as the ponderous man's tottering passage easily brushed him aside.

"I sh'll stop her, of course," Lion told him. "It is the standard method, don't y' know. When she is almost upon us, I sh'll fire a sot over her bow."

"What?" the Leader reprised with even more alarm, hurrying after, altogether appalled.

"Lud," remarked Fox, clapping a hand over his eyes.

"Ahoy, the *Lady Beatrice!*" Robert suddenly called out from the coble.

Caught in indecision, the Leader's body twisted back and forth. Whatever was he to do next? . . . discover who in the world had come calling at such a benighted time, or attempt to wrestle down a friend intent upon using a dueling pistol to stop a fully rigged French brig?

The others of the Black Masks were troubled with no such vacillation. By the time the viscount called again, to a man they had gathered at the gunwales.

"Throw down a ladder!" the viscount again shouted up to the collection of very familiar appearing armor now peering down at his small party from the collier deck.

"I say, Brumley, isn't that your cousin at the rudder?" Wolf called back over his shoulder as the Loyalists watched the small fishing vessel toss up fore and aft lines to several of the hired seamen.

Astonishment stole away the Leader's torment.

"Robert?" he exclaimed, hurrying to join the others, then peering, too, over the gunwales. "Why, it is! But whatever is he doing here when he is supposed to be . . . ?" Suddenly, his eyes rounded. "And where is Horatia?" he cried down to the coble in alarm.

"That's her, ain't it?" Lion suddenly, and quite star-

tlingly, pointed out just after the several folds of his chin
draped over the Leader's haute piece. "See there, Brumley?
She's b'side the other chit jus' behind the sail," he told him,
gesturing with a slosh of his Pusser's, then casually throwing back the last of it and sagging against the gunwales.

"Harry! Thank God," the Leader cried, seizing his
friend's shoulders. "Horatia, come up here this instant!
Now, Lion, I must insist that you remain with the rest of
us and not try to stop Paine's ship single-handed."

"Nons'nce," Lion replied, brushing away the Leader's
restraint. "It's the standard method, don't y' know. Ahoy,
Horatia, m'dear!" he then shouted down in the coble's direction, wiggling a thick set of fingers before lurching to
his feet.

In moments he was once again lunging toward the bowsprit.

"Harry, wait! Stop!"

"Not a bit of it," Lion responded over his shoulder as
the four from the coble began to make their way up the
collier's rope ladder. "The brig's upon us, Brumley. I must
be about m' king's business."

"Harry!"

"Uncle . . . !" Tia then called in the best tones of a governess, her head just peeking above the gunwales.

"Lud," the Leader sighed, stopping short in his tracks
to wipe a hand across his eyes. "Unmanned and unmasked."

"Uncle, stay right where you are," Tia scolded, throwing
one olive-stockinged leg over the gunwales. "I am well
aware of what you are planning and, rest assured, I have a
great deal to say to you about it."

"Horatia, my dear," the Leader soothed, at once turning
in her direction and at the same time twisting back toward

Lion's retreating shuffle again. "Lion, stop! Lud, this whole bumblebroth has gotten to be the outside of enough! What the deuce am I to do now?"

The four from the coble only just managed to make it aboard the *Lady Beatrice* before the brigantine captain's tricorn leaped into the sea, riding upon Lion's pistol ball.

It must be said, of course, and to his credit, that Lion's plan did stop the French brigantine. Within moments of the tricorn's disappearance over the side, seamen were scuttling like manic crabs up the weblike shrouds, their deft hands quickly reefing the brig's royals, brig sail, and studding sails to effectively arrest the ship's progress. Only the twentieth part of a moment later, the order was heard shouted all the way to the deck of the collier to bring the brig alongside the impudent, worm-eaten coal barge and to open all gunports.

Bad enough, Tia thought, becoming quite incensed at the brig's threatening maneuvering, but even worse and most rag-manneredly, she decided as even her earlobes scorched, the whole was spoken in a most improper idiom. It really was too much.

Aside her, his arm supporting her against the deck's unsteady roll, Robert was paying the brig little attention. Instead, he nodded toward the collier captain. Within seconds the coal transport began to rapidly close the distance between itself and the brig. Another surreptitious nod sent nearly half the hired crew scattering in a dozen directions . . . marbles struck by a commanding agate.

"Bouncing baubles, they shall blow us from the water!" Wolf cried, snapping shut a scarlet-plumed helm.

"Oh, this is the outside of enough!" Tia began, dragging

her gaze away from the brig's preparations for war and taking hold of the edge of Walmsley's haute piece. "Uncle, you must listen—"

"Yes, I suppose I should," her uncle quickly interrupted, drawing her into his arms and smoothing back her damp, collapsed *à la grêque*. "Or at least sought good advice . . . or, God save me, heeded the Enforcer. But, lud, dearest, it is far too late for that, don't you see?"

"But, Uncle . . ."

"No, now Horatia, dearest, I fear that I simply cannot stop to chat now. I should like to, of course," he said, gingerly cupping her cheek with one gauntleted hand. "There is much you must be wondering . . . much to explain. But I must get to my men, you see," he told her emphatically, afterward putting her hands away from him. "Take care of her, cousin," he admonished the viscount.

"Always," Robert said.

Nodding, the earl then turned toward Dex and Margaret.

"Well, Mr. Clark, I am persuaded that you must know the whole of it by now," he said, his eyes heavy within their lids.

"I do, milord," Dex responded with a firm nod, his gaze steady upon the earl's tired face.

Again Walmsley nodded his acceptance. "I would have you also know that it was never our intention to cause the destruction . . ."

"I am aware of that, milord."

"You are?" Walmsley questioned, his weary voice taking on an edge of hope. "Well, imagine that. Of course, that is neither here nor there, is it? The damage, however unintentional, was done. I am burdened by my part in it."

"Then why not consider, milord, taking ease in your solution?" Dex suggested with a knowing grin.

The earl's eyes widened within their eyeholes. "Sir, I beg your pardon! Think you that *I* provided your father with that addition to his bank account?" he harrumphed, what flesh was exposed abrading. "Why, no indeed, sir!" he exclaimed. "Not a bit of it."

At his response, Dex's eyes gleamed above a warm smile. "In that case, then, it is I who must ask your forgiveness, milord," he murmured with the utmost humility. "Obviously, I have drawn incorrect conclusions."

"Well, let that be a lesson to you, my boy," the earl gruffly replied, scratching beneath his chin.

Suddenly a shout rang out from the forecastle. "Forward into the fray!" Lion cried, emerging from the crush of Loyalists to wobble forward, all the while pumping his spent pistol in the brig's direction.

"Lud," the earl sighed, drawing forth a whip-thin rapier. "Well, my dears, the time seems to have arrived."

"Oh, Uncle, no!" Tia cried as the ships drew abreast of one another, each crew's offering of epithets rising steadily to at last crescendo into a roar.

"Tia, brace yourself," Robert warned, planting his feet and drawing her tightly against him as several of the hired crew swung grappling hooks away from the collier to clutch viciously at several spots along the brig's gunwales.

No sooner had that been done than the two ships shuddered into contact.

"Oh, Uncle, put an end to this!" Tia pleaded as she regained her footing, her lids leaking tears over the breast of her cousin's caped drab coat.

"I would, of course," the earl amiably replied, "but . . . you see, it seemed the perfect plan at the time, my dear. Truly it did. But who could foresee . . . And now . . . well, Fullerton is damnably full of Pusser's, and . . . 'pon rep,

Robert, I fear the whole thing has gotten quite out of hand . . ."

"Yes, it has, hasn't it?" Robert smiled.

Tia's gaze bored into the viscount's, appalled. "How can you be so cavalier about this, cousin?" she cried, pushing away. "There is going to be bloodshed in but a few moments! Oh, Uncle Brumley, can you not call everyone back?"

"Can't, my dears," the earl told them, turning away with an apologetic smile. And then he straightened to his full height. "I am the Leader of these Loyalists, you see," he admitted, his shoulders seeming to square visibly. "Responsible for them. I must be with them to take what comes no matter that we have once again made mice feet of our foray."

"Oh, dear Uncle Brumley . . . ," Tia breathed, once again subsiding into the sanctuary of Robert's several capes.

"Now, Horatia, my dear, save your tears," Walmsley chided gently, giving her forehead a brisk kiss. "And yourselves as well if you would do a kindness for me here at the last. Go back to the coble, all of you," he ordered, shaking his cousin's hand. "At any moment the French shall open fire with those four-pounders, and this collier shall be blown to bits. I shall leave this life content that I have served my king if I can but know that my loved ones are not at risk. Go now."

Having stated his final wishes, after a brief bow toward Dex and Margaret, the earl turned again and entered the milling mass. Moments later he emerged at the head of the clustered Loyalists, happily just in time to help a gabbling Fox restrain Lion from climbing out onto the collier's slim bowsprit.

"We must do something to stop this!" Tia whispered, her eyes wide with tears as she watched the Loyalists draw forth their weapons. "He shall get himself killed!"

"You wound me, cousin," the viscount replied, looking down at her along his narrow nose. "Do you really think I would allow that to happen?"

"You are one man, Robert," Tia replied. "I fail to see how you can prevent it."

"Steps have already been taken," the viscount responded.

"Against fourteen guns?"

"They shall not fire on the collier, love," Robert soothed, unsheathing a knife from his boot.

"What shall prevent that?" Tia demanded to know.

Aside her, Robert sighed. "What prevents it is the collier's being so close aside the brig," he responded. "The French cannot fire their guns without danger to their own ship, you see. We are safe until they cut the grappling lines . . . and, before you say it, cousin, no, they shan't do that either."

"Why?"

"Because the lines are being guarded . . . see?"

Beneath his arm, Tia's head tipped slightly in the direction the viscount's finger was waggling. Near each grappling hook stood a well-armed seaman. Instantly her attention returned.

"And you have known this the entire time?" she asked with an edge of pique to her voice.

"I told you to trust me, Tia, and I meant it. Now, stay here with Miss Tutweiler," the viscount commanded, firmly putting her away from him. "And that is an order, cousin, not a suggestion. Are you coming, Dex?"

"I, you say . . . ?" he questioned with a grin, both brows

shooting up, "come with you, a peer? . . . and to fight for Loyalists?"

Turning back, Robert smiled. "No . . . to fight for friends."

Dex shrugged. "Ah, well, I didn't have anything better to do today anyway," he replied. Taking off his cloak, loosening his cravat, he then followed the viscount into the crush of men.

"Oh, Tia, shall they be all right?" Margaret asked, touching the corner of her handkerchief to her delicate upper lip.

"Yes, certainly they shall," Tia told her around a constricted breath, feeling what remained of her Grecian style slide damply down to her sable collar. "If they have anything else in mind, I simply shan't allow it."

Only the twentieth part of a moment later, the Black Masks surged forward like a pack on the scent across the ships' joined bulwarks, crashing into the French with a great clatter of breastplates, swords, and dislodged basinets. In response, the two women fell upon one another's necks.

Tia bit at her lower lip. It was really not at all the thing, she decided, spinning away from the cacophony, the flash of metal, and the cries. No matter what Robert's assurances, someone was bound to be killed. And then her eyes grew round. It might be him! she suddenly realized, her heart thumping up into her throat. No! she cried out in her thoughts, whirling back toward the sounds of battle, reaching out to squeeze Margaret even tighter than before. Cousin, if you dare, I shall . . . !

And then she straightened. No, I shall not. It would serve him right, the varlet! she vowed. How dare he make her realize how very important he was to her, how very much

she cared for him and had always done, and then not be
there to keep her from falling in love with someone else?
It was the outside of enough! How was she to know what
to do about it all? she wondered, brushing away a new
freshet of tears. What if she were never able to talk to him
about how she felt?

He wouldn't dare! . . . she reiterated, taking Margaret's
cold hand and settling her against the side of the collier's
longboat.

. . . Still, I wish he were here beside me again, she conceded, sniffing loudly . . . .

. . . And I wish he had left behind the handkerchief from
his right waistcoat pocket . . .

And then her lips thinned with chagrin.

Fiddle, she thought, sagging, too, against the longboat's
length. What she really wished for at that particular moment was a tot of that Pusser's Lord Harry had been sloshing out of his silver cup all over the collier's deck.

Twenty-four

It was not long into the conflict when it became apparent to Tia that something quite extraordinarily odd was going on.

"Margaret, have you noticed it?" she asked when, to her, it was becoming blatantly apparent, her voice a most unladylike shout over the battle's din.

"Noticed what?" came the other's reply, the sound muffled by two tightly pressed gloves.

Tia gestured in the brig's direction. "The fact that for all this battle's ferocity, not one drop of blood is being shed."

"Oh, truly, Tia?" Margaret hopefully inquired, releasing some of the pressure against her full pink lips.

"Only look, Margaret," Tia coaxed. "See? Not one that I can see bears even a scratch." Suddenly, a remembrance sprang into her thoughts. "Just as Robert promised," she added, the afterthought stirring pensive wrinkles across her brow. "Of course, he always keeps his promises," she murmured, scowling toward the struggle again.

The fight lengthened. Tia held her gaze steadily upon it, concentrating on the play of weapon against weapon, helping one man with the twist of one slight shoulder, another with the thrust of one small hand. And as she watched, an even stranger occurrence began to separate itself from the progress of events. Slowly, it became apparent that the crew of the collier were fighting not only for the Loyalists, but also for the French!

Uncertain of her conclusion, Tia blinked. Then, narrowing her gaze, intensifying her scrutiny, she looked again, certain that if she but singled out one of the collier crewmen to follow for a time, she would put a fair test to her observation. Quickly she selected a likely man. As she watched, he first parried a French rapier thrust that would have pierced Lord Digby's shoulder, then just as deftly engaged the spade of her uncle's gardener, easily overcoming the elderly retainer's impassioned scoops to tangle him within several handy loops of coiled hemp.

Her brow furrowing, she shifted her regard to another man. Under her watchful gaze, with the greatest of agility, he leaped over the swipe of a Frenchman's broad, curved cutlass, then, after it had buried itself deep into one of the mainsail blocks, pirouetted about to deflect the sweep of Lord Fullerton's cup away from the skull of the brigantine's bosun. It was true, then. Again and again the pattern replayed; again and again what could have brought calamity was turned into nothing more harmful than a cup of tea with one of Henri's scones.

The conclusion Tia was forced to draw was inescapable. For reasons only the crew appeared to know, they were serving to keep the two other factions from doing real harm to one another. But why? Who were they, and how had they come to be involved?

Her brow now creasing in a manner that was most unfashionable, she quickly began to scan the brig's deck for signs of the viscount, hoping to catch his eye and convey to him one of the silent signals they had developed over their years together that she very much needed to speak with him. She spotted Dex quite easily, standing his ground upon the quarterdeck with his sword cane against the deft rapier of the tall French captain, whipping his weapon into a blur as the two dueled about the brig sail boom, first clashing on the port side, then ducking beneath to fall into a defensive stance on the starboard. Nearby, her uncle led a shuffling dance about the ship's wheel with a common seaman, appearing to hold his own against his opponent as, at differing times, one or the other of them would tire, then rejuvenate, only to again yield the upper hand. She soon determined, however, that she would have to look elsewhere for her cousin.

She searched again, scanning the deck all the way to the forecastle. Lord Digby was there, dueling against his entanglement in the foresail shrouds, dodging the repetitive passage of dear, ancient Lord Walpole who clung to the foremast, circling it round and round in his escape of a French musket bayonet's dogged prod. On the main deck, Lord Fullerton now lay draped over and quite soundly asleep between several spokes of the brig's main jeer-capstan, while beside him Lord Etheridge waged war with an emerald silk neckcloth which had snagged most rag-manneredly upon the visor of his scarlet-plumed basinet. Robert, however, was becoming more and more conspicuous by his absence.

Uncertainty grew into an obstacle within Tia's throat she simply could not dislodge.

Suddenly Margaret seized her arm. "Heaven forfend!" she gasped just above a whisper. "Oh, Tia, look!" she breathed, pointing back in the direction of the brig's quarterdeck.

Tia did . . . and every drop of blood in her veins drained into her toes.

Her dear Uncle Brumley had been driven to one knee.

"Uncle!" Tia gasped, her body frozen, her gaze riveted to the earl's dear portly frame, to the dance of blade against blade, all thoughts of the whereabouts of her cousin forgotten as the Frenchman slowly began to eat away at the last of her uncle's strength.

Frantically her eyes began to sweep the area, looking for someone from the hired crew who was aware of the earl's deteriorating situation, who would step forward and deflect the sudden flurry of the seaman's rapier point, yet no one seemed to notice . . . no one! Only Dex, still focused upon his struggle with the captain, was near enough to come to her uncle's rescue. Yet, in his concentration, he was yet in ignorance.

Dear God! Tia thought, her hands fisting before her mouth. "Dex!" she cried, desperate to be heard above the battle sounds. "Dex! Oh, please, turn around! Please!"

Yet even as she cried out, a powerful stroke of the seaman's rapier swept the Earl of Walmsley's sword from his quavering hand. The twentieth part of a moment later, the Frenchman brought the point of his blade to the hollow just at the base of Brumley's neck.

"Uncle . . . oh, no!" Tia gasped, her eyes huge in their fierce concentration, her fingers rising to rest upon that very same spot.

And then a shadow fell over the desperate scene.

And he was there . . . the Enforcer! . . . standing like an avenging demon upon the quarterdeck. Slowly, his fists rose to rest upon his hips, revealing a shiny coil of his leather whip beneath the black silk cape flowing about his mirrored Hessians. His face was grim beneath his half mask; his eyes glittered with the frolic of reflected sunlight rising from the uneasy sea.

"Hold, Frenchman," he commanded, his words snapping like sail in a changing wind.

Tia's heart careened off every bone in her rib cage. Beside her, Margaret screamed.

Instantly Dex responded to the sound, whirling about.

"You!" he cried, immediately spotting the Enforcer, a strength born of outrage quickly dispatching the captain over the stern gunwales. "I told you what I would do if I ever saw you again," he growled, beginning to stalk forward, his weapon menacingly upraised.

"Yes . . . you vowed to finish what lies between us, I believe," the Enforcer responded with a slight smile. "Yet I admit that I have little time for it," he continued, divesting his broad shoulders of his silken cape. "You will forgive me, I hope, for once again thwarting you." And in one fluid movement, the Enforcer seized his whip, sent it snaking about the wrist of the seaman threatening her uncle, then snapped the handle around to lay a stunning blow just to the side of Dex's head. At the very moment that Dex dropped to his knees, the Frenchman's sword flew upward out of his hand to disappear overboard beneath a swelling wave.

Directly after, however, the point of the French captain's rapier imbedded itself just beneath the skin of the Enforcer's cheek. At his sudden stilling, every other conflict taking place on the brigantine's deck simply ceased.

Nearby, Dex slowly shook his senses back into place, retrieved his sword, then struggled once again to his feet. Catching his first glimpse of his former opponent, he narrowed his gaze and gaped.

"How . . . ?" he voiced aloud as he stared at the resurrected captain, rubbing at the swollen knob at the side of his head.

"How?" the captain repeated with a slight chuckle. *"C'est simple, monsieur.* You pushed me over the stern," he informed him. *"C'est stupide, n'est-ce pas?* I fell upon the *galerie* just outside my own quarters."

Drawing in a deep breath, Dex smiled and shook his head. "And with that intelligence, have managed to reveal to all how little I know about ships. Accept my apology, captain," he said, making an admiring leg. "My thanks, too, for capturing this bounder known hereabouts as the Enforcer. I shall take over from here."

Disturbingly, the captain's blade retreated not even a whit, "Ah, so this is the one?" he replied, his eyes now focused on the Enforcer, their dark cores sparkling with interest.

"The same," Dex told him, raising the point of his sword blade to rest firmly against the Enforcer's silk-clad chest. "You may withdraw now, sir. I have him."

Again the captain laughed low and without mirth. "But I, *monsieur,* have you both," he replied, stroking one side of his long, well-coiffed moustache. "It is a great *coup,* is it not? . . . one captive who shall be an example to all of what happens when one attacks a French ship, and the other the most feared of all the monarchists? The Convention shall enjoy your trials, I think.

"Mes enfants!" he suddenly called to his complement of seamen. "Gather the weapons. You three by the jeer-capstan! . . . find pistols and take these gentlemen below."

Instantly, the Enforcer caught Dex's gaze. "Now would be a good time for you to make your move," he suggested in low undertones, staring hard at him from within his half mask.

"Why, of course," Dex sneered equally softly, warily sliding his gaze away to assess the three Frenchmen starting for the quarterdeck stairs. "Why would I even hesitate to pit my one blade against an entire crew of Frenchmen?"

"You wouldn't," the Enforcer calmly breathed.

"Indeed!" Dex chuckled softly and with not a whit of mirth. "And why not, sir?"

"Because you are valiant."

"What?"

"And loyal."

"Oh, I say! . . ." Dex sputtered with growing affront.

"You took your sweet time about it, of course," the Enforcer finished with a sudden grin that sent Dex's jaw dropping to the tops of his feet, "but you did finally tear yourself away from Sunderland . . . and, by God, you *did* damn well show up wherever the hell we were."

Once Dex's jaw had snapped shut, his fist lashed out. Only the tic of an eye later, not much remained undamaged of the captain's arrogantly groomed moustache. Sagging into unconsciousness, the Frenchman's sword clattered to the deck.

Immediately, the Enforcer turned toward the gathering. "Disarm them," he commanded, his voice like a sea-swept Wave.

In moments, the crew of the collier had restrained the three oncoming Frenchmen, and the assortment of knives, pistols and swords had been secured.

The show of obedience sent Tia's brows aloft. So the men her uncle had hired as crew were the Enforcer's! she understood at last . . . and present, as she, herself, had proved, not to take sides in the conflict, but solely to prevent the two factions from coming to harm! Had that always been the case? she wondered . . . since the formation of the Loyalist group? Yet if that were so, how could the Enforcer be the evil man of his reputation?

The answer was simple, she realized. He could not.

And, knowing this, clasping her arms about her waist, Tia smiled.

Until another question occurred. If the hired crew of the collier were the Enforcer's, how had Robert seemed to know what they were about? And where, under heaven, was he, anyway? . . . the varlet!

Suddenly, a murmuring rose up from the deck of the brigantine, cutting Tia's speculation short. Curious, she once again scanned the mass of gathered men, quickly to be drawn toward a slight stirring that had begun near the door leading toward the captain's cabin beneath the quarterdeck. As she watched, a young lad opened the door wide, then reached back within the shadowed opening to support the feeble, shuffled entrance of a stooped, white-haired man.

"Oh, Margaret," Tia breathed, "that can be none other than Thomas Paine!"

"Indeed!" her friend responded. "How very intriguing! He is quite old, is he not? . . . for one so notorious?"

"Which I am persuaded only teaches us that it takes long years to build such a standing," Tia smiled. "But, hush now, dearest. Let us see if we can detect what Mr. Paine is saying."

Leaning across the gunwales, the two intently sharpened their hearing.

". . . And you are he who planned this kidnapping?" the elderly American asked of the powerful black-clad man who had seen him settled upon the aft ladder casing and then knelt to a more accommodating vantage before him.

"Unhappily, no," the Enforcer smiled. "I fear that a plot of that magnitude could only be conceived by that man," he stated, gesturing back toward the Leader's sudden start.

With all eyes now upon him, the earl began to harrumph. "Oh, but . . . ! Well, you see . . . ," he began, stumbling forward from the gathered Masks' midst, "truly, sir, and this I do hope you might find it in your heart to believe, we . . . that is, the Black Masks and I . . . would never have allowed you to come to harm. Why, we pride ourselves on the fact that we have never shed anyone's blood, do we not, gentlemen?" he asked, turning slightly around as his fingers began to intertwine.

The response was instantaneous and gratifying. Murmurs of "We do, indeed! Here, here!" and "Not a drop has hit the ground!" quickly justified the Leader's claim.

Slowly, Mr. Paine's lips stretched, the slight smile that formed drawing the upper of them into contact with his nose's unusually long, teardrop-shaped tip.

"Then I suppose I must offer you my grudging admiration," he finally said, offering the earl his skeletal hand. "I am not a man who is easily thwarted from my intentions as you must be aware, yet I am persuaded that in this instance, at last I must allow that I have been confounded."

Above him, Walmsley's chest rounded. "Why, yes . . . ," he responded on a rather startled grin, "so you must, sir." And then he loudly harrumphed again. "But it is for the best, don't you know. Can't have you gadding about the country stirring up rebellion."

Nodding, the American sighed. "Yet I did wish to see my bridge one last time," he whispered, catching the Enforcer's gaze with hopeful, rheumy eyes.

The Enforcer smiled gently, but finally shook his head. "It is too dangerous for you here now, I fear. Perhaps later . . . in a few years . . ."

Mr. Paine waved aside the suggestion's completion. "I

do not have them, sir. Once I leave these waters, I shall never cross the ocean again."

"Then I am truly sorry," the Enforcer replied.

"As am I," Mr. Paine responded, taking the lad's hand to stagger once again to his feet.

Immediately, the Enforcer rose to lend his own support.

"Well, Sir Leader," the American stated, straightening to as much as he could of his full height, "I am at your mercy. Where is this 'ghaut' in which you will imprison me? Shall it be for a long time, do you think? And before I am completely cut away from the world, shall you at least grant me the company of those two lovely ladies?"

Walmsley's answer was to thrust out his lower lip in thought and to scratch at a particularly annoying itch directly above his ear.

"Well, sir?" Mr. Paine finally urged.

"Brumley . . . ?" Fox questioned, stepping to his side.

"Yes, what shall you do?" Falcon queried.

The question restored the earl's presence of mind. "Well, I certainly shall not introduce a convicted traitor to the ladies, that I can tell you," he suddenly vowed with a firm nod. "One of them is my niece, don't you know."

"A most pretentious suggestion," Fox chided, stepping forward.

"The outside of enough!" Raptor agreed.

"And a quite reasonable precaution on your part, Brumley, to my way of thinking," Wolf responded, positioning himself firmly at Walmsley's other side.

The earl, as befit his rank of Leader duly elected and sworn into office with proper secret ceremony, accepted their support as his due and, of course, with great dignity.

"And it is my further consideration," he continued, "that a man of such scurrilous character should not even set foot upon the soil of our beloved England, even if those feet are bound. Why, what would we want with such trouble?" he asked, throwing up his hands.

"What, indeed!" arose from all around.

"There are impressionable children to be influenced, after all . . . ," he argued.

"A-and whole families of feeble minds," Falcon timidly asserted, hiding afterward behind Wolf's towering scarlet-plumed helm.

"Er, yes . . . whole families of them," Walmsley agreed, afterward rubbing at his eye.

Mr. Paine's responding chuckle was as dry as winter leaves. "A most unhappy circumstance, to be sure," he finally, and most soberly, concurred.

"And not to be toyed with lightly," the Leader replied. "No, I see it all quite clearly now, my friends. Our plan was a disaster in the making. It is my opinion, gentlemen, that grievous harm would befall our beloved England should we proceed. We cannot allow that to happen. Black Masks, we must with all haste send Mr. Paine on his way."

A bevy of smiles stretched every black mouth hole belonging to the Society.

"A most sensible plan, Brumley! . . ." Fox exuberantly agreed.

". . . Well reasoned . . . ," Raptor analyzed in his warbling voice.

". . . And brilliantly said," Wolf sighed, wafting a fluttering of emerald green lace.

"Well, then, gentlemen," the Leader concluded, "I suggest that we each go our separate ways. You have my apologies for the inconvenience, sir," he said, offering a slight bow to Mr. Paine.

Slowly, and with a great creaking of joints, the gesture was returned. "And you, milord, have my thanks."

Suddenly, a shuffling sounded to the rear of the gathering.

"Ahoy, there!" Lion groggily asked, rolling his heavy mass away from the capstan cap to sag against a stay. "Have we boarded her yet?"

"We did, my friend," the Leader replied, his mouth hole spread wide.

"Well, who won?"

"Everyone."

Hanging from the line, Lion's brows knit with consternation.

"Lud," Fox responded, throwing up his hands.

As the lad and the Enforcer escorted Mr. Paine back below deck, on the collier, Tia wrung yet another volley of tears from the hem of her orange Melton traveling cape.

Twenty-five

"Dearest, do stop fidgeting," the countess requested in the Abbey drawing room the following day, all the while attending to the selection of the proper shade of silk thread to be added to the rose taking shape within her tambour frame. "Robert shall finish his *amende honorable* in Brumley's study soon enough."

At her remark, Tia's gaze slid toward the countess to pause briefly before it dropped.

"I know, Mama," she then quietly responded from her station by one of the room's tall, lancet windows, a bright wedge of winter sunshine bathing her blue sarcenet.

"La, Horatia, I cannot understand it," her mother continued, tugging her selection free from the neat twist in which it was bound. "How could you let yourself fall into such debasement? . . . after all that had been decided? Do you see now why I objected to your taking off on that wretched trip?"

"Yes, Mama," Tia responded, watching yet another cormorant soar up from beyond the distant cliffs.

"I knew it was a mistake to let you go off on a foolish search for the sender of that horrid valentine! Do you see what your hoydenish behavior has gotten you? A husband, Horatia! Of all things, a husband!"

"Hardly a sentence of death, cousin," Robert suddenly

interjected from the doorway, splendidly attired in buff inexpressibles, polished Blüchers, and a dark navy cutaway.

At his appearance, Tia whirled around. "Robert," she breathed.

"Hello, Tia," her cousin replied with a soft smile. "Cousin Sophie," he then added with an elegantly executed leg.

"Do come in, Robert," the countess replied, returning once again to her tambour frame.

Stepping forward into the cool shadows, Tia's heart began to race.

"I was not certain you would come today," she said softly. "I did not see you on the journey back to the harbor . . . not during the skirmish, either, now that I think of it."

"I went below immediately after gaining the brig's bulwarks, Tia. Given the Loyalists' state of mind yesterday . . . ," he told her, afterward interrupting himself to chuckle softly, *"and* state of inebriation . . . I thought it prudent to do what I could to assure Mr. Paine's safety."

"That was kind in you, Robert," she offered with a warm smile. Then, however, and for a few moments only, she chewed on the inside of her cheek. "H-have you finished your discussion?" she finally ventured on an unsteady exhalation, fingering the broad apple green bow tied just beneath her breasts.

"Yes I have, and try not to look so grim, cousin," Robert replied with a teasing laugh, striding forward to take her cold hands. "Brumley and I have not been discussing our rather delicate situation the entire time."

Clinging tightly to his fingers, Tia smiled reluctantly, then slightly relaxed. "Indeed. You will forgive me, but I find that most difficult to believe."

"Yet true nevertheless," Robert assured her, peering warmly down into her wary hazel eyes. "I had to give him an account of our travels, of course. It was necessary in order to demonstrate to him without question our need to quickly marry. However, in the course of my narration, I was able to offer several explanations that served to settle his mind a bit, and I did tell him what we had discovered about Wilson."

"Did you?" Tia remarked, her head slightly tipping. "How did he react?"

"He gave me permission to speak to you, then immediately departed to find Beale and assure him that he still has the Society's utmost confidence."

"Dear Uncle Brumley," Tia replied, smiling in spite of herself.

"Yes. But, come now, cousin," Robert commanded, squeezing her hands. "There are matters which must be settled between us. Ring for your cape and hat. I am certain that the countess will excuse us while we walk for just a bit."

"Mama?" Tia inquired, trembling slightly on a deeply drawn breath.

Near the fire, the countess's lips thinned. "What choice do I have?" she responded tartly, puncturing one petal of her silken rose. And then she pierced her cousin with her worried gaze. "If this were anyone but you, Robert—!"

"But it is not, Sophie," Robert interrupted, kneeling before her and bringing her slender fingers to his lips. "It *is* I."

Slowly, the countess covered Robert's fingers with her other hand. For the first time in her life, Tia saw tears form in her mother's eyes.

"She is my child, cousin," the countess whispered.

"I know," Robert tenderly replied, stretching forward to place a soft kiss aside her cheek. At last he stood and turned away, squaring his shoulders as he faced Tia again. "Well, cousin? This shan't become any easier later in the day."

"No . . . well I know it," Tia admitted, nodding her assent. "I shall ring for Nancy."

"And I shall wait, Tia. I shall always wait," Robert told her, a gleam of purpose arising in his woodland eyes.

Not long after, the two cousins found themselves on the rugged cliffs just to the south of Whitby, their view overlooking Saltwick Bay framed by the stunted, stubborn presence of a lone juniper tree. How they had gotten there was a befuddlement for Tia. For the life of her she could not recall their passing. Embarrassed by her rag-mannered inattention, she glanced toward the viscount. When he did not return her gaze, she turned again to watch a pair of cormorants soar upward on a rising current, then suddenly hang above the treacherous rocky outcroppings of Saltwick Nab like stringless marionettes. It had grown warm for February; absently, she untied the lacings of her cape.

Next to her side, Robert drew in a breath.

"Tia, will you marry me?"

The sudden question made Tia gasp. Instantly, her gaze leapt to his face. "I . . . I am sensible of the great honor you do me . . ."

"Tia, deuce take it, cut line!" Robert growled, slashing the air with his hand. "This is me, remember? I need no inane niceties."

"Robert, I . . ."

"No, I . . . Tia, please forgive me," he implored, removing his beaver to tunnel a complement of fingers through his hair. "Please . . . let me start again."

"Oh, Robert . . . ," Tia breathed, tears pricking at her eyes.

"Tia, do you at least care for me?" he interrupted with an intensity that stole away the rest of her sentence.

"Yes! Yes, of course I do!" she told him, seizing his arms. "But . . ."

Beneath her fingers, Robert stiffened. " 'But.' Damnable word. Perhaps you had better explain why it was necessary to use it."

Dropping her gaze, Tia shook her head and squeezed her waist. "Oh, Robert," she sighed, two limp strands of hair sliding down to her cape. "I am not at all sure I can."

Suddenly, the viscount sighed. "And I am not making it easy for you, am I?" he replied, smiling ruefully as he gently enfolded her into his arms. "Poor Tia . . . forgive me. In my self-absorption, I have forgotten that you have had a very difficult four days."

"That is very true, you know," Tia agreed, putting her arms about his familiar form and pressing her nose into his cutaway. "I have."

"You have, indeed. Where a mere four days ago, you were secure in your choice to remain a spinster," he stated, rubbing one shoulder and the side of her neck, "now you have discovered that your cousin and dearest friend is an odious man; worse, you must marry the beast."

"Exactly so," Tia concurred, nodding up to him before again burying her face. "Oh, not the part about your being a beast, you understand," she suddenly added.

"Of course."

"But the other . . ."

". . . I understand perfectly, Tia. A moment embroiled in a compromising situation, and, suddenly, a husband on the near horizon. Most oversetting."

"It is, Robert," Tia whuffled into navy serge. "Indeed it is."

"I do think it must be pointed out, however, that in the midst of the whole scandal broth, you did discover at least one pleasant thing."

"Whatever was that?" Tia asked, quite improperly sniffing and dabbing at her cheeks with her sleeve.

"That you are not above the human condition, Tia," the viscount responded.

"Oh, true, cousin!" Tia exclaimed, peering up at him again. "And it came as a great surprise to me, too, I must say. Whoever would have thought that I, too, possess . . ."

"Say it, Tia."

"That I possess feelings, Robert! . . . *those* feelings!" she cried, clutching at his lapels. "And I have no idea what to do!"

His arms still comfortingly surrounding her, the viscount laughed. "The solution is simple, cousin, if your feelings are for me."

"Of course they are!" Tia exclaimed, raising her gloved fingers up to cup his familiar, beloved cheek. "How could there be any question of that after what happened between us at Blackamore Grange? But . . ."

"Ah, that damnable 'but' again," her cousin sighed, shaking his head. "What is it, Tia? Can it be possible that I do not possess all of them?"

"Oh, Robert! . . ."

Drawing in a deep breath, the viscount squeezed her again. "Well, that certainly answers that question, I should think."

"Robert . . ."

"Is it Dex, Tia?" the viscount asked levely, one finger raising her face to his.

Tia's eyes widened with surprise. "Dex! Why, of course not!"

"Good . . . because right at the moment he is at the Grange asking for Miss Tutweiler's hand."

"He is? Oh, truly, cousin?" Tia exclaimed, brightening considerably. "Is he indeed? But this is all that is wonderful! I must send a note to Margaret immediately . . ."

"No, you must not," Robert countered quellingly. "You must only stick to the matter at hand, if you please. So, it is the Enforcer, then. Did he make love to you?"

"What?" his cousin queried in astonishment.

"It is a simple question, Tia," Robert stated, staring hard into her eyes. "Did he make love to you when the two of you were alone?"

Within his warm embrace, Tia trembled slightly. "I . . . ," she began, biting her lip. "Oh, Robert, to be honest about it, I truly am not at all certain."

"Oh?" her cousin responded with a half grin, dramatically elevating one brow.

"Well . . . no," Tia was forced to admit. "Oh, of a certainty, he did not do to me what you did in the bedchamber at Blackamore, but . . ."

"But . . . ?"

"But we . . ."

"Yes, Tia . . . ?"

"We . . . well, Robert . . . we kissed."

Again the viscount drew in a deep, sustained breath.

"I see," he finally commented, drawing his lips together. "I can only conclude, then, that with that one kiss, the Enforcer managed to obliterate what you might have felt for me."

"Oh, no!" Tia exclaimed, seizing hold of his cravat. And

then her whole being seemed to sink. "And that is my problem, you see."

"And at last we have reached the heart of the matter, I perceive," the viscount replied, squeezing her tightly against his broad frame. "Poor Tia," he soothed. "Tell me, my dear, is it possible that you are a spinster who has just discovered herself in love with two men?"

"Oh, yes, Robert, that is it exactly!" Tia cried, new tears beginning to spill down her smooth, downy cheeks. "It is quite true! And I do love you . . . I do! I didn't understand it before, but now I am quite certain."

"I love you, too, my darling," Robert replied, kissing her forehead and hugging her close, "and always have done. But you could never see it, could you?"

"No," Tia smiled, stroking his jaw. "Though how it escaped me I shall never be able to say."

"You simply did not wish to see it, my love," Robert supplied, slipping a strand of hair behind her ear.

"No, I suppose not," Tia agreed, "but now it seems the most reasonable of things. I love you, Robert."

"Tia," Robert sighed, tucking her damp face against his neck. "If what you say is true, then will you *please* marry me?" he asked again, his voice husky in his overwhelming need.

"Yes, Robert," Tia whispered. "I will . . . I must. But . . ."

At her pause, the viscount's shoulders sagged. "Do you think, cousin," he asked with great deliberation, "that you could never again say that word?"

Smiling, Tia poked his white silk waistcoat. "I am quite serious, you varlet!" she exclaimed. "I know we must marry for propriety's sake. More, I want to marry you and make you happy for the rest of your life. But how is that to happen if I am never able to forget . . . ?"

"Forget what?" Robert asked her, a slow gleam beginning to dance within the forest hues staring so intently down into her own hazel gaze.

"F-forget . . . ," she stumbled, biting at her lower lip.

"The way he held you, Tia?" the viscount suggested into her distress. "Did he hold you like this?" he added, shifting her slightly until the length of her body came into full contact with his.

Tia's lips parted on a softly drawn gasp. "Yes."

"I thought as much. And when he touched you, Tia," he continued, lifting his hand to her cheek, then trailing his fingers along her jaw to her throat, only to stroke them slowly on down the length of her pulse beat, "was it like this?" he asked, murmuring his question into her hair as his hand finally sank to the warm round of her breast and, finding it, paused to gently shape and caress.

"Yes . . . ," Tia sighed, her body drifting on an exquisite tide. "Oh, Robert, just like that!"

"And his kiss, Tia," the viscount asked huskily, giving her no respite, his breath now warm and sweet against her lips, "was this his kiss?"

"Robert . . . ," Tia sighed as their mouths caught in a tender collide, "Robert . . ."

And it was the same . . . a gentle, hungry devouring, a beginning and a completion, an absorption of being into being . . . the same.

Good heavens, the same!

"You!" she gasped, bending away to gape up at him. "You are . . . he! . . . the same!" she cried, pushing herself free from his compelling body, a new freshet of tears coursing along drying tracks she had yet to brush from her face.

"But . . . no, you cannot be!" she exclaimed, her fingers next skimming across her bodice, fumbling about underneath her sleeve. "Oh, fiddle, cousin," she burst out finally, "it is ever the same. Where in the world have I put my handkerchief?"

Smiling, her cousin unbuttoned, then held wide his cutaway.

"Here, of course," he offered, "in the right-hand pocket of my waistcoat, my love . . . where it always has been and ever shall be."

It was moments before Tia realized that she had drawn forth a black silk half mask to blot against her streaming cheeks.

Twenty-six

"You are not too happy about this, are you?" the viscount asked after Tia had gasped and flung the half mask away from her as if it had sprouted eight legs.

"How am I to answer a question like that?" she cried, throwing up her hands. "On the one hand, there is you, my comfortable, familiar cousin . . . my childhood friend," she exclaimed, beginning to pace back and forth along the bluff in front of him, "and yet on the other there is the Enforcer . . . mysterious, dangerous . . . a wholly overwhelming man. And, suddenly, I find myself in love with both of them, for entirely different reasons! . . . only to then discover that they are actually one and the same! What do you imagine I would think about a circumstance such as that, cousin?" she cried at a most improper volume, planting her fists at the sides of her waist.

"Perhaps that when Tia Hilton shops at the marriage mart, *she* comes home with two for the price of one?" he suggested with a slow half grin. "Quite a bargain in my opinion."

Tia critiqued that assessment with her most quelling glower.

"Begin at the beginning, cousin," she commanded, her words carefully spaced. "How, under heaven, did all of this . . . did *any* of it come about?"

Settling himself on a wind-polished boulder, the viscount smiled. "Tia, it was an attempt on my part to leave two very fine, proud groups of life-long acquaintances with their manhood intact while at the same time preventing them from killing each other."

"The Freedom Brigade and the Black Masks, you mean."

"Exactly," the viscount nodded, afterward motioning Tia onto the rock beside him. "It was not long after the Brigade formed, and then the Masks to counter them, that I realized something more than just pleading for a return of reason would have to be done. Passions were running quite high at the time."

"Yes, I remember," Tia commented, leaning close beside him and accepting his arm about her waist. "What did you do?"

"I gathered others from about the county who felt as I did and formed my own group."

"The hired hands on the collier!" Tia exclaimed, ineffectively snapping her gloved fingers.

"The same," the viscount affirmed. "Very good, Tia."

"But how did they come to be there, Robert?" Tia quite reasonably asked. "On the collier, I mean? You were still lying unconscious on the moors when Uncle Brumley must have been looking for a crew to hire. How did they know to sign on?"

"Fortunately, Wilson's blow was not as debilitating as it looked, Tia," Robert informed her, giving her waist a slight squeeze. "I regained consciousness quite rapidly, thanks in great part to Nancy's ministrations. Only moments later, of course, I had changed into my Black Mask's garb and Romney was on his way back to Whitby with directions to watch the Masks and to make himself a part of whatever it was they were planning."

"Romney?" Tia queried, looking up at her cousin.

"Mm-hmm," Robert affirmed, giving her nose a gentle tweak. "Did you not recognize him, cousin? He was serving as the collier captain."

"The captain!" Tia cried, twisting toward him. "But the captain was all bent and limping!" she added with a bit of heat. Then, picturing the wizened man in her mind's eye, her gaze narrowed around sparkles of suspicion. "He was wearing an eye patch."

"Romney has always enjoyed a good disguise," the viscount commented, granting her observation an agreeable nod. "He was a most satisfactory ghost as well."

"Ghost?" Tia giggled in surprise.

"Just so," Robert confirmed, grinning broadly. "It is how we assured that the ruins of Byland Abbey were not blown to dust by Fullerton. We were a rather quelling rainstorm once as well. We formed a bucket brigade from Ethan Burnside's frozen pond to the top of his barn on the night the Masks came to burn it down. We created quite a deluge," he chuckled softly before shaking his head. "Upon another occasion my own store of Whitby jet prevented the market's collapse and Fenster Ogilvie's ruination. The crew saved Hiram Bottonby's Scottish blackface, too, with the aide of the castle's sheep dogs."

"Oh, no!" Tia gasped, placing fingertips to her lips. "What happened?"

"Let us just say that the Loyalists were unmasked," the viscount suggested.

"Never say so!" Tia giggled, and then a sudden thought occurred. "Your handiwork must have been displayed at the Sinnington Mill as well, then!" she exclaimed, tossing back several of her trailing strands.

"No, no," Robert denied, holding up his free hand and shaking his head. "I was in London at the time that particular dish of suds took place. Just as I was when the Penfield mine exploded, if you recall. No, unfortunately, Tia, I could not be here to stop everything, nor could Romney discover all of the Black Masks' schemes."

"But, for the most part," Tia concluded, "when you were here you kept them from serious harm, all the while giving them the perception that they had struck a blow for the monarchy. How very clever of you, Robert," she added, smiling up at him warmly, "and how very good."

Beside her, the viscount shook his head. "Not good enough, I am afraid. I could not always stop them, Tia. Dear God, when I think what might have happened at Penfield!"

"But it did not, dear," Tia soothed, reaching up to stroke his cheek.

"No," Robert replied, relaxing again. "But it could have. That is why, as the Enforcer, I forbade them to try anything when I was not about."

"Was that why you developed such a frightening reputation for the Enforcer, cousin?" Tia asked.

"Partly . . ." Robert nodded, "and partly to keep the Freedom Brigade from ever waging a campaign of their own. That, at least, was successful. The Masks, however, are a devilishly stubborn group!"

Beside him, Tia grinned. "Dear Uncle Brumley," she agreed. "And dear *you*," she told him, stretching upward to kiss him softly on the mouth, "for doing so much to keep him safe."

Groaning softly, the viscount pulled her close. "May I

take it, then, that I am forgiven?" he asked, smiling against her lips.

"You are, cousin," Tia replied, kissing him once again.

"And shall you still wish to marry me?" he asked again, pausing in his question just long enough to ride his tongue along the tender inner flesh of her upper lip.

"Oh, yes," she responded breathlessly, and then she paused. "Only as long, of course, as you promise to always love me like Robert does, but kiss me like the Enforcer!"

Drawing back a bit, the viscount began to laugh. "I imagine that might be arranged." Suddenly, he sobered somewhat. "But what is this I see?" he asked, catching her chin within his warm fingers and peering steadily into her eyes. "Your lips are smiling, cousin, but there is still a sadness lingering behind your gaze. Tia, you have known me all your life. Surely you cannot still be giving credence to what the countess has said. Do you not yet know that you would never come to any harm by my hand?"

Tia's gaze widened with surprise, and then she smiled. "Yes, I do know that now," she said softly, squeezing him about the waist. "I do admit that at first I was very confused and . . . uncertain. But when I was forced to leave you behind to go with the kidnappers and learned from them how you had protected me, I came to understand that Mama was wrong. All men are not cut from the same cloth. You are not my father . . . just as you are not dear Uncle Brumley, or Lord Digby . . . or any other man. You are you. Robert. The man I love with all my heart."

The viscount nodded, but continued to study her. Suddenly his lips pursed.

"But . . ."

"What?" Tia responded, tilting her head.

"But, what?" the viscount elucidated. "But, what, Tia? Forgive me, my dear, but there is still a 'but' in your eyes."

At that, Tia broke into a soft chuckle. "Yes, I suppose there is," she affirmed with a slow nod. "How could you think there would not be when . . ."

"Yes?" the viscount interrupted, concern sharpening his well-modulated voice.

"Well . . ."

"Tia!" his lordship cried.

"Oh, very well, Robert," she exclaimed, bounding to her feet, "how could you think there would not be when I still do not know the sender of that horrid valentine!"

The viscount immediately subsided. "Ah, that," he commented as she began to pace, tucking his clasped hands between his knees. "Well, as to that, cousin, I suppose that now is as good a time as any to tell you that . . ."

"To tell me what, cousin?"

"Well . . . to tell you that . . . I did," he admitted, looking up at her with a charmingly contrite grin.

Tia's stalking half boots instantly fused to the cliff.

"You, cousin?" she breathed, staring at him in shock, her hazel eyes growing huge. *"You* sent it to me? But why?"

"Because I could see no other course left to me, that's why!" Robert exclaimed, rising swiftly to seize her shoulders in a tight grip. "I had spent a lifetime waiting for you to stop seeing me as a childhood chum, Tia," he told her. "I had to do something that would at once jar you loose from the path Cousin Sophie had set you upon, and at the same time place you in my sole company for a time so that I might have at least a chance to convince you that there was more to me than you realized."

Suddenly, once again Tia set her fists to the sides of her

hips. "Then you *did* say something to Squire Tutweiler, didn't you?" she accused. "It *was* because of something you said that Margaret was not allowed to accompany us."

"Absolutely," the viscount replied.

"What did you tell him?" Tia insisted upon knowing.

"You don't want to know," Robert replied.

"Yes, I do."

"No, you don't."

"Tell me, Robert," Tia insisted, crossing her arms beneath her breasts.

"Oh, very well," he groused, suddenly looking up at her and breaking into a wide grin. "I merely told the squire that the last female to accompany you upon one of your escapades was Miss Alicia Evans."

"You didn't!" Tia cried, planting her fists on her hips.

In response, the viscount began to chuckle.

"You bounder!" Tia evaluated as her cousin's arms suddenly snaked about her and pulled her against his length.

"It worked, did it not?" The viscount grinned before bending to her ear and beginning to nibble a course down along her pulse's path.

"You scoundrel!" Tia sighed, gasping slightly at the exquisite sensation of then being kissed over every square inch of her face.

"So did the valentine," Robert made sure to point out as his hands began to make free with whatever portions of her anatomy happened to lie within reach.

"Varlet," she breathed when the viscount stopped suddenly, then, loosening his neckcloth, began to lead her toward a stunted copse of juniper on the other side of the boulders sheltering a bit of needle-strewn ground just to the formation's lee.

At her whispered word, Robert paused. "Your servant,

ma'am," he responded, turning back toward her, his voice husky and low, all the love in his heart there for her to see in his woodland eyes' comfortable, familiar green. "Always, Tia . . . forever."

With great tenderness, then, he showed her. Just as he had always done since either of them could remember, the viscount reached out and slipped another strand of hair behind his cousin's ear.

Exactly two months later, Robert Baldwin, Viscount Bainbridge, took Lady Horatia Hilton to be his wife in the chapel of Whinstone Abbey, thus making her the first of the Walmsley heiresses since Henry's Dissolution to actually marry someone. Happily, upon their leaving for a wedding trip to the Continent, life on the moors returned to normal. Except for one small detail, however, it must be said. From the moment of the wedding ceremony's conclusion, no cormorant ever circled Whinstone Abbey's eastern tower again.

It was of no moment, however, the townsfolk decided once the great birds' absence had been duly noted and endlessly discussed. After all, the curse had been broken, had it not? And what need had a fine village such as theirs with a musty old legend when the rumored identity of the Enforcer and a suspected new heir to the Walmsley fortune had just presented themselves to be bruited about? A bit of all right, that Bainbridge, the town agreed, saluting him when it crossed their minds with a collective pint of ale and a hearty huzza. Yes, indeed . . . a bit of all right without a doubt.

Spring soon after made its way to the Blackamore on a warm sou'westerly from the Dales; contentment, except for the occasional activities of a few pesky secret Societies, you understand, once again settled over Whitby like a warm, comfortable shawl.

Author's Note

Those of you who have visited the lovely seaside town of Whitby at the edge of the North York Moors know that there is, indeed, an abbey located on the bluffs above the town; but it is not the Whinstone Abbey of my story. St. Hilda's Abbey is the real one, beautiful in its time, but unfortunately now in ruins. It did not fall to Henry VIII, however, without leaving its mark. From its brethren came the oxherd Caedmon who was destined to become England's first religious poet; and from the Synod of Whitby, which took place in AD 663, the date of Easter was standardized,

I must also confess that there is no legend concerning cormorants associated with St. Hilda's either. The true legend tells of St. Hilda ridding the area of snakes by cutting off their heads and turning them into stone. Interesting that there actually *are* coiled, snakelike stones to be found on the nearby shores. Proof of the legend, do you think? . . . or, as those very unromantic scientists tell us, are they but fossilized ammonites, a type of Cephalopod long extinct?

A word, too, about Thomas Paine. The history I presented to you in my story actually happened, with two exceptions: the bridge did exist, however Mr. Paine never tried to return to England to see it after leaving France; and the actual date of his return to America was September, 1802, not the following February, a date I invented, of course, for my plot's convenience. I had no choice in my fact-bending, however. This is, after all, a romance abou a valentine. And consider this: while Tia and Robert wer traipsing around the Blackamore meddling in everyone affairs, what better intrigue could I have invented to kee those dear Black Masks occupied?

I hope you enjoyed the story. Let me know! I'd love t hear what you think. You may write to me c/o Zebra Books Please include a self-addressed stamped envelope if yo wish a response.